THE EROTIC NOVELS OF ANNE RICE WRITING AS A. N. ROQUELAURE

The Claiming of Sleeping Beauty

•

Beauty's Punishment

•

Beauty's Release

Since 1983, A. N. Roquelaure has envisioned (for the uninhibited reader) a hypnotic and seductive adult fairy tale in the Sleeping Beauty novels. Now, the author of this exquisite erotic trilogy reveals her true identity—beckoning the reader into a sensuous world of forbidden dreams and dark-edged desires . . . a world in which traditional ideas of submission and dominance and gender preference are thrown to the winds . . . a world made irresistibly inviting by the adventurous spirit and imagination of the unrivaled Anne Rice.

an

erotic novel of

discipline,

love and surrender,

for the enjoyment

of men

and women

The Sequel to
The Claiming of
Sleeping Beauty
and Beauty's
Punishment

BEAUTY'S RELEASE

A. N. Roquelaure

A PLUME BOOK

PLUME

Published by the Penguin Group

Penguin Putnam Inc., 375 Hudson Street, New York, New York 10014, U.S.A.

Penguin Books Ltd, 27 Wrights Lane, London W8 5TZ, England

Penguin Books Australia Ltd, Ringwood, Victoria, Australia

Penguin Books Canada Ltd, 10 Alcorn Avenue, Toronto, Ontario, Canada M4V 3B2

Penguin Books (N.Z.) Ltd, 182–190 Wairau Road, Auckland 10, New Zealand

Penguin Books Ltd, Registered Offices: Harmondsworth, Middlesex, England

Published by Plume, a member of Penguin Putnam Inc.

Previously published in a Dutton edition.

First Plume Printing, November, 1990

First Plume Printing, This Edition, May, 1999

20 19 18 17 16 15 14 13 12 11

REGISTERED TRADEMARK—MARCA REGISTRADA

Roquelaure, A. N.

Beauty's release.

Sequel to: The claiming of Sleeping Beauty and

Beauty's Punishment

I. Title.

PS3568.0696B44   1985   813'.54   85-1486

ISBN 0-452-28145-8

Printed in the United States of America

Designed by Nancy Etheredge

BOOKS ARE AVAILABLE AT QUANTITY DISCOUNTS WHEN USED TO PROMOTE PRODUCTS
OR SERVICES. FOR INFORMATION PLEASE WRITE TO PREMIUM MARKETING DIVISION,
PENGUIN PUTNAM INC., 375 HUDSON STREET, NEW YORK, NEW YORK 10014.

CONTENTS

(v)

CONTENTS

(vi)

CONTENTS

CONTENTS

THE
STORY
THUS
FAR

In
THE CLAIMING
OF SLEEPING BEAUTY

AFTER HER century-long slumber, the Sleeping Beauty opened her eyes at the kiss of the Prince to find her garments stripped away and her heart as well as her body under the rule of her deliverer. At once, Beauty was claimed as the Prince's naked pleasure slave to be taken to his Kingdom.

With the grateful consent of her parents, and dazed with desire for the Prince, Beauty was then brought to the Court of Queen Eleanor, the Prince's mother, to serve as one of hundreds of naked Princes and Princesses, all playthings of the Court until such time as they would be rewarded and sent home to their Kingdoms.

Dazzled by the rigors of the Training Hall, the Hall of Punishments, the ordeal of the Bridle Path, and her own mounting passion to please, Beauty remained the undisputed favorite of the Prince and the delight of her sometime Mistress, the lovely young Lady Juliana.

Yet she could not ignore her secret and forbidden infatuation with the Queen's exquisite slave, Prince Alexi, and finally the disobedient slave, Prince Tristan.

After glimpsing Prince Tristan among the disgraced of the castle, Beauty, in a moment of seemingly inexplicable rebellion, brought upon herself the very same punishment destined for Tristan: to be sent away from the voluptuous Court to the degradation of harsh labor in the nearby village.

In
BEAUTY'S PUNISHMENT

Sold on the village auction block at dawn, Tristan soon found himself tethered and harnessed to the carriage of a handsome young Master, Nicolas, the Queen's Chronicler. And Beauty, put to work in Mistress Lockley's Inn, became the plaything of the Captain of the Guard, the Inn's chief lodger.

But within days of their separation and sale, Beauty and Tristan were both seduced by the iron discipline of the village. The sweet terrors of the Place of Public Punishment, the Punishment Shop, the Farm and the Stable, the Soldiers' Night at the Inn enflamed them as well as frightening them, causing them to forget their former selves utterly.

Even the harsh judgment of the runaway slave, Prince

Laurent, his body bound to a Punishment Cross for exhibit, only served to tantalize them.

And, as Beauty gloried in chastisements at last equal to her spirit, Tristan became hopelessly enamored of his new Master.

Yet no sooner had the pair met and confided their shameless happiness to each other than a band of powerful enemy soldiers attacked the village, kidnapping Beauty and Tristan along with other choice slaves, including Prince Laurent, to be taken by sea to the land of a new Master, the Sultan.

Within hours of the attack, the stolen Princes and Princesses learned that they would not be ransomed. By agreement between their sovereigns, they had been condemned to serve in the Sultan's palace until such time as they would be safely returned to their Queen for further judgment.

Kept in long, rectangular golden cages in the hold of the Sultan's ship, the slaves accepted their new destiny.

As our story continues, it is night on the quiet vessel and the long voyage is nearing its close.

And Prince Laurent is alone with his thoughts about his slavery. . . .

BEAUTY'S
RELEASE

LAURENT: CAPTIVES AT SEA

NIGHTTIME.

But something had changed. As soon as I opened my eyes, I knew we were close to land. Even in the shadowy silence of the cabin, I could smell the living things of the land.

And so the journey is coming to an end, I thought. And we will finally know what awaits us in this new captivity in which we are destined to be even lower, and more abject, than before.

I was as relieved as I was frightened, as curious as I was filled with dread.

And by the light of the one night lantern, I saw Tristan

lying awake, his face tense as he peered into the darkness. He too knew that the voyage was almost ended.

The naked Princesses still slept, however, looking like exotic beasts in their golden cages. The piquant little Beauty was a yellow flame in the gloom, Rosalynd's curly black hair draped her white back to the curve of her plump little buttocks. And above, the long, delicate-boned Elena lay on her back, her straight brown hair combed out over her pillow.

Lovely flesh, these three, our tender fellow prisoners: Beauty's rounded little arms and legs begging to be pinched as she lay snuggled in her sheets; Elena's head thrown back in the total abandon of sleep, her long slender legs wide apart, one knee against the bars of the cage; Rosalynd turned on her side as I looked at her, her large breasts falling gently forward, nipples darkly pink and erect.

And to my far right the black-haired Dmitri, vying with the blond Tristan in muscular beauty, Dmitri's face oddly cold in slumber, though by day he was often the kindest and most accepting of us all. We Princes, caged as securely as the women, probably looked no more human, no less exotic.

And each of us wore the stiff little covering of gold mesh between our legs, forbidding us the slightest examination of our own hungry organs.

We had come to know each other very well during the long nights at sea when our guards were not near enough to hear our whispers. And in our quiet hours of thinking and dreaming, perhaps we had come to better know ourselves.

"Do you feel it, Laurent?" Tristan whispered. "We are near to the shore."

Tristan was the anxious one, the one who grieved for his lost Master, Nicolas, yet watched everything around him.

"Yes," I answered under my breath, with a little glance at him. Flash of his blue eye. "It can't be long."

"I only hope . . ."

"Yes?" I said again. "What is there to hope for, Tristan?"

". . . that they don't separate us."

I didn't answer. I lay back and closed my eyes. What did it matter to talk about it when soon all things would be revealed? And we could do nothing to alter them.

"Whatever happens," I said dreamily, "I'm glad the voyage is ended. I'm glad we'll soon to be put to some use again."

After the initial tests of our passion, we had not been used again by our captors. And for a fortnight we had been tortured by our own desires, the boyish attendants only laughing gently at us and quickly binding our hands when we dared to touch the delicate wedge-shaped casings of mesh that imprisoned our privates.

We had all suffered equally, it seemed, with nothing to distract us in the hold of the ship but the sight of one another's nakedness.

And I couldn't help but wonder if these young caretakers, so thoughtful in every other regard, realized how relentlessly we had been schooled in the appetites of the flesh, how our Masters and Mistresses in the Queen's Court had taught us to crave even the crack of the strap to alleviate the fire within us.

Not a half day of the old servitude had passed without thorough use of our bodies, and even the most obedient of us had received constant chastisement. And those sent down from the castle to the penance of the village had known little rest either.

But those were different worlds, as Tristan and I had often agreed during our whispered nighttime conversations. In both the village and the castle, we had been expected to speak, if only to say, "Yes, My Lord," or, "Yes, My Lady." And we had been given express commands and sent now and then to do errands unaccompanied. Tristan had even conversed at length with his cherished master, Nicolas.

But we had been warned before we ever left the Queen's domain that these servants of the Sultan would treat us as if we were mute animals. Even if we could understand their strange foreign tongue, they would never speak to us. And in the Sultan's land any lowly pleasure slave who attempted speech would merit immediate and severe punishment.

The warnings had been borne out. All during the voyage, we had been petted, stroked, pinched, and guided about in tender and condescending silence.

When, out of desperation and boredom, Princess Elena had spoken aloud, begging to be let out of the cage, she had been quickly gagged, her ankles and wrists bound against the small of her back, her undulating body suspended on a chain from the cabin ceiling. And there she remained, the attendants scowling at her in shock and outrage, until she had given up her vain and muffled protests.

And how kindly and carefully she had been taken down afterwards. Her silent lips had been kissed, her hurting wrists and ankles oiled until the red marks of the leather cuffs were gone from them.

The young silk-robed boys had even brushed her sleek brown hair and massaged her buttocks and back with their strong fingers, as if such irascible little beasts as we must be soothed in this manner. Of course, they had stopped soon enough when they realized the soft shadow of brown curly hair between Elena's legs was moist, and that she could not help but move her hips against the silk of the grooming mattress, so excited was she by their touch.

With little scolding gestures and shakes of the head, they had made her kneel up, holding her wrists again as they fitted her little vagina with its inflexible metal covering, the chains coming round her thighs and quickly clasped tight. Then she had been put in her cage, arms and legs tied to the bars with thick satin ribbons.

Yet this display of passion had not angered them. On the contrary, they had stroked her wet sex before covering it, smiling at her as if to approve her heat, her need. Yet all the moaning in the world had not brought mercy from them.

And the rest of us had only watched in lustful silence, our own starved organs pulsing vainly. I wanted to climb into her cage and tear off the little shield of gold mesh and stab my cock in the wet little nest made for it. I wanted to open her mouth with my tongue. I wanted to squeeze her heavy breasts in my hands, suckle the small coral-colored nipples, and see her flushed red with throbbing pleasure as I rode her to the finish. But these were but painful dreams. Elena and I could only look at each other, as I hoped in silence that sooner or later we might be allowed the ecstasy of each other's arms.

The dainty little Beauty was also most intriguing, and the buxom Rosalynd with her big mournful eyes absolutely luscious, but it was Elena who was full of cleverness and dark disdain for what had befallen us. During our whispered talks, she laughed at our fate, tossing her heavy brown hair over her shoulder as she spoke.

"Who has ever had three such marvelous choices, Laurent?" she asked. "The Sultan's palace, the village, the castle. I tell you, in any one I can find delights to suit me."

"But, darling, you don't know what it will be like in the Sultan's palace," I said. "The Queen had hundreds of naked slaves. In the village there were hundreds at labor. What if the Sultan has even more than that—slaves from all the realms of the East and the West, so many slaves he can use them for footstools?"

"Do you think he does?" she asked excitedly. Her smile became charmingly insolent. Such wet lips and exquisite teeth. "Then we must find some way to distinguish ourselves, Laurent." She leaned her chin on her hand. "I don't want to be just one of a thousand suffering little Princes and Princesses. We must see that the Sultan knows who we are."

"Dangerous thoughts, my love," I said, "when we can

neither speak nor be spoken to, when we are pampered and punished as simple little beasts."

"We'll find a way, Laurent," she said, with a mischievous wink. "Nothing ever frightened you before, did it? You ran away just to see what it would be like to be captured, didn't you?"

"You're too quick-witted, Elena," I said. "What makes you think I didn't run in fear?"

"I know you didn't. No one ever ran away from the Queen's castle in fear. It's always done in the spirit of adventure. I did it myself, you see. That is why I was sentenced to the village."

"And was it worthwhile, my dear?" I asked. Oh, if only I could kiss her, make her pour her high spirits into my mouth, pinch her little nipples. It was a great cruelty that I'd never even been near her during our days in the castle.

"Yes, it was worth it," she said thoughtfully. She had been in the village a year when the raid happened, a female farm slave of the Lord Mayor, working in his country gardens, searching out weeds in the grass with her teeth on her hands and knees, the gardener a stout and severe man, never without a strap in his hand.

"But I was ready for something new," she said, turning over on her back, letting her legs go apart as she always did. I couldn't stop staring at the thick brown hair of her sex under the woven gold shield. "And then the Sultan's soldiers came as if I had summoned them with my imagination. Remember, Laurent, we have to do something to distinguish ourselves."

I laughed to myself. I liked her spirit.

But then I liked all of them: Tristan, a beguiling mixture of strength and need, who bore his suffering in silence; and Dmitri and Rosalynd, both contrite and dedicated to pleasing, as if they had been born slaves instead of royalty.

But Dmitri could not control his agitation or his lust, could not hold still for punishment or use, though his mind was filled with nothing but high thoughts of love and submission. He had spent his short village sentence pilloried in the Place of Public Punishment, awaiting his whippings on the Public Turntable. And Rosalynd too knew no semblance of control unless shackled tightly. Both had hoped the village would purge their fears, allow them to serve with the finesse they admired in others.

As for Beauty, well, next to Elena she was the most enchanting, the most unusual slave. Cold she seemed, yet undeniably sweet, thoughtful and rebellious. Now and then through the dark nights at sea I saw her staring at me through the bars of her cage with a puzzling expression on her strong little face, her lips spreading easily in a smile when I acknowledged her.

When Tristan wept, she would say softly in his defense: "He loved his Master." And she would shrug as if she found it sad but incomprehensible.

"And you loved no one?" I had asked her one night.

"No, not really," she said. "Only other slaves now and then. . . ." And there came that provocative look that made my cock rise at once. There was something savage in her, something untouched, for all her seeming fragility.

But now and then she seemed to brood on her resistance. "What would it mean to love them?" she asked once, almost as if talking to herself. "What would it mean to yield the heart completely? The punishments, I love. But to love one of the Masters or Mistresses. . . ." She looked afraid suddenly.

"It troubles you," I said sympathetically. The nights at sea worked on all of us. The isolation worked on all of us.

"Yes. I long for something I have not had," she whispered. "I deny it, but I long for it. Maybe it is only that I haven't found the proper Master or Mistress. . . ."

"The Crown Prince, it was he who brought you to the Kingdom. Surely you found him a truly magnificent Master."

"No, not at all," she said dismissively. "I can barely remember him. He did not interest me, you see. What would happen if I were mastered by someone who interested me?" And her eyes took on a strange glitter, as if seeing for the first time a whole new realm of possibility.

"I can't tell you," I had said, feeling suddenly at a loss. Up until that moment I was sure that I had loved my Mistress, Lady Elvera. But now I wasn't entirely certain. Maybe Beauty spoke of a deeper, finer love than I had ever known either.

The fact was, *Beauty interested me*. She who lay beyond my grasp upon her silken bed, her naked limbs as perfect as a sculpture in the semi-dark, her eyes full of half-revealed secrets.

Yet all of us, despite our differences, our talk of love, were true slaves. That was certain.

We had been opened up and inalterably changed by our servitude. No matter what our fears and conflicts, we were not the blushing, awestruck beings we had once been. We swam, each at his or her own pace, in the dazzling current of erotic torment.

And as I lay thinking, I sought to understand the important differences between the castle life and the village life, and to guess what this new captivity in the Sultanate promised us.

LAURENT: MEMORIES OF THE CASTLE AND THE VILLAGE

I HAD SERVED well for a year in the castle, property of the strict Lady Elvera, who had had me whipped each morning as a matter of course, while she took her breakfast. She was a proud and quiet raven-haired woman with slate-gray eyes, who spent her hours at delicate embroidery. I had kissed her slippers afterwards in thanks for the whipping, hopeful for the smallest crumb of praise—that I had taken the blows well or that she found me handsome still. Seldom did she speak a word. Seldom did she look up from her needle.

In the afternoons, she took her work to the gardens, and there I coupled with Princesses for her amusement.

I had first to catch my pretty prey, which meant a hard chase through the flower beds, and then the blushing little Princess must be carried back and laid at My Lady's feet for inspection, after which my real performance commenced and must be carried through perfectly.

Of course, I had loved these moments—pumping my heat into the shy and quivering body beneath me, even the most frivolous Princess shaken by the chase and the capture, and both of us burning under My Lady's steady gaze as she nevertheless went on with her sewing.

Pity I had never covered Beauty during this time. Beauty had remained the Crown Prince's favorite until she fell from grace and was sent down to the village. Only the Lady Juliana was allowed to share her. But I had glimpsed her on the Bridle Path and longed to have her gasping under me. How finely tuned a slave she had been even in the first few days, her form as she marched beside Lady Juliana's horse quite impeccable. Her hair was golden as wheat as it hung down beside her heart-shaped face; her blue eyes flashed with burnt pride and undisguised passion. Even the great Queen was jealous of her.

But, looking back on all of it now, I did not for a moment doubt Beauty when she said she had not loved those who claimed her affections. I could have seen, had I looked, that her heart wore no chains then.

But what had been the particular quality of my life in the halls of the castle? My heart did wear chains. But what had been the essence of my bondage?

I was a Prince, though bound to serve—a high-born being temporarily deprived of his privileges and made to undergo unique and difficult trials of the body and the soul. Yes, that was the nature of the humiliation: that I should be privileged again after it was over, that I was the equal of those who enjoyed my nakedness and reprimanded me severely for the slightest show of will or pride.

It was never so clear to me as when Princes from other lands came to visit and to marvel at this custom of keeping royal pleasure slaves. How it had flayed me to be presented to these guests.

"But how do you make them serve?" they would ask, half astonished, half enchanted. You never knew whether they yearned to serve or command. Do all beings have both inclinations at war within them?

The inevitable answer to their timid questions was a mere demonstration of our fine training; that we must kneel before them, offering our naked organs for their examination, our upturned backsides to be whipped.

"It is a game of pleasure," My Lady would say matter-of-factly. "And this one, Laurent, a beautifully mannered Prince, amuses me in particular. He will one day rule a rich realm." She would pinch my nipples slowly, then lift my cock and balls in her open hand to display them to the amazed guest.

"But still, why does he not struggle, resist?" the visitor might ask, possibly masking his deeper feelings.

"Think on it," My Lady would say. "He is quite well stripped of the accoutrements that would make him a man in the outside world, only the better to expose the fleshly accoutrements that make him a man for my service. Imagine yourself as naked, as defenseless, as thoroughly subjugated. You might serve, too, rather than risk a gamut of even more ignominious corrections."

What newcomer had not asked for his own slave before nightfall?

Red-faced and trembling, I had crawled to obey many an order given in an unfamiliar and unpracticed voice. And these were Lords I should some day receive in my own Court. Would we remember these moments? Would anyone dare to mention them?

And so it was with all the naked slave Princes and Princesses of the castle. Nothing but the highest quality for this utter debasement.

"I think Laurent will serve another three years at least," Lady Elvera would say airily. How remote she was, how eternally distracted. "But then the Queen makes these decisions. I shall weep when he goes. I think perhaps it is his size that most entices me. He is taller than the others, bigger-boned, yet his face is noble, don't you think?"

She would snap her fingers for me to come near, and then run her thumb down my cheek. "And the organ," she might say, "it is extremely thick but not overly long. That is important. How the little Princesses squirm under him. I simply must have a strong Prince. Tell me, Laurent, how might I punish you in some new fashion, something perhaps that I have not thought of?"

Yes, a strong Prince in temporary subjugation, a monarch's son, with all his faculties engaged, sent here to be a pupil of pleasure and pain.

But to incur the wrath of the Court and to be sent to the village? That was an altogether different ordeal. And one that I had barely tasted, though what I did come to know was the very quintessence of it.

Only two days before my capture by the Sultan's thieves, I had run away from Lady Elvera and the castle. And I do not know why I did it.

Certainly, I adored the Lady. I did. No doubts really. I admired her imperiousness, her endless silences. She could only have pleased me more had she whipped me herself more often, rather than ordering it done by other Princes.

Even when she gave me to the guests or the other Lords and Ladies, there was the special joy of returning to her, of being taken again into her bed, being allowed to lap at the narrow triangle of black hair between her white thighs as she sat there against the pillow, her hair down, her eyes narrow and indifferent. It had been a challenge to melt her glacial heart, to make her throw back her head and cry out in pleasure finally like the most lascivious little Princess in the garden.

Yet I had run away. And it had come over me suddenly, the impulse—that I should dare to do it, just get up and go off into the forest and let them search for me. Of course they'd find me. I never doubted they would. They always found the runaways.

Maybe I had lived too long in fear of doing it, of being captured by the soldiers and sent to labor in the village. It was tempting me suddenly, like the plunge from a great cliff.

And I had mastered all my other faults by this time; I had attained a rather boring perfection. I never ' hied from the strap. I had grown so to need it that my flesh quivered warmly at the mere sight of it. And I always caught the little Princesses quickly in the garden chase, lifting them high by their wrists and carrying them back over my shoulder, their hot breasts thudding against my back. It had been an interesting challenge to master two and three in a single afternoon with the same stamina.

But this matter of running away. . . . Maybe I wanted to know my Masters and Mistresses better! Because, when I became their captured fugitive, I would feel their power to the marrow of my bones. I would feel all that they could make me feel, completely.

Whatever the reason, I waited until the Lady had fallen asleep in her garden chair, and then I stood up and rushed to the garden wall and climbed over it. This was no little bid for attention on my part. I would make it an indisputable attempt at escape. And, without glancing back, I fled over the mown fields towards the forest.

Yet never had I felt so naked, so utterly the slave as in those moments when I appeared to be in rebellion.

Every leaf, every tall blade of grass stroked my exposed flesh. A new shame astonished me as I roamed beneath the dark trees, creeping past the watchtowers of the village.

When night came on, I felt that my nude skin was glowing like a light, that the forest would not conceal me. I belonged to the intricate world of power and submission and had tried wrongly to steal away from its obligations. And the forest knew it. Brambles scratched my calves. My cock hardened at the slightest sound in the brush.

And o, the final horror and thrill of capture, as the soldiers spotted me in the dark and drove me onward with shouts until they had me surrounded.

Rude hands grabbed at my arms and legs. I was carried low to the ground by four of the men, my head hanging and my limbs outstretched, merely an animal who had given good sport, brought into the torchlit camp amid cheers and hoots and laughter.

And in the blazing moment of inescapable justice, everything was further clarified. I was no high-born Prince anymore. I was a stubborn and lowly thing to be whipped and raped repeatedly by the spirited soldiers until the Captain of the Guard appeared and ordered me bound to the thick wooden Punishment Cross.

And it was during that ordeal that I had again seen Princess Beauty. She had already been sent down to the village and chosen by the Captain of the Guard as his little plaything. Kneeling in the dirt of the camp, she was the only woman there, her fresh pink and milk-white skin all the more delectable for the dust clinging to it. She had magnified all that happened to me with her intense gaze.

And no wonder I still fascinated her: I was a true fugitive, and the only one of us in the Sultan's ship who had earned the Punishment Cross.

In earlier castle days, I had glimpsed such mounted runaways myself. I had seen them put in the cart to be taken to the village, their legs spread wide on the crossbar, their heads bent back over the top of the cross so that they looked straight up into the sky, mouths stretched by the black leather band that held their heads in this position. I had been terrified for them, marveling that even in this disgrace their cocks were hard as the wood to which their bodies were tethered.

And then I was the condemned one. I had passed into the tableau to be bound in the same excruciating fashion, eyes heavenward, my arms doubled behind the rough stake, my open thighs stretched wide and aching, my cock as hard as any I'd ever beheld.

And Beauty was but one of a thousand witnesses.

Through the village streets I was paraded to the slow beat of the drum for common crowds that I could hear and not see, each turn of the cart's wheels jarring the wooden phallus implanted in my backside.

It had been as delicious as it was extreme, the greatest of all degradations. I had felt myself luxuriating in it even as the Captain of the Guard whipped my bare chest, my open legs, my naked belly. And how divinely easy it had been to plead through uncontrollable groans and undulations, knowing full well that I would never be heeded. How it had titillated my soul to know there was not the slightest hope of mercy for me.

Yes, in those moments, I had known the full power of my captors, but I had also known my own power—that we who are bereft of all privileges may yet goad and guide our punishers into new realms of heat and loving attentiveness.

There was no desire to please now, no passion to accomplish. Only divine and anguished abandon. I had rocked my buttocks shamelessly on the phallus that jutted into me from the cross, receiving the quick blows of the Captain's leather strap like kisses. I had struggled and wept to my heart's content without a particle of dignity.

The only flaw in the magnificent scheme, I suppose, was that I could not see my tormentors unless they stood directly above me, which only happened rarely.

And at night, when I was mounted high in the village square, and I could hear them gathered on the platform below me—feel them pinching my sore backside, spanking my cock—I wished I could see the contempt and humor on their faces, their utter superiority to the lowest of the low which I had become.

I liked being condemned. I liked being this grim and frightening exhibit of folly and suffering, even as I quaked at the sounds that signaled a fresh whipping, as the tears spilled uncontrollably down my face.

It was infinitely richer than being the scarlet-faced and

trembling plaything of Lady Elvera. Finer even than the sweet sport of mounting Princesses in the garden.

And finally, there were special rewards for the painful angle of my vision as well. The young soldier, after whipping me at the stroke of nine o'clock, had mounted the ladder beside me, and looked down into my eyes, and kissed my gagged mouth.

I had been unable to show how much I adored him, unable even to close my lips around the thick band of leather that gagged me and held my head in place. But he had clasped my chin and sucked on my upper lip, then my lower lip, running his tongue into my mouth under the leather, and then he promised me in a whisper that I should be whipped again very well at midnight; he would see to it himself. He liked the task of whipping bad slaves.

"You've a good tapestry of pink stripes on your chest and belly," he said. "But you're going to be even prettier. And then there is the Public Turntable for you at sunup, when you'll be unbound and made to kneel over, and the village Whipping Master will do his work on you for the morning crowd. How they will love it, a big strong Prince such as you."

Again he kissed me, sucking on my lower lip, running his tongue along my teeth. I had heaved against the wood, against my bonds, my cock a shaft of exquisite hunger.

I had tried in every unspoken way known to me to show my love for him, his words, his affection.

How strange it all was, that he might not understand it. But it didn't matter. It didn't matter if I was gagged forever, and could never tell anyone. What mattered was that I had found my perfect place and must never rise above it. I must be the emblem of the worst punishment. If only my sore cock, my swollen cock, could know a moment's respite, just a moment's. . . .

And, as if reading my thoughts, he had said:

"Now I have a little gift for you. We want to keep that handsome organ in good form after all, and that is not done through laziness." And I heard near him a woman's laughter. "She's one of the lovelier village girls," he said, brushing my hair out of my eyes. "Would you like to have a good look at her first?"

Oooh, yes, I tried to answer. And I saw her face above me—bouncing red curls, sweet blue eyes, blushing cheeks, and lips that came down to kiss me.

"See how pretty she is?" he asked in my ear. And to her he said: "You may go ahead, dearest."

I felt her legs hooked over mine, her starched petticoats tickling my flesh, her wet little crotch rubbed against my cock, and then the hairy little sheath opening as she came down on me very tight. I was moaning louder than it seemed possible to moan. And the young soldier smiled above me and lowered his head again to bestow his wet, sucking kisses.

O, lovely hot little pair. I thrashed uselessly under my leather bonds. But she made the rhythm for both of us, riding me up and down, the heavy cross shaking, my cock erupting into her.

I hadn't seen anything after that, not even the sky.

I vaguely remembered the young soldier coming and saying it was midnight and time for my next good whipping. And, if I was a very good boy from now on, and my cock stood well to attention for every whipping, he might have another village girl for me the next night. It was his opinion a punished runaway ought to have a girl often. It only made his suffering worse.

I had smiled gratefully under the gag of black leather. Yes, anything to make the suffering worse. And how was I to be a good boy, by twitching and struggling and making noises to show my suffering, by thrusting my hungry cock into the empty air? I was more than willing to do it. I wished I knew how long I would be on exhibit. I wished I could remain so forever, a permanent symbol of baseness, worthy only of scorn.

Now and then I had thought, as the strap licked at my nipples and my belly, of how Lady Elvera had looked when they had brought me to the castle gates on the cross.

Looking up, I had seen her with the Queen in the open window. And I had wept desperately, my tears overflowing. She was so very pretty! And that she would give me the worst now was why I worshiped her.

"Take him away," My Lady had said with an almost bored air, her voice carrying over the empty courtyard. "And see that he is well whipped and sold to a good, cruel Master or Mistress."

Yes, it was a new game of necessary discipline with new rules in which I discovered a depth of submission undreamed of.

"Laurent, I shall come down myself to see you sold," she had said as I was being taken away. "I shall make certain you are given absolute drudgery."

Love, real love for Lady Elvera, had underscored all of it. But Beauty's later ruminations in the hold of the ship confused me.

Had the passion for Lady Elvera been all that love could be? Or was it merely the love one can have for any accomplished Mistress? Was there more to be learned in the crucible of heat and sublime pain? Maybe Beauty was more discriminating, more honest . . . more demanding.

Even with Tristan, one had the feeling that the love of his Master had been given too quickly, too freely. Had Nicolas, the Queen's Chronicler, really been worthy of it? When Tristan spoke of this man, did he illuminate any particular? What came through Tristan's laments was the fact that the man had invited the love with moments of remarkable intimacy. I wondered if, for Beauty, such an invitation would in itself have been sufficient.

Yet in the village it had been bittersweet to think of my lost Lady Elvera as I stretched and twisted on the Punishment Cross, the strap doing its work. But it was also bittersweet to think of pert little Princess Beauty back in the soldiers' camp, who had stared at me in frank amazement. Was she on to the secret? That I had willed it? Would she herself dare such things? They had said at the castle that she had brought the village punishment upon herself. Yes, I liked her very much even then, bold and tender little darling.

But my life as punished runaway had ended before it began. I had never seen the auction block.

Within moments of that last midnight whipping the raid on the village had commenced. The Sultan's soldiers thundered through the little cobblestone streets.

My leather gag and bonds were cut, and my aching body thrown over a speeding horse before I could even glimpse my captor.

Then the hold of the ship, this little cabin hung with jeweled tentwork and brass lanterns.

And the gold oil had been rubbed in my abraded skin, the perfume combed through my hair, and the stiff mesh covering had been chained over my cock and balls so that I could not touch them. And the confines of the cage. And the timid and respectful questions of the other captive slaves: Why had I run away and how had I endured the Punishment Cross?

And the echo of the warning of the Queen's emissary before we left her Kingdom:

"In the Sultan's palace . . . you will no longer be treated as beings with high reason. . . . You will be trained as valuable animals are trained, and you must never, heaven help you, try to speak or to evince anything more than the simplest understanding."

And I wondered now, as we drifted offshore, if in this strange land the diverse torments of the castle and the village might somehow be reconciled.

We had been abject by royal command, then abject by royal condemnation. Now in an alien world, far from those who knew our history or our stations, we would be abject by our very nature.

I opened my eyes, seeing again the one small night lantern hanging from its brass hook amid the tentwork drapery of the ceiling. Something was changed. We had dropped anchor.

And there was much movement above. All the crew it seemed had been roused. And steps were approaching. . . .

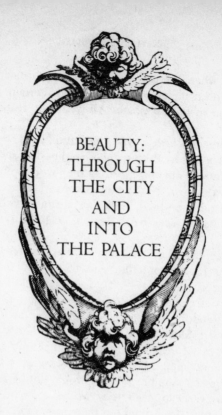

BEAUTY:
THROUGH
THE CITY
AND
INTO
THE PALACE

Beauty OPENED her eyes. She had not been sleeping, and she knew without having to see through a window that it was morning. The air in the cabin was unusually warm.

An hour ago she had heard Tristan and Laurent whispering in the dark, and she had known the ship was at anchor. And she had been only slightly afraid.

After that, she had slipped in and out of thin erotic dreams, her body wakening all over like a landscape under the rising sun. She was impatient to be ashore, impatient to know the full extent of what was to happen to her, to be threatened in ways that she could understand.

Now, when she saw the lean, comely little attendants flooding into the room, she knew for certain that they had come to the Sultanate. All would be realized soon enough.

The precious little boys—they could be no more than fourteen or fifteen, despite their height—had always been richly dressed, but this morning they wore embroidered silk robes, and their tight waist sashes were made of rich striped cloth, and their black hair gleamed with oil, and their innocent faces were dark with an unusual air of anxiety.

At once, the other royal captives were roused, and each slave was taken from the cage and led to the proper grooming table.

Beauty stretched herself out on the silk, enjoying her sudden freedom from confinement, the muscles in her legs tingling. She glanced at Tristan and then at Laurent. Tristan was suffering too much still. Laurent, as always, looked faintly amused. But there was not even time now to say farewell. She prayed they would not be separated, that whatever happened they would come to know it together, and that somehow their new captivity would yield moments when they might be able to talk.

At once the attendants rubbed the gold pigmented oil into Beauty's skin, strong fingers working it well into her thighs and buttocks. Her long hair was lifted and brushed with gold dust, and then she was turned on her back gently.

Skilled fingers opened her mouth. Her teeth were polished with a soft cloth. Waxen gold was applied to her lips. And then gold paint was brushed onto her eyelashes and eyebrows.

Not since the first day of the journey had she or any of the slaves been so thoroughly decorated. And her body steamed with familiar sensations.

She thought hazily of her divinely crude Captain of the Guard, of the elegant but distantly remembered tormentors of the Queen's Court, and she felt desperate to belong to someone again, to be punished for someone, to be possessed as well as chastised.

It was worth any humiliation, that, to be possessed by another. In retrospect, it seemed she had only been a flower in full bloom when she was thoroughly violated by the will of another, that in suffering for the will of another she had discovered her true self.

But she had a new and slowly deepening dream, one that had begun to flame in her mind during the time at sea, and that she had confided only to Laurent: the dream that she might somehow find in this strange land what she had not found before; someone whom she might truly love.

In the village, she had told Tristan that she did not want this, that it was harshness and severity alone she craved. But the truth was that Tristan's love for his Master had deeply affected her. His words had swayed her, even as she had spoken her contradictions.

And then had come these lonely nights at sea of un-fulfilled yearning, of pondering too much all the twists of fate and fortune. And she had felt strangely fragile think-ing of love, of giving her secret soul to a Master or Mis-tress, more than ever off balance.

The groom combed gold paint into her pubic hair, tugging each curl to make it spring. Beauty could hardly keep her hips still. Then she saw a handful of fine pearls held out for her inspection. And into her pubic hair these went, to be affixed to the skin with powerful adhesive. Such lovely decorations. She smiled.

She closed her eyes for a second, her sex aching in its emptiness. Then she glanced at Laurent to see that his face had taken on an Oriental cast with the gold paint, his nipples beautifully erect like his thick cock. And his body was being ornamented, as befitted its size and power, with rather large emeralds instead of pearls.

Laurent was smiling at the little boy who did the work, as if in his mind he was peeling away the boy's fancy clothes. But then he turned to Beauty, and, lifting his

hand languidly to his lips, he blew her a little kiss, un-
noticed by the others.

He winked and Beauty felt the desire in her burning
hotter. He was so beautiful, Laurent.

"O, please don't let us be separated," she prayed. Not
because she ever thought she would possess Laurent—
that would be too interesting—but because she would be
lost without the others, lost. . . .

And then it hit her with full force: She had no idea
what would happen to her in the Sultanate, and absolutely
no control over it. Going into the village, she had known.
She had been told. Even coming into the castle, she had
known. The Crown Prince had prepared her. But this was
beyond her imagining, this place. And beneath her con-
cealing gold paint she grew pale.

The grooms were gesturing for their charges to rise.
There were the usual exaggerated and urgent signs for
them to be silent, still, obedient, as they stood in a circle
facing each other.

And Beauty felt her hands lifted and clasped behind
her back as if she were a senseless little being who could
not even do that much herself. Her groom touched the
back of her neck and then kissed her cheek softly as she
compliantly bowed her head.

Still, she could see the others clearly. Tristan's genitals
had also been decorated with pearls, and he gleamed from
head to toe, his blond locks even more golden than his
burnished skin.

And, glancing at Dmitri and Rosalynd, she saw that
they had both been decorated with red rubies. Their black
hair was in magnificent contrast to their polished skin.
Rosalynd's enormous blue eyes looked drowsy under their
fringe of painted lashes. Dmitri's broad chest was tightened like that of a statue, though his strongly muscled
thighs quivered uncontrollably.

Beauty suddenly winced as her groom added a bit more
gold paint to each of her nipples. She couldn't take her
eyes off his small brown fingers, enthralled by the care
with which he worked, and the way that her nipples hard-

ened unbearably. She could feel each of the pearls clinging to her skin. Every hour of starvation at sea sharpened
her silent craving.

But the captives had another little treat in store for
them. She watched furtively, her head still bowed, as the
grooms drew out of their deep, hidden pockets new and
frightening little toys—pairs of gold clamps with long
chains of delicate but sturdy links attached to them.

The clamps Beauty knew and dreaded, of course. But
the chains—they really agitated her. They were like leashes
and they had small leather handles.

Her groom touched her lips for quiet and then quickly
stroked her right nipple, gathering a nice pinch of breast
into the small gold scallop-shell clamp before he snapped
it shut. The clamp was lined with a bit of white fur, yet
the pressure was firm. And all of Beauty's skin seemed
to feel the sudden nagging torment. When the other clamp
was just as tightly in place, the groom gathered the handles of the long chains in his hands and gave them a tug.
This was what Beauty had feared most. She was brought
forward sharply, gasping.

At once the groom scowled, quite displeased with the
openmouthed sound, and spanked her lips with his fingers
firmly. She bowed my head lower, marveling at these two
flimsy little chains, at their hold upon these unaccountably
tender parts of her. They seemed to control her utterly.

She watched with her heart contracting, as the groom's
hand tightened again and the chains were jerked, and she
was pulled forward once more by her nipples. She moaned
this time but she did not dare to open her lips, and for
this she received his approving kiss, the desire surging
painfully inside her.

"O, but we cannot be led ashore like this," she thought.
She could see Laurent, opposite, clamped the same as she
was, and blushing furiously as his groom tugged the hated
little chains and made him step forward. Laurent looked
more helpless than he had in the village on the Punishment Cross.

For a moment, all the delightful crudity of village punishments came back to her. And she felt more keenly this delicate restraint, the new quality of servitude.

She saw Laurent's little groom kiss his cheek approvingly. Laurent had not gasped or cried out. But Laurent's cock was bobbing uncontrollably. Tristan was in the same transparently miserable state, yet he looked, as ever, quietly majestic.

Beauty's nipples throbbed as if they were being whipped. The desire cascaded through her limbs, made her dance just a little without moving her feet, her head suddenly light with dreams of new and particular love again.

But the business of the grooms distracted her. They were taking down from the walls their long, stiff leather thongs; and these, like all other objects in this realm, were heavily studded with jewels, which made them heavy instruments of punishment, though, like strips of sapling wood, they were quite flexible.

She felt the light sting on the back of her calves, and the little double leash was pulled. She must move up behind Tristan, who had been turned towards the door. The others were probably lined up behind her.

And quite suddenly, for the first time in a fortnight, they were to leave the hold of the ship. The doors were opened, Tristan's groom leading him up the stairs, the thong playing on Tristan's calves to make him march, and the sunlight pouring down from the deck was momentarily blinding. There came with it a great deal of noise—the sound of crowds, of distant shouts, of untold numbers of people.

Beauty hurried up the wooden stairs, the wood warm under her feet, the tugging of her nipples making her moan again. What precious genius, it seemed, to be led so easily by such refined instruments. How well these creatures understood their captives.

She could scarcely bear the sight of Tristan's tight, strong buttocks in front of her. It seemed she heard Laurent moan behind. She felt afraid for Elena and Dmitri and Rosalynd.

But she had emerged on the deck and could see on either side the crowd of men in their long robes and turbans. And beyond the open sky, and high mud-brick buildings of a city. They were in the middle of a busy port, in fact, and everywhere to right and left were the masts of other ships. The noise, like the light itself, was numbing.

"O, not to be led ashore like this," she thought again. But she was rushed behind Tristan across the deck and down an easy, sloping gangplank. The salt air of the sea was suddenly clouded with heat and dust, the smell of animals and dung and hemp rope, and the sand of the desert.

The sand, in fact, covered the stones upon which she suddenly found herself standing. And she could not help but raise her head to see the great crowds being held back by turbaned men from the ship, hundreds and hundreds of dark faces scrutinizing her and the other captives. There were camels and donkeys piled high with wares, men of all ages in linen robes, most with their heads either turbaned or veiled in longer, flowing desert headdresses.

For a moment Beauty's courage failed her utterly. It was not the Queen's village, this. No, it was something far more real, even as it was foreign.

And yet her soul expanded as the little clamps were tugged again, as she saw gaudily dressed men appear in groups of four, each group bearing on its shoulders the long gilded rods of an open, cushioned litter.

Immediately, one of these cushions was lowered before her. And her nipples were pulled again by the mean little leashes as the thong snapped at her knees. She understood. She knelt down on the cushion, its rich red and gold design dazzling her slightly. And she felt herself pushed back on her heels, her legs opened wide, her head bowed again by a warm hand placed firmly on her neck.

"This is unbearable," she thought, moaning as softly as she could, "that we will be carried through the city itself.

Why were we not taken secretly to His Highness the Sultan? Are we not royal slaves?"

But she knew the answer. She saw it in the dark faces that pressed in on all sides.

"We are only slaves here. No royalty accompanies us now. We are merely expensive and fine, like the other merchandise brought from the hold of the ships. How could the Queen let this happen to us?"

But her fragile sense of outrage was at once dissolved as if in the heat of her own naked flesh. Her groom pushed her knees even wider apart, and spread her buttocks upon her heels as she struggled to remain utterly pliant.

"Yes," she thought, her heart palpitating, her skin breathing in the awe of the crowd, "a very good position. They can see my sex. They can see every secret part of me." Yet she struggled with another little flair of alarm. And the gold leashes were quickly wound around a golden hook at the front of the cushion, which made them quite taut, holding her nipples in a state of bittersweet tension.

Her heart beat too fast. Her little groom further frightened her with all his desperate gestures that she be silent, that she be good. He was being fussy as he touched her arms. No, she must not move them. She knew that. Had she ever tried so hard to remain motionless? When her sex convulsed like a mouth gasping for air, could the crowd see it?

The litter was lifted carefully to the shoulders of the turbaned bearers. She grew almost dizzy with an awareness of her exposure. But it comforted her just a little to see Tristan kneeling on his cushion just ahead, to be reminded that she was not alone here.

The noisy crowd made way. The little procession moved through the huge open place that spread out from the harbor.

Overcome with a sense of decorum, she dared not move a muscle. Yet she could see all around her the great bazaar—merchants with their bright ceramic wares spread out upon multicolored rugs; rolls of silk and linen in stacks; leather goods and brass goods and ornaments of silver and gold; cages of fluttering, clucking birds; and food cooking in smoking pots under dusty canopies.

Yet the whole market had turned its chattering attention to the captives who were being carried past. Some stood mute beside their camels, just staring. And some—the young bareheaded boys, it seemed—ran along beside Beauty, glancing up at her and pointing and talking rapidly.

Her groom was at her left, and with his long leather thong he made some small adjustment of her long hair, and now and then fiercely admonished the crowd, driving it backwards.

Beauty tried not to see anything but the high mud-brick buildings coming closer and closer.

She was being carried up an incline, but her bearers held the litter level. And she struggled to keep her perfect form, though her chest heaved and pulled at the mean little clamps, the long gold chains that held her nipples shivering in the sunlight.

They were in a steep street, and on either side of her windows opened, people pointed and stared, and the crowd streamed along the walls, their cries growing suddenly louder as they echoed off the stones. The grooms drove them back with even stricter commands.

"Ah, what do they feel as they look at us?" Beauty thought. Her naked sex pulsed between her legs. It seemed to feel itself so disgracefully opened. "We are as beasts, are we not? And these wretched people do not for a moment imagine that such a fate could befall them, poor as they might be. They wish only that they might possess us."

The gold paint tightened on her skin, tightened particularly on her clamped nipples.

And try as she might, she could not keep her hips entirely still. Her sex seemed to churn with desire and move her entire body with it. The glances of the crowd touched her, teased her, made her ache in her emptiness.

But they had come to the end of the street. The crowd streamed out into an open place where thousands more stood watching. The noise of voices came in waves. Beauty could not even see the end of this crowd, as hundreds jostled to get a closer look at the procession. She felt her heart pound even harder as she saw the great golden domes of a palace rising before her.

The sun blinded her. It flashed on white marble walls, Moorish arches, giant doors covered in gold leaf, soaring towers so delicate that they made the dark, crude, stone castles of Europe seem somehow clumsy and vulgar.

The procession turned to the left sharply. And, for an instant, Beauty glimpsed Laurent behind her, then Elena, her long brown hair swaying in the breeze, and the dark, motionless figures of Dmitri and Rosalynd. All obedient, all still upon their cushioned litters.

The young boys in the crowd seemed to be more frenzied. They cheered and ran up and down, as though the proximity of the palace somehow heightened their excitement.

Beauty saw that the procession had come to a side entrance, and turbaned guards with great scimitars hanging from their girdles drove the crowd back as a pair of heavy doors were opened.

"O, blessed silence," Beauty thought. She saw Tristan carried beneath the arch, and immediately she followed.

They had not entered a courtyard as she had expected. Rather they were in a large corridor, its walls covered in intricate mosaics. Even the ceiling above was a stone tapestry of flowers and spirals. The bearers suddenly came to a halt. The doors far behind were closed. And they were all plunged into shadow.

Only now did Beauty see the torches on the walls, the lamps in their little niches. A huge crowd of young dark-faced boys, dressed exactly like the grooms from the ship, surveyed the new slaves silently.

Beauty's cushion was lowered. At once, her groom clasped the leashes and pulled her forward onto her knees on the marble. The bearers and the cushions quickly disappeared through doors that Beauty hardly glimpsed. And she was pushed down onto her hands, her groom's foot firm on the back of her neck as he forced her forehead right to the marble flooring.

Beauty shivered. She sensed a different manner in her groom. And, as the foot pressed harder, almost angrily, against her neck, she quickly kissed the cold floor, overcome with misery that she couldn't know what was wanted.

But this seemed to appease the little boy. She felt his approving pat on her buttocks.

Now her head was lifted. And she saw that Tristan was kneeling on all fours in front of her, the sight of his well-shaped backside further teasing her.

But as she watched in stunned silence, the little gold-link chains from her clamped nipples were passed through Tristan's legs and under his belly.

"Why?" she wondered, even as the clamps pinched her with renewed tightness.

But immediately she was to know the answer. She felt a pair of chains being passed between her own thighs, teasing her lips. And now a firm hand clasped her chin and opened her mouth, and the leather handles were fed to her like a bit that she must hold in her teeth with the usual firmness.

She realized this was Laurent's leash, and she was now to pull him along by the damnable little chains just as she herself was to be pulled by Tristan. And if her head moved in the slightest involuntary way, she would add to Laurent's torment just as Tristan added to hers as he pulled the chains given him.

But it was the spectacle of it that truly shamed her.

"We are tethered to one another like little animals led to market," she thought. And she was further confused by the chains stroking her thighs and the outside of her pubic lips, by their grazing her taut belly.

"You little fiends!" she thought, glancing at the silk robes of her groom. He was fussing with her hair, forcing her back into a more convex position so that her rear was higher. She felt the teeth of a comb stroking the delicate hair around her anus, and her face flooded with a hot stinging blush.

And Tristan, did he have to move his head, making her nipples throb so?

She heard one of the grooms clap his hands. The leather thong came down to lick at Tristan's calves and the soles of his naked feet. He started foward, and she immediately hurried after him.

When she raised her head just a little to see the walls and ceiling, the thong smacked the back of her neck. Then it whipped the undersides of her feet just as Tristan's were being whipped. The leashes pulled at her nipples as if they had life of their own.

And yet the thongs smacked faster and louder, urging all the slaves to hurry. A slipper pushed at her buttocks. Yes, they must run. And, as Tristan picked up speed, so did she, remembering in a daze how she had once run upon the Queen's Bridle Path.

"Yes, hurry," she thought. "And keep your head properly lowered. And how could you think you would enter the Sultan's Palace in any other manner?"

The crowds outside might gape at the slaves, as they probably did at the most debased of prisoners. But this was the only proper position for sex slaves in such a magnificent palace.

With every inch of floor she covered, she felt more abject, her chest growing warm as she ran out of breath, her heart, as ever, beating too fast, too loudly.

The hall seemed to grow wider, higher. The drove of grooms flanked them. Yet still she could see arched doorways to the left and right and cavernous rooms tiled in the same beautifully colored marbles.

The grandeur and the solidity of the place worked their inevitable influence upon her. Tears stung her eyes. She felt small, utterly insignificant.

And yet there was something absolutely marvelous in the feeling. She was but a little thing in this vast world yet she seemed to have her proper place, more surely than she had had in the castle or even in the village.

Her nipples throbbed steadily in the fur-lined grip of the clamps, and occasional flashes of sunlight distracted her.

She felt a tightness in her throat, an overall weakness. The smell of incense, of cedar wood, of Eastern perfumes, suddenly enveloped her. And she realized that all was quiet in this world of richness and splendor; and the only sound was that of the slaves scurrying along and the thongs that licked them. Even the grooms made no sound, unless the singing of their silk robes was a sound. The silence seemed an extension of the palace, an extension of the dramatic power that was devouring them.

But as they progressed deeper and deeper into the labyrinth, as the escort of grooms dropped back a bit, leaving only the one little tormentor with his busy thong, and the procession went round corners and down even wider halls, Beauty began to see out of the corner of her eye some strange species of sculpture set in niches to adorn the corridor.

And, suddenly, she realized that these were not statues. They were living slaves fitted into the niches.

At last, she had to take a good look, and struggling not to lose her pace, she stared from right to left at these poor creatures.

Yes, men and women in alternation on both sides of the hall, standing mute in the niches. And each figure had been wrapped tightly from neck to toe in gold-tinted linen, except for the head held upright by a high ornamented brace and the naked sex organs left exposed in gilded glory.

Beauty looked down, trying to catch her breath. But she couldn't help looking up again immediately. And the spectacle became even clearer. The men had been bound with legs together, genitals thrust forward, and the women had been bound with legs apart, each leg completely wrapped and the sex left open.

All stood motionless, their long, shapely, gold neck

braces fixed to the wall in back by a rod that appeared to hold them securely. And some appeared to sleep with eyes closed, while others peered down at the floor, despite their slightly lifted faces.

Many were dark-skinned, as the grooms were—and showed the luxuriant black eyelashes of the desert peoples. Almost none were fair as Tristan and Beauty were. All had been gilded.

And in a silent panic, Beauty remembered the words of the Queen's emissary, who had spoken to them on the ship before they left their sovereign's land: "Though the Sultan has many slaves from his own land, you captive Princes and Princesses are a special delicacy of sorts, and a great curiosity."

"Then surely we can't be bound and placed in niches such as these," Beauty thought, "lost among dozens and dozens of others, merely to decorate a corridor."

But she could see the real truth. This Sultan possessed such a vast number of slaves that absolutely anything might befall Beauty and her fellow captives.

As she hurried along, her knees and hands getting a little sore from the marble, she continued to study these figures.

She could make out that the arms had been folded behind the back of each one, and that the gilded nipples too were exposed and sometimes clamped, and that each figure had his or her hair combed back to expose the ears which wore jeweled ornaments.

How tender the ears looked, how much like organs!

A wave of terror passed over Beauty. And she shuddered to think of what Tristan was feeling—Tristan, who so needed to love one Master. And what about Laurent? How would this look to him after the singular spectacle of the village Punishment Cross?

There came the sharp pull of the chains again. Her nipples itched. And the thong suddenly dallied between her legs, stroking her anus and the lips of her vagina.

"You little devil," she thought. Yet as the warm tingling

sensations passed all through her, she arched her back, forcing her buttocks up, and crawled with even more sprightly movements.

They were coming to a pair of doors. And with a shock, she saw that a male slave was fixed to one door and a female slave to the other. And these two were not wrapped, but rather completely naked. Gold bands around the foreheads, the legs, waist, neck, ankles, and wrists held each flat to the door with knees wide apart, the soles of the feet pressed together. The arms were fixed straight up over the head, palms outward. And the faces were still, eyes cast down, and the mouths held artfully arranged bunches of grapes and leaves that were gilded like the flesh so that the creatures looked very much like sculptures.

But the doors were opened. The slaves passed these two silent sentinels in a flash.

And the pace slowed as Beauty found herself in an immense courtyard, full of potted palm trees and flower beds bordered in variegated marble.

Sunlight dappled the tiles in front of her. The perfume of flowers suddenly refreshed her. She glimpsed blossoms of all hues, and for one paralyzing instant she saw that the vast garden was filled with gilded and caged slaves as well as other beautiful creatures fixed in dramatic positions atop marble pedestals.

Beauty was made to stop. The leashes were taken from her mouth. And she saw her groom gather up her own leashes as he stood beside her. The thong played between her thighs, tickling her, forcing her legs a little apart. Then a hand smoothed her hair tenderly. She saw Tristan to her left and Laurent to her right, and she realized that the slaves had been positioned in a loose circle.

But all at once the great crowd of grooms began to laugh and talk as though released from some enforced silence. They closed in on the slaves, hands pointing, gesturing.

The slipper was on Beauty's neck again, and it forced

her head down until her lips touched the marble. She could see out of the corner of her eye that Laurent and the others were bent in the same lowly posture.

In a wash of rainbow colors the silk robes of the grooms surrounded them. The din of conversation was worse than the noise of the crowd in the streets. Beauty knelt shuddering as she felt hands on her back and on her hair, the thong pushing her legs even wider. Silk-robed grooms stood between her and Tristan, between her and Laurent.

But suddenly a silence fell that utterly shattered the last of Beauty's fragile composure.

The grooms withdrew as if swept aside. And there was no sound except the chattering of birds, and the tinkling of wind chimes.

Then Beauty heard the soft sound of slippered feet approaching.

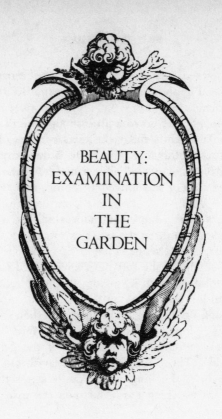

BEAUTY:
EXAMINATION
IN
THE
GARDEN

I T WAS NOT one man who
entered the garden, but a group of three. Yet two stood
back in deference to one who advanced alone and slowly.

In the tense silence, Beauty saw his feet and the hem
of his robe as he moved about the circle. Richer fabric,
and velvet slippers with high upturned curling toes, each
decorated by a dangling ruby. He moved with slow steps,
as if he was surveying everything carefully.

Beauty held her breath as he approached her. She
squinted slightly as the toe of the wine-colored slipper
touched her cheek, and then rested upon the back of her
neck, then followed the line of her spine to its tip.

She shivered, unable to help herself, her moan sounding loud and impertinent to her own ears. But there was no reprimand.

She thought she heard a little laugh. And then a sentence spoken gently made the tears spring to her eyes again. How soothing was the voice, how unusually musical. Maybe the unintelligible language made it seem more lyrical. Yet she longed to understand the words spoken.

Of course, she had not been addressed. The words had been spoken to one of the other two men, yet the voice stirred her, almost seduced her.

Quite suddenly she felt the chains pulled hard. Her nipples stiffened with a tingling that sent its tentacles down into her groin instantly.

She knelt up, unsure, frightened, and then was pulled to her feet, nipples burning, her face flaming.

For one moment the immensity of the garden impressed her. The bound slaves, the lavish blooms, the blue sky above shockingly clear, the large assemblage of the grooms watching her. And then the man standing before her.

What must she do with her hands? She put them behind her neck, and stood staring at the tiled floor, with only the vaguest picture of the Master who faced her.

He was much taller than the little boys—in fact, he was a slender giant of a man, elegantly proportioned, and he seemed older by virtue of his air of command. And it was he who had pulled the chains himself and still held the handles.

Quite suddenly he passed them from his right hand to his left. And with the right hand, he slapped the undersides of Beauty's breasts, startling her. She bit down on her cry. But the warm yielding of her body surprised her. She throbbed with the desire to be touched, slapped again, for an even more annihilating violence.

And in the moment of trying to collect her wits, she had glimpsed the man's dark wavy hair, not quite shoulder length, and his eyes, so black they seemed drawn in ink, with large shining beads of jet for the irises.

"How gorgeous these desert people can be," she thought. And her dreams in the hold of the ship suddenly rose to mock her. Love him? Love this one who is but a servant like the others?

Yet the face burnt through her fear and agitation. It seemed an impossible face suddenly. It was almost innocent.

The ringing slaps came again, and she stepped back before she could stop herself. Her breasts were flooded with warmth. At once, her little groom thrashed her disobedient legs with the thong. She steadied herself, sorry for the failure.

The voice spoke again and it was as light as before, as melodious and almost caressing. But it sent the little grooms into a flurry of activity.

She felt soft, silken fingers on her ankles and on her wrists, and before she realized what was happening, she was lifted, her legs raised at right angles to her body and spread wide by the grooms who held her, her arms forced straight up in the air, her back and head supported firmly.

She shivered spasmodically, her thighs aching, her sex brutally exposed. And then she felt another pair of hands lift her head, and she peered right into the eyes of the mysterious giant of a Master, who smiled at her radiantly.

O, too handsome he was. Instantly, she looked away, her lids fluttering. His eyes were tilted upwards at the outsides, which gave him a slightly devilish look, and his mouth was large and extremely kissable. But, for all the innocence of the expression, a ferocious spirit seemed to emanate from him. She sensed menace in him. She could feel it in his touch. And, with her legs held wide apart as they were, she passed into a silent panic.

As if to confirm his power, the Master quickly slapped her face, causing her to whimper before she could stop herself. The hand rose again, this time slapping her right cheek, and then the left again, until she was suddenly crying audibly.

"But what have I done?" she thought. And through a mist of tears she saw only curiosity in his face. He was studying her. It wasn't innocence. She had judged wrongly. It was merely fascination with what he was doing that flamed in him.

"So it's a test," she tried to tell herself. "But how do I pass or fail?" And shuddering, she saw the hands rising again.

He tilted her head back and opened her mouth, touching her tongue and her teeth. Chills passed over her. She felt her whole body convulse in the hands of the grooms. The probing fingers touched her eyelids, her eyebrows. They wiped at her tears, which were spilling down her face as she stared at the blue sky above her.

And then she felt the hands at her exposed sex. The thumbs went into her vagina, and she was pulled impossibly wide as her hips rocked forward, shaming her.

It seemed she would burst with orgasm, that she couldn't contain it. But was this forbidden? And how would she be punished? She tossed her head from side to side, struggling to command herself. But the fingers were so gentle, so soft, yet firm as they opened her. If they touched her clitoris, she would be lost, incapable of restraint.

But mercifully, they let her go, tugging at her pubic hair, and only pinching her lips together quickly.

In a daze, she bowed her head, the sight of her nakedness thoroughly unnerving her. She saw the new Master turn and snap his fingers. And through the tangle of her hair she saw Elena hoisted instantly by the grooms just as she had been.

Elena struggled for composure, her pink sex wet and gaping through its wreath of brown hair, the long delicate muscles of her thighs twitching. Beauty watched in terror as the Master proceeded with the same examination.

Elena's high, sharply angled breasts heaved as the Master played with her mouth, her teeth. But when the slaps came Elena was utterly silent. And the look on the Master's face further confused Beauty.

How passionately interested he seemed, how intent upon what he was doing. Not even the cruel Master of Postulants at the castle had seemed so dedicated as this one. And his charm was considerable. The rich velvet robe was well tailored to his straight back and shoulders. His hands had a beguiling grace of movement as he spread Elena's red pubic mouth and the poor Princess pumped her hips disgracefully.

At the sight of Elena's sex growing full and wet and obviously hungry, Beauty's long starvation at sea made her feel desperate. And when the Master smiled and smoothed Elena's long hair back from her forehead, examining her eyes, Beauty felt raging jealousy.

"No, it would be ghastly to love any of them," she thought. She couldn't give her heart. She tried not to look anymore. Her own legs throbbed, the grooms holding them back as firmly as ever. And her own sex swelled unbearably.

But there were more spectacles for her. The Master came back to Tristan. And now he was lifted into the air, and his legs spread wide in the same manner. Out of the corner of her eye, Beauty saw that the little grooms struggled under Tristan's weight, and Tristan's beautiful face was crimson with humiliation as his hard and thrusting organ was examined closely by the Master.

The Master's fingers played with the foreskin, played with the shiny tip, squeezing out of it a single drop of glistening moisture. Beauty could feel the tension in Tristan's limbs. But she dared not look up to see his face again as the Master reached to examine it.

In a blur she saw the Master's face, saw the enormous ink-black eyes, and the hair swept back over the ear to reveal a tiny gold ring stabbing the ear lobe.

She heard him slapping Tristan, and she closed her eyes tight as Tristan finally moaned, the slaps seeming to resound through the garden.

When she opened her eyes again it was because the Master had laughed softly to himself as he passed in front of her. And she saw his hand rise almost absently to squeeze her left breast lightly. The tears sprang to her eyes, her mind struggling to understand the outcome of his examinations, to push away the fact that he drew her more than any being who had hitherto claimed her.

Now, to her right and slightly in front of her, it was Laurent who must be raised up for the Master's scrutiny. And, as the enormous Prince was lifted, she heard the Master make some quick verbal outburst which brought laughter from all the other grooms immediately. No one needed to translate it for her. Laurent was too powerfully built, his organ was too splendid.

And she could see now that it was fully erect, well trained as it was, and the sight of the heavily muscled thighs spread wide apart brought back to her delirious memories of the Punishment Cross. She tried not to look at the enormous scrotum, but she could not help herself.

And it seemed that the Master had been moved by these superior endowments to a new excitement. He smacked Laurent hard with the back of his hand several times in amazingly rapid succession. The enormous torso writhed, the grooms struggling to keep it still.

And then the Master removed the clamps, letting them drop to the ground, and pressed both of Laurent's nipples as Laurent moaned loudly.

But something else was happening. Beauty saw it. Laurent had looked at the Master directly. He had done it more than once. Their eyes had met. And now as his nipples were squeezed again, very hard it seemed, the Prince stared right at the Master.

"No, Laurent," she thought desperately. "Don't tempt them. It won't be the glory of the Punishment Cross here. It will be those corridors and miserable oblivion." Yet it absolutely fascinated her that Laurent was so bold.

The Master went round him and the grooms who held him, and now he took the leather thong from one of the others and spanked Laurent's nipples over and over again. Laurent couldn't keep quiet, though he had turned his head away. His neck was corded with tension, his limbs trembling.

And the Master seemed as curious, as fastened upon his test as ever. He made a gesture to one of the others. And, as Beauty watched, a long gilded leather glove was brought to the Master.

It was beautifully worked with intricate designs all the way down the leather length of the arm to the large cuff, the whole gleaming as if it had been covered in a salve or unguent.

As the Master drew the glove over his hand and down his arm to the elbow, Beauty felt herself flooded with heat and excitement. The Master's eyes were almost child-like in their studiousness, the mouth irresistible as it smiled, the grace of the body as he approached Laurent now entrancing.

He moved his left hand to the back of Laurent's head, cradling it, his fingers curled in Laurent's hair as the Prince stared straight upward. And with the gloved hand, the right hand, he pushed upward slowly between Laurent's open legs, two fingers entering his body first, as Beauty stared unabashedly.

Laurent's breathing grew hoarse, rapid. His face darkened. The fingers had disappeared inside his anus, and now it seemed the whole hand worked its way into him.

The grooms moved in a little on all sides. And Beauty could see that Tristan and Elena watched with equal attention.

The Master, meanwhile, seemed to see nothing but Laurent. He was staring right at Laurent's face, and Laurent's face was twisted in pleasure and pain as the hand moved its way deeper and deeper into his body. It was in beyond the wrist, and Laurent's limbs were no longer shuddering. They were frozen. A long, whistling sigh passed through his teeth.

The Master lifted Laurent's chin with the thumb of his

left hand. He bent over until his face was very close to Laurent's. And in a long, tense silence the arm moved ever upward into Laurent as the Prince seemed to swoon, his cock stiff and still, the clear moisture leaking from it in the tiniest droplets.

Beauty's whole body tightened, relaxed, and again she felt herself on the verge of orgasm. As she tried to drive it back, she felt herself grow limp and weak, and all the hands holding her were in fact making love to her, caressing her.

The Master brought his right arm forward without withdrawing it from Laurent. And in so doing, he tilted the Prince's pelvis upward, further revealing the enormous balls, and the glistening gold leather as it widened the pink ring of the anus impossibly.

A sudden cry came out of Laurent. A hoarse gasp that seemed a cry for mercy. And the Master held him motionless, their lips nearly touching. The Master's left hand released Laurent's head and moved over his face, parting his lips with one finger. And then the tears spilled from Laurent's eyes.

And very quickly, the Master withdrew his arm and peeled off the glove, casting it aside, as Laurent hung in the grasp of the grooms, his head down, his face reddened.

The Master made some little remark, and again the grooms laughed agreeably. One of the grooms replaced the nipple clamps, and Laurent grimaced. The Master immediately gestured for Laurent to be placed on the floor, and the chains of Laurent's leashes were suddenly fixed to a gold ring on the back of the Master's slipper.

"O, no, this beast can't take him away from us!" Beauty thought. But that was the mere surface of her thoughts. She was terrified that it was Laurent and Laurent alone who had been chosen by the Master.

But they were all being put down. And suddenly Beauty was on hands and knees, neck pressed low by the soft velvety sole of the slipper, and she realized that Tristan and Elena were beside her and all three of them were being pulled forward by their nipple chains and whipped by the thongs as they moved out of the garden.

She saw the hem of the Master's robe to her right, and behind him the figure of Laurent struggling to keep up with the Master's strides, the chains from his nipples anchoring him to the Master's foot, his brown hair veiling his face mercifully.

Where were Dmitri and Rosalynd? Why had they been discarded? Would one of the other men who had come in with the Master take them?

She couldn't know. And the corridor seemed endless.

But she didn't really care about Dmitri and Rosalynd. All she cared about truly was that she and Tristan and Laurent and Elena were together. And, of course, the fact that he, this mysterious Master, this tall and impossibly elegant creature, was moving right alongside of her.

His embroidered robe brushed her shoulder as he moved ahead, Laurent struggling to keep pace with him.

The thongs licked at her backside, licked at her pubis, as she rushed after them.

At last, they came to another pair of doors, and the thongs drove them through into a large lamp-lighted chamber. She was bid to stop by the firm pressure of a slipper on her neck once more, and then she realized that all the grooms had withdrawn and the door had been shut behind them.

The only sound was the anxious breathing of the Princes and Princesses. The Master moved past Beauty to the door. A bolt was thrown, a key turned. Silence.

Then she heard the melodious voice again, soft and low, and this time it was speaking, in charmingly accented syllables, her own language:

"Well, my darlings, you may all come forward and kneel up before me. I have much to say to you."

BEAUTY: MYSTERIOUS MASTER

A TUMULTUOUS SHOCK to be spoken to.

At once the group of slaves obeyed, coming round to kneel up in front of the Master, the golden leashes trailing on the floor. Even Laurent was freed now from the Master's slipper and took his place with the others.

As soon as they were all still, kneeling with their hands clasped to the backs of their necks, the Master said:

"Look at me."

Beauty did not hesitate. She looked up into his face and found it as appealing and baffling now as it had been in the garden. It was a better-proportioned face than she had realized, the full and agreeable mouth finely shaped, the nose long and delicate, the eyes well spaced and radiantly dominant. But, again, it was the spirit that magnetized her.

As he looked from one to another of the captives, Beauty could feel the excitement coursing through the little group, feel her own sudden elation.

"O, yes, a splendid creature," she thought. And memories of the Crown Prince who had brought Beauty to the Queen's land and of her crude Captain of the Guard in the village were suddenly threatened with complete dissolution.

"Precious slaves," he said, eyes fixing on her for a brief, electric moment. "You know where you are and why you are here. The soldiers have brought you by force to serve your Lord and Master." So mellifluous the voice, the face so immediately warm. "And you know that you will serve always in silence. Dumb little creatures you are to the grooms who attend you. But I, the Sultan's steward, cherish no such illusions that sensuality obliterates high reason."

"Of course not," Beauty thought. But she didn't dare to voice her thoughts. Her interest in the man was deepening rapidly and dangerously.

"Those few slaves I pick," he said, his eyes traveling again, "those I choose to perfect and offer to the Sultan's Court are always apprised of my aims, and my demands, and the dangers of my temper. But only in the secrecy of this chamber. In this chamber I want my methods to be understood. My expectations to be fully clarified."

He drew closer, towering over Beauty, and his hand reached for her breast, squeezing it as he had done before, just a little too hard, the hot shiver passing down into her sex immediately. With the other hand he stroked the side of Laurent's face, thumb grazing the lip as Beauty turned to watch, utterly forgetting herself.

"That you will not do, Princess," he said, and at once he slapped her hard and she bowed her head, her face stinging. "You will continue to look at me until I tell you otherwise."

Beauty's tears rose at once. How could she have been so foolish?

But there was no anger in his voice, only a soft indulgence. Tenderly, he lifted her chin. She stared at him through her tears.

"Do you know what I want of you, Beauty? Answer me."

"No, Master," she said quickly. Her voice alien to her.

"That you be perfect, for me!" he said gently, the voice seeming so full of reason, of logic. "This I want of all of you. That you be nonpareils in this vast wilderness of slaves in which you could be lost like a handful of diamonds in the ocean. That you shine by virtue not merely of your compliance but by virtue of your intense and particular passion. You will lift yourself up from the masses of slaves who surround you. You will seduce your Masters and Mistresses by a lustre that throws others into eclipse! Do you understand me!"

Beauty struggled not to sob in her anxiousness, her eyes on his, as if she could not look away even if she wanted to. But never had she felt such an overwhelming desire to obey. The urgency of his voice was wholly different from the tone of those who had educated her at the castle or chastised her in the village. She felt as if she was losing the very form of her personality. She was slowly melting.

"And this you will do for me," he said, his voice growing even more soft, more persuasive, more resonant. "You will do it as much for me as for your royal Lords. Because I desire it of you." He closed his hand around Beauty's throat. "Let me hear you speak again, little one. In my chambers, you will speak to me to tell me that you wish to please me."

"Yes, Master," she said. And her voice once again seemed strange to her, full of feelings she hadn't truly known before. The warm fingers caressed her throat, seemed to caress the words she spoke, coax them out of her and shape the tone of them.

"You see, there are hundreds of grooms," he said, narrowing his eyes as he looked away from her to the others, the hand still clasping her. "Hundreds charged with preparing succulent little partridges for Our Lord the Sultan, or fine muscular young bucks and stags for him to play with. But I, Lexius, am the only Chief Steward of the Grooms. And I *must* choose and present the finest of all playthings."

Even this was not said with anger or urgency.

But as he looked again at Beauty, his eyes widened with intensity. The semblance of anger terrified her. But the gentle fingers massaged the back of her neck, the thumb stroking her throat in front.

"Yes, Master," she whispered suddenly.

"Yes, absolutely, my little love," he said, crooning to her. But then he became grave, and his voice became small, as if to command greater respect by speaking its words simply.

"It is absolutely out of the question that you do not distinguish yourselves, that after one glimpse of you the great luminaries of this house do not reach out to pluck you like ripe fruit, that they do not compliment me upon your loveliness, your heat, your silent, ravening passion."

Beauty's tears flowed again down her cheeks.

He withdrew his hand slowly. She felt suddenly cold, abandoned. A little sob caught in her throat, but he had heard it.

Lovingly, almost sadly, he smiled at her. His face was shadowed and strangely vulnerable.

"Divine little Princess," he whispered. "We are lost, you see, unless they notice us."

"Yes, Master," she whispered. She would have done anything to have him touch her again, hold her.

And the rich undertone of sadness in him startled her, enchanted her. O, if only she could kiss his feet.

And, in a sudden impulse she did. She went down on

the marble and touched her lips to his slipper. She did it over and over. And she wondered that the word "lost" had so delighted her.

As she rose again, clasping her hands behind her neck, she lowered her eyes in resignation. She should be slapped for what she had done. The room—its white marble, its gilded doors—was like so many facets of light. Why did this man produce this effect in her? Why. . . .

"Lost." The word set up its musical echo in her soul.

The Master's long, dark fingers came out and touched her lips. And she saw him smiling.

"You will find me hard, you will find me impossibly hard," he said gently. "But now you know why. You understand now. You belong to Lexius, the Chief Steward. You musn't fail him. Speak. All of you."

He was answered by a chorus of "Yes, Master." Beauty heard even the voice of Laurent, the runaway, answering just as promptly.

"And now I shall tell you another truth, little ones," he said. "You may belong to the most High Lord, to the Sultana, to the Beautiful and Virtuous Royal Wives of the Harem. . . ." He paused, as if to let his words sink in. "But you belong just as truly to me!" he said, "as to anyone! And I revel in every punishment I inflict. I do. It is my nature, as it is yours to serve—my nature, when it comes to slaves, to eat from the very same dish as my Masters. Tell me that you understand me."

"Yes, Master!"

The words came out of Beauty like an explosion of breath. She was dazed with all he had said to her.

She watched him intently as he turned now to Elena, and her soul shrank, though she did not turn her head a fraction of an inch or move her steady gaze from him. Yet still, she could see that he was kneading Elena's fine breasts. How Beauty envied those high, jutting breasts! Nipples the color of apricot. And it hurt her further that Elena moaned so bewitchingly.

"Yes, yes, exactly," said the Master, the voice as intimate as it had been with Beauty. "You will writhe at my touch. You will writhe at the touch of all your Masters and Mistresses. You will give up your soul to those who so much as glance at you. You will burn like lights in the dark!"

Again a chorus of "Yes, Master."

"Did you see the multitude of slaves who make up the ornaments of this house?"

"Yes, Master," from all of them.

"Will you distinguish yourselves from the gilded herd by passion, by obedience, by putting into your silent compliance a deafening thunder of feeling!"

"Yes, Master."

"But now, we shall begin. You will be properly purified. And then to work immediately. The Court knows that new slaves have come. You are awaited. And your lips are once again sealed. Not under the sternest punishment are you to make a sound with them parted. Unless otherwise commanded you crawl on hands and knees, buttocks up and forehead near to the very ground, almost touching it."

He walked down the silent row. He stroked and examined each slave again, lingering for a long time on Laurent. Then with an abrupt gesture, he ordered Laurent to the door. Laurent crawled as he had been told to do, his forehead grazing the marble. The Master touched the bolt with the thong. Laurent at once slid it back.

The Master pulled the nearby bell cord.

BEAUTY: THE RITES OF PURIFICATION

A<small>T ONCE</small> the young grooms appeared and silently took the slaves in hand, quickly forcing them on hands and knees through another doorway into a large, warm bathing place.

Amid delicate tropical flowering plants and lazing palms, Beauty saw steam rising from the shallow pools in the marble floor and smelled the fragrance of herbs and spiced perfumes.

But she was spirited past all of this into a tiny private chamber. And there she was made to kneel with legs wide apart over a deep, rounded basin in the floor through which water ran fast from hidden founts and down the drain continuously.

Her forehead was once again lowered to the floor, her hands clasped upon the back of her neck. The air was warm and moist around her. And immediately the warm water and soft scrub brushes went to work upon her.

It was all done with much greater speed than at the bath in the castle. And within moments, she was perfumed and oiled and her sex was pumping with expectation as soft towels caressed her.

But she was not told to get up. On the contrary, she was bid to be still by a firm pat of the hand on her head, and she heard strange sounds above her.

Then she felt a metal nozzle entering her vagina. Immediately her juices flowed at the long-awaited sensation of being entered, no matter how awkwardly. But she knew this was merely for cleansing—it had been done other times to her—and she welcomed the steady fount of water that suddenly gushed into her with delicious pressure.

But what startled her was the unfamiliar touch of fingers on her anus. She was being oiled there, and her body tensed, even as the craving in her was doubled. Hands quickly took hold of the soles of her feet to keep her firmly in place. She heard the grooms laughing softly and commenting to one another.

Then something small and hard entered her anus and forced its way in deep as she gave a little gasp, pressing her lips tightly together. Her muscles contracted to fight the little invasion, but this only sent new ripples of pleasure through her. The flush of water into her vagina had stopped. And what happened now was unmistakable: A stream of warm water was being pumped into her rectum. And it did not wash back out of her as did the douching fluids. It filled her with ever-increasing force, and a strong hand pressed her buttocks together as if bidding her not to release the water.

It seemed a whole new region of her body came to life, a part of her that had never been punished or even really examined. The force of the flow grew stronger and stronger. Her mind protested that she could not be invaded in this final way, that she could not be rendered so helpless.

She felt she would burst if she did not let go. She wanted to expel the little nozzle, the water. But she dared not, she could not. This must happen to her now and she accepted it. It was part of this realm of more refined pleasures and manners. And how dare she protest? She began to whimper softly, caught between a new pleasure and a new sense of violation.

But the most enervating and taxing part was yet to come, and she dreaded it. Just when she thought she could bear no more, that she was full to overflowing, she was lifted upright by her arms, and her legs were pulled even wider apart, the little nozzle in her anus plugging her and tormenting her.

The grooms smiled down at her as they held her arms. And she looked up fearfully, shyly, afraid of the utter shame of the sudden release that was inevitable. Then the nozzle was slipped out, and her buttocks were spread apart, and her bowels quickly emptied.

She squeezed her eyes shut. She felt warm water poured over her private parts, front and back, heard the loud full rush in the basin. She was overcome with something like shame. But it wasn't shame. All privacy and choice had been taken from her. Not even this act was to be hers alone anymore, she understood. And the chills passing through her body with every spasm of release locked her into a delirious sense of helplessness. She gave herself over to those who commanded her, her body limp and unprotesting. She flexed her muscles to help with the emptying, to complete it.

"Yes, to be purified," she thought. And she experienced a great undeniable relief, the awareness of her body cleansing itself becoming exquisite as she shuddered.

The water continued to flow over her, over her buttocks, her belly, down into the basin, washing away all the waste. And she was dissolving into an overall ecstasy that seemed a form of climax in itself. But it wasn't. It was just beyond her reach, the climax. And as she felt her mouth open in a low gasp, she rocked back and forth on the brink, her body pleading silently and vainly with those who held her. All the invisible knots were gone from her spirit. She was without the slightest strength, and utterly dependent upon the grooms to support her.

They stroked her hair back from her forehead. The warm water washed her again and again.

And then she saw, as she dared to open her eyes, that the Master himself was there. He was standing in the doorway of the room and he was smiling at her. He came forward and he lifted her up out of this moment of indescribable weakness.

She stared at him, stunned that it was he who held her as the others covered her in towels again.

She felt as defenseless as she had ever been, and it seemed an impossible reward that he led her out of the little chamber. If she could only embrace him, only find the cock under his robes, only. . . . The elation of being near him escalated immediately into pain.

"O, please, we have been starved and starved," she wanted to say. But she only looked down demurely, feeling his fingers on her arm. That was the old Beauty speaking the words in her head, wasn't it? The new Beauty wanted to say only the word "Master."

And to think that only moments ago she had been considering love for him. Why, she loved him already. She could breathe the fragrance of his skin, almost hear his heart beat as he turned her and directed her forward. His fingers clasped her neck as tightly as they had before.

Where was he taking her?

The others were gone. She was set on one of the tables. She shivered in happiness and disbelief as he himself began to rub more perfumed oil into her. But this time there was to be no covering of gold paint. Her bare flesh would shine under the oil. And he pinched her cheeks with both hands to give them color as she rested back on her heels, her eyes wet from the steam and from her tears, watching him dreamily.

He seemed deeply absorbed in his work, his dark eyebrows knit, his mouth half open. And, when he applied gold leash clamps to her nipples, he pressed them tight for an instant with a little tightening of his lips that made her feel the gesture all the more deeply. She arched her back and breathed deeply. And he kissed her forehead, letting his lips linger, letting his hair brush her cheek.

"Lexius," she thought. It was a beautiful name.

When he brushed her hair it was almost with angry, fierce strokes, and chills consumed her. He brushed it up and wound it on top of her head. And she glimpsed the pearl pins that he used to fasten it. Her neck was naked now, like the rest of her.

As he put the pearls through her ear lobes, she studied the smooth dark skin of his face, the rise and fall of his dark lashes. He was like a finely polished thing, his fingernails buffed to look like glass, his teeth perfect. And how deftly yet gently he handled her.

It was over too fast, and yet not fast enough. How long could she writhe, dreaming of orgasm? She cried because there had to be some release, and when he put her on the floor her body ached as never before, it seemed.

Gently, he pulled the leashes. She bent down, forehead to the ground, as she crept forward, and it seemed to her that she had never been more completely the slave.

If she had any ability left to think, as she followed him out of the bath, she thought that she could no longer remember a time when she had worn clothes, walked and talked with those who did, commanded others. Her nakedness and helplessness were natural to her, more natural here in these spacious marble halls than anywhere else, and she knew without a doubt that she would love this Master utterly.

She could have said it was an act of will, that after talking with Tristan she had simply decided. But there was too much that was unique about the man, even in the delicate way that he himself had groomed her. And the place itself, it was like magic to her. And she had thought she loved the harshness of the village!

Why must he give her away now? Take her to others? But it was wrong to question. . . .

As they moved along the corridor together, she heard for the first time the soft breathing and sighs of the slaves who decorated the niches on either side of them. It seemed a muted chorus of perfect devotion.

And a confusion of all sense of time and place overcame her.

BEAUTY:
THE FIRST
TEST
OF
OBEDIENCE

W HEN THEY paused at a
door, she dared to kiss his slipper. And for this he rewarded her by touching her hair and whispering under
his breath:

"Little pet, you please me very much. But now comes
the first real test. See that you outshine those before
you."

Her heart skipped a beat. And when she heard him
knock on the door before her, she held her breath altogether.

In a moment, the door opened. Two male servants
admitted her and the Master. And again, she was moving

fast across a polished floor, and a dim sound coming from a distance distracted her.

Women's voices, laughter. It came in waves. It froze her soul suddenly.

Her Master had stopped her with a little pull on the leashes. He was talking pleasantly with the two men. How civilized it all sounded. As if she didn't kneel there with the clamps on her nipples, her hair swept up to expose her naked neck, her face burning.

And how many such slaves had these men seen? What was another without a name, remarkable only perhaps for the unusual blond coloring?

But the little conversation was finished. The Master gave a jerk of the chains again and led Beauty to a wall, where suddenly she saw a small opening before her.

It was a passage, but one that could not be entered except on hands and knees, and at the far end she could see bright sunlight. The feminine laughter and talk echoed through the passage loudly.

She shrank back, frightened of the passage, frightened of the voices. It was the harem. It had to be. What had he called it, the Harem of Beautiful and Virtuous Royal Wives? And she must enter it this way, alone, without the Master? Like a little beast released into an arena?

Why had he chosen this for her? Why? She was suddenly paralyzed with fear. She feared the women more than she could have ever explained. After all, they weren't Princesses of her own class, or hardworking Mistresses who would treat her harshly of necessity. She had no idea really what they were, except they were different from anything she had ever known. What would they do to her, expect of her?

It seemed the most horrid of humiliations that she would be given over to them—women who were kept veiled and secluded for the pleasure of their husband. Yet they seemed more dangerous even than the men of the palace. She could not fathom it.

She shrank back even farther, and she heard the two

men laugh above her. The Master at once bent down and placed the two soft leather handles of her leashes into her mouth. He adjusted her head, put a little hair in place, pinched her cheek.

She tried not to cry.

And then firmly and confidently he pushed her buttocks forward, his hand very strong and hot against the thin streaks of warmth left by the weak and delicate thong, and she struggled to obey, sobbing silently with the little gag of the handles in her teeth.

There was no choice. Had he not told her what was expected? And, once she entered the passage, she could not stop. It would be too utterly disgraceful.

But just when her courage did fail her again, when a particularly loud volley of noise rolled through the passage, she felt his lips against her cheek. He was kneeling beside her himself. He slid his hand beneath her breasts, gathering them tenderly in his long fingers. And he whispered in her ear.

"Do not fail me, lovely one."

And breaking from the warmth of his touch, she went at once into the opening. Her cheeks were stinging with humiliation as she realized she carried her own leashes in her mouth, that she was crawling of her own will through this hollow passage of polished stone—polished by other hands and knees, surely—that she must emerge in this abject manner.

But faster and faster she moved, towards the light and towards the voices. And there was some faint hope in her that, no matter how dreadful this might be, the passion in her might somehow be used to advantage. Her sex swelled, pumped with life. If only there weren't so many, so very many. . . . When had she ever been given to so many?

Within seconds she emerged into the light.

She crept out onto the floor and into the dizzying ring of chatter and laughter.

On all sides bare feet approached her. And the long

veils that fell down around them were gossamer and shimmering, the sunlight exploding on golden anklets and toe rings set with emeralds and rubies.

Beauty crouched low, fearful of the commotion, the frenzy, but instantly a dozen small hands had hold of her and lifted her until she was standing. All around her were gorgeous women. She glimpsed olive-skinned faces with kohl-rimmed eyes, tresses tumbling over bare shoulders. The billowing pantaloons they wore were almost transparent, only the lower part of the crotch covered in darker, thicker fabric. And the fitted bodices of heavier silk only thinly veiled their full breasts, their dark nipples. But the most enticing parts of their costumes were the broad tight girdles that seemed to imprison their tiny waists, and to rein in all the sensuality that smoldered beneath the colorful diaphanous wrapping.

Beautifully shaped arms they had, enhanced with winding snake bracelets, and there were rings on their fingers as well as their toes, and here, a brilliant glittering jewel embedded behind the delicate curve of a tiny nostril.

How enchantingly lovely these creatures were—savage-eyed counterparts of the lean and graceful men. But this made them seem all the more treacherous and frightening to Beauty. They looked wildly licentious compared to the heavily draped women of Europe. Ready for the bed, they seemed, and yet Beauty felt purely, stunningly naked as she stood at their mercy.

They closed in upon her.

Her wrists were pinioned behind her back, her head turned this way, her legs pried apart, as riffs of laughter and shrieking deafened her.

And everywhere she glanced she saw the large black eyes, thick eyelashes, long curls unwinding on half-naked shoulders.

But there was not a moment even for her to get her bearings. She winced and shivered as they poked at her ears, touched her breasts, her belly.

And she was panting and sobbing under her breath as

the group rushed her forward, their long pantaloons tickling her legs, into the center of the room where the sunlight poured in upon heaps of silk-covered pillows and low, padded couches.

It was an opulent pleasure den, this room. Why did they need her to torment?

But immediately, she was thrown down on her back upon one of these couches, her arms stretched above her. And the women gathered on their knees, surrounding her. Once again, her legs were pried apart, and a cushion was thrust under her buttocks to raise her for examination.

She was as powerless as she had been in the hands of the grooms before, but the feminine faces that peered down at her were full of wild jubilation. Excited words flew back and forth. Fingers stroked her breasts. She looked up into the expectant eyes, panic-stricken, unable to shield herself.

And as her legs were turned out, knees pressed flat, she felt fingers pulling at her sex, once again opening it, widening it.

She struggled to be quiet, but her tortured sex was brimming. As she pumped her hips on the scarlet cushion, the women only squealed louder. She could not count the hands that grasped her inner thighs, each stroke of a finger further maddening her. Long hair spilled down on her naked breasts, on her belly.

And it seemed that even the light lyrical voices stroked her and heightened her suffering.

But why did they stare at her, she wondered. Had they never seen a woman's organs before? Had they never seen their own organs? Useless to try to understand. Those who could not get a close look stood up and leaned over the shoulders of the others.

And as she writhed in the hands that held her, she saw that some one of them had placed a mirror before her sex, and the reflection of her private, secret parts shocked her.

But now one of the women forced aside the others,

and, as she took hold of Beauty's nether lips, she peeled them back harshly. Beauty twisted and arched her back. She felt she was being turned inside out. And she moaned as the fingers pinched at her clitoris, folding back the little hood of flesh that covered it. Beauty could hardly control herself any longer. She sobbed, and her hips rode up off the silk of the pillow and remained suspended in the air by virtue of the tension in her.

The crowd of women seemed to grow quieter, more fascinated. Suddenly one of the wives took Beauty's left breast in her hand and removed the little gold clamp, and scratched at the marks left in the skin and then played with the nipple roughly.

Beauty shut her eyes. Her body had no weight. It had become pure sensation. She worked her limbs in the hands that held her, but this was not true motion. It was pure feeling.

She felt the woman's hair fall down on her naked chest. Then another woman had taken the clamp from her right breast, and she felt hot playful fingers examining her there also.

Meanwhile the hand that widened her vagina continued to probe, to feel beneath the clitoris, to pull upon it. The juices exploded inside, and Beauty felt them trickling out, and she felt the hot fingers examining the moisture.

Suddenly a wet mouth closed on her left breast. And another on her right. And both women sucked hard as the fingers pinched at her pubic lips. And Beauty was no longer conscious of anything but exquisite desire rolling up towards the long-awaited orgasm.

At last, she went over the edge, her face and breasts throbbing with fire, and she felt her hips go rigid in the air, her vagina convulsing on the emptiness, grasping for the fingers that stroked her clitoris as she felt it grow harder and harder.

She cried out—a long hoarse cry. And the orgasm went on and on, the mouths suckling her, the fingers stroking her.

It seemed she would float forever in this sea of tenderness, this sea of delicate violation. And as she sobbed shamelessly, not conscious now of any injunction to be quiet, she felt a mouth close on hers, she felt the cries taken into another.

Yes, yes, she said mutely with her whole body, the woman's tongue going into her mouth, her breasts exploding as they were bitten and licked, her hips lunging as if to swallow the probing fingers.

And then as it overflowed, as it passed out of her with a thousand rippling reverberations, she felt herself embraced by the softest arms, kissed by the softest lips, the long delicate tresses veiling her.

She breathed deeply, whispered aloud, "Yes, Yes, I love you, love you all." But the mouth was still kissing her, and no one heard these words; they, like all else, were mere glorious, sensual reverberation.

But her Mistresses were not satisfied. They would not let her rest.

They took the pins out of her hair and they lifted her.

"Where are you taking me?" she cried out before she could stop herself. She looked up, trying frantically to catch the lips that had just withdrawn from her mouth. But she saw only smiling faces.

She was carried across the chamber, her body shocked and throbbing still, her breasts aching to be suckled again.

And in a moment, she saw the answer to her question. A finely made bronze statue stood gleaming in the center of the garden: the statue of a god, it seemed, with knees bent and arms outstretched to the side, and head thrown back in laughter. From its naked loins jutted a cock, and Beauty knew that they meant to impale her on it.

She almost laughed in her happiness. She felt herself placed on the hard, smooth, sun-warmed bronze, dozens of soft little hands supporting her. She felt the cock enter her wet vagina, her legs winding over the bronze thighs, her arms up to go around the neck of the deity. The cock filled her, stabbed at the mouth of her uterus sending a new contraction of pleasure through her. She pushed down, her vulva sealed against the bronze, and rocked on the cock, the orgasm rising again.

"Yes, Yes," she cried out, seeing everywhere their rapt faces. She threw back her head. "Kiss me!" she cried. And she opened her mouth hungrily. At once, they responded as if they understood. The lips found her mouth, her breasts, the curls again tickling her, and she flung herself back into their arms away from the god, only her pubis still sealed to him, needing only his cock as they suckled her.

The orgasm was blinding, obliterating. Her hands held tight to soft, silken arms, to warm, tender necks. Her fingers were tangled in the long, fine hair. She was smothered in flesh and smothered in happiness.

And when it was finished, when she could stand it no longer and she was withdrawn from the god, she fell back on silken pillows, her body wet and feverish, her vision dazed, the creatures of the harem purring and whispering as they continued to kiss her and stroke her.

LAURENT:
FOR
THE LOVE
OF
THE MASTER

Tristan and I had seen them give the purge to Beauty and Elena. And I had thought, "They cannot do that to us." But they did it.

When they had shaved the hair from our faces and our legs, they took Tristan and me into the bath chamber together. Beauty was already gone. The Master had taken her away.

And Tristan and I knew what was coming. But I wondered if they didn't delight in tormenting us more than the women. They made us kneel facing each other and made us put our arms around each other, as if they liked the picture of it. As if it wasn't necessary to separate us for the sake of delicacy. They wouldn't let our cocks touch. When we tried that, they whipped us with those humiliating little thongs that couldn't have struck a decent blow on a gnat. All the thongs did was remind me of what it was like to be really beaten.

And yet they helped to keep the fires burning, as if holding Tristan wasn't enough.

Over Tristan's shoulder, I watched the groom lower the brass pipe and insert the end of it into his backside. And, at the same moment, I felt the nozzle enter me. Tristan tensed, his bowels filling as mine were filled, and I held to him, trying to steady him.

I wanted to tell him I had had it done before, once, at the castle, at the request of a royal guest before a night of the most humiliating games, and, though it was unnerving, it was not so terrible. But of course I didn't dare to whisper even in his ear. I just held him and waited, the warm water jetting into me, the grooms busy washing us all over as if this other thing, this cleansing of our insides, wasn't happening.

I stroked Tristan's neck and kissed him below the ear when the worst moment came and the nozzles were withdrawn and we were emptied. His whole body went rigid against me, but he was kissing my neck too, gnawing at my flesh a little, and our cocks brushed each other, stroked each other.

But the grooms were so busy pouring the warm water over our backsides and washing away the waste that for a moment they didn't see what we were doing. I pressed Tristan to me, feeling his belly against mine, his cock bulging against me, and I almost came then, not caring anymore what any of them wanted of us.

But they separated us. They forced us apart and held us back away from each other as the emptying went on, and the water flowed over us. And I was weak all over, belonging to them inside and out, belonging to the roar of the water in this echo chamber of a room, to their hands, to the whole procedure and the way it was done, as if it had been done to thousands before us.

If they punished us for touching, well, that would be

my fault. And I wished there was a way to tell Tristan that I regretted getting him into trouble.

But they were too busy, apparently, to punish us.

One purge was not enough, as it had been for the women. We had to have another, and once again they let us hold each other, and the nozzles went in and the water was pumping up into me, and one of the grooms whipped my cock a little with the thong as the purge continued.

My mouth was next to Tristan's ear. And he was kissing me again, which was lovely.

I thought, "I cannot stand this deprivation much longer. It's worse than anything else they've done to us." And I might well have done something indiscreet again, just pushed my cock against his belly, anything.

But then our new Lord and Master, Lexius, appeared, and I felt a little shock when I saw him in the doorway.

Fear. When had anyone at the castle ever made me feel the wallop of it like this? It was maddening. He stood with his hands clasped behind his back, surveying us as they finished with the towels, and his face had a cold cheerfulness to it, as if he was proud of his selections.

When I looked right at him, he didn't show the slightest disapproval. And looking up into his eyes, I thought of that glove going up into my rear—the sensation of being widened and impaled on his arm, and the others watching.

And that, mixed with the shame of having been purged, was almost too much for me.

It wasn't just fear, fear that he would put on the glove again and do that; it was damnable pride that he had done it only to me, and that only I had been tethered to his slipper.

I wanted to please the devil, that was the horror of it. And it made it worse that he had worked the same spell on the others. Elena he had made into a trembling virgin at his command. Beauty he had reduced to obvious adoration.

Now, if the grooms told him that Tristan and I had touched. . . . But they didn't. They dried us off. They brushed our hair. The Master gave some little command, and we were put down on our hands and knees and made to follow him into the main bath again. He gestured for us to kneel up in front of him.

I could feel his eyes moving over me, see him looking over Tristan. Then came another command—his voice like a whip itself stroking my flesh—and the grooms quickly brought out the leather and gold ornaments. They lifted my balls and buckled a broad jeweled ring around my cock, keeping my balls pushed forward.

It had been done before at the castle, but never had I been so hungry.

And then the clamps for the nipples again, only this time they didn't have leashes attached. They were small and tight, and little weights dangled from them.

I couldn't help but wince when they were put on. And Lexius saw it, heard it. I didn't dare look up, but I saw him turn towards me and I felt his hand suddenly on my head. He stroked my hair. Then he tapped the weight dangling from my left nipple and made it swing on its hook, and I winced again, and blushed again, remembering what he had said about silently showing our passion.

It wasn't hard to do. I felt clean and polished inside and out and with no means of combating his power over me. The passion gnawed in my loins and the tears rolled down my face, suddenly.

He pressed the back of his hand against my lips, and I kissed it immediately. Then he did the same to Tristan, and it seemed Tristan made a more graceful art of the kiss, his whole body yielding to it. I felt my tears get thicker, come faster and hotter.

What was happening to me in this strange palace? Why in these simple preliminaries was I reduced to this? After all, I was the runaway, the rebel.

But here I was, dropping on silent command to my hands and knees beside Tristan, our foreheads to the floor, and we were both following Lexius out of the bath into the corridor.

We came to a large garden full of low fig trees and flower beds, and I saw immediately what was going to happen to us. But to make certain we understood, Lexius touched us under our chins with the thong to make us raise our heads and look in front of us, and then he took us, still on our hands and knees, on a little journey along the path so that we could study more thoroughly the slaves who decorated the garden.

They were male slaves, at least twenty of them, their natural skin color unchanged, each mounted on a smooth wooden cross that was planted in the earth amid the flowers and the grass, under the low tree branches.

But the crosses weren't like the village Punishment Cross. They had high crossbars that went under the arms of the slaves which were tied behind them. Wide, curved hooks of polished brass held the weight of the spread-apart thighs, and the soles of the feet of each slave were pressed together, ankles tethered.

Their heads hung forward so that they could see their own erect cocks, and their wrists were bound to the cross in back by chains connected to the large gilded phalluses protruding from their backsides. Not a one looked up or dared to move as we made our little walk in the garden.

And I saw that silent servants, heavily robed and moving with obsequious speed, were spreading brightly colored carpets on the grass and setting low tables upon them, as if for a banquet. Brass lamps were being hung in the trees and torches placed along the walls that enclosed the place.

Cushions were laid all about. And silver and gold jugs of wine were already set in place, and on the tables were trays of goblets. It was clear a meal would be served here at nightfall.

I could imagine the feel of the crossbar under my arms, imagine the smooth cold brass of the hooks curving around my legs, the penetration of the phallus. In the lamplight the vision of the mounted slaves would be stunning. And here the Lords would dine with these sculptures to delight them if they chanced to look up—and what might follow? Would we be taken down, raped?

But it was a very long time before nightfall. I didn't want to be on this cross, suffering, waiting—seeing the gleaming torsos of the others, their primed cocks—no, this was too much, I thought. I can't bear this.

Our tall, elegantly haughty Master led us to the very center of the garden. The air was warm and sweet, just a little breeze. There was Dmitri, already mounted; and another, fair-skinned European slave with dark red hair, probably a Prince taken from our benevolent Queen; and two empty crosses waiting for Tristan and me.

The grooms appeared and lifted Tristan as I watched, and mounted him efficiently and quickly. They didn't insert the phallus until they had his thighs comfortably fitted into the curve of the brass hooks, and when I saw the size of the phallus I winced. In an instant, his wrists were chained to the end of the thing, with the upright wood of the cross between them. His cock couldn't have been any harder.

As the grooms went to combing his hair and binding his feet in place, I realized I had only seconds to do something rash if I was going to do it. I looked up at the Master's still face. His lips were parted as he studied Tristan. His cheeks were slightly red.

I was still on all fours. I moved closer to him until I was against his robe, and then slowly, deliberately, I sat back on my ankles and looked up at him. A strange expression crossed his face, a prelude to rage that I had dared to do this. I whispered without moving my lips so that the grooms couldn't hear me.

"What have you got under that robe," I said, "that you torment us like this? You're a eunuch, aren't you? I don't see any hair on your pretty face. That's what you are, aren't you?"

I thought I could see the hair of his head stand on end. The grooms were polishing Tristan's muscles with clear oil and carefully wiping away what the skin did not absorb.

But that was just a little blaze in the corner of my eye.

I was staring up at the Master.

"Well, are you a eunuch?" I whispered, barely moving my lips. "Or have you got something under those fancy robes worth ramming into me!" I laughed with my lips closed, a real evil-sounding laugh. I was really amusing myself. And I knew that it could well go awry. But the look on his face—the pure astonishment—was worth it.

He colored beautifully, the rage cresting, then melting under his control. His eyes narrowed.

"You're a handsome bastard, you know, eunuch or no eunuch!" I hissed.

"Silence!" he thundered.

The grooms were startled. The word echoed throughout the garden. Then his voice crackled as he gave some quick commands. The grooms, terrified, finished with Tristan and hurried off silently.

I had bowed my head, but now I looked up again.

"You dare!" he whispered. And it was an interesting moment because he was whispering exactly the way I had. He couldn't dare speak to me aloud any more than I could speak to him.

I smiled. My cock was pumping with juice, just ready to spill.

"I'll cover you, if you prefer!" I whispered. "I mean if it doesn't work, that thing you have—"

The slap came so fast I didn't see it. He knocked me off balance. I was on all fours again. I heard a whistling sound, something that struck fear for reasons I couldn't remember. I glanced up and saw he was pulling out a long leather leash from his girdle. It had been wound around his waist, hidden in the folds of velvet. It had a little loop on the end of it, just big enough for a regular cock, not mine, I didn't think.

He grabbed me by the hair of my head and pulled me up. I felt the pain like a burn. He smacked me twice, hard, and I saw the garden in flashes of color as my head turned. Tumult in paradise. I felt his fingers raking my balls, pulling them up, and the cock strap went round and was buckled tight. Good fit, actually. And the leash dragged my whole pelvis forward, my knees scraping on the grass, as I tried to gain my balance.

My head was forced down by him until he could get the almighty slipper on the back of my neck, and then it was down to the ground again, though the leash ran under my chest, and he pulled it roughly, forcing me to hurry on all fours after him.

I wished I could look back at Tristan. I felt as if I'd betrayed him. And I thought suddenly I'd made a hideous mistake, that I'd wind up in one of the corridors, or something worse. But it was too late now. The strap tightened on my cock as he pulled me harder towards the doors of the palace.

BEAUTY:
THE
WATCHER

BEAUTY AWAKENED in a half swoon. They were gathered all around her still, the wives of the harem, talking idly.

They had long, beautiful feathers in their hands—peacock feathers and other brightly colored plumes with which they now and then stroked her breasts and her organs.

A little pulse throbbed in her moist sex. She felt the feathers lazing on her breasts, then stroking her sex more roughly but slowly.

Did they want nothing for themselves, these gentle creatures? Sleep took her again, and then again released her.

She opened her eyes, saw the sun pouring through the high latticed windows, saw the tentwork above aswarm with bits of embroidery, bits of mirrored glass, gold thread. She saw their faces near her, their white teeth, their soft rose-dark lips; heard their low, rapid speech, their laughter. From the folds of their garments perfume rose. The feathers continued to play with her as if she were a toy, a thing to tease idly.

And gradually from this forest of beautiful creatures, she fixed upon one stately figure—a woman who stood apart from the rest, her body half hidden by a high ornamental screen, one hand clutching the border of cedar wood as she stared down at Beauty.

Beauty closed her eyes, luxuriating in the warmth of the sun, the bed of cushions, the feathers. Then she opened them again.

The woman was still there. Who was she? Had she been here before?

Remarkable face, even in a sea of remarkable faces. Lush mouth, tiny nose, and blazing eyes that were somehow different from the eyes of the others. Her deep brown hair was parted in the middle, and it fell down below the shoulders in heavy banks of curls that created a triangle of darkness around the face, only a few ringlets on the forehead suggesting disarray, human imperfection. A thick circlet of gold wound round her forehead to hold in place a long rose-colored veil that appeared to float over her dark hair and fall behind her figure like a rose-tinted shadow.

Heart-shaped the face was, yet severe, very severe. The expression was one of seeming rage that was almost bitter.

Some faces would be ugly with this expression, Beauty thought, but this face was enhanced by the intensity. And the eyes—why, they were violet-gray. That was what was so strange. They weren't black. And yet they were not pale eyes; they were vibrant, and searching, and suddenly full of conflict as Beauty looked up into them.

The woman drew back a little behind the screen, as if

Beauty had driven her back. But the move defeated her purpose. All heads turned now to see her. No one made a sound at first. Then the women rose and bowed in greeting to her. Every one in the room—except Beauty, who dared not move—bowed to the woman.

"She must be the Sultana," Beauty thought, and she felt a tightening in her throat to see the violet eyes focused so sharply on her. The clothes were very rich, Beauty realized this now. And the earrings the woman wore— two immense oval ornaments heavily carved with violet enamel in relief—how lovely.

The woman didn't move or answer the greetings murmured to her. She remained half hidden by the screen, and she stared at Beauty.

Gradually the women resumed their former places. They sat beside Beauty and once again laid the feathers on her, stroked her. One of them leaned against her, warm and fragrant like a giant cat, and let her fingers play with Beauty's tiny tight pubic locks idly. Beauty blushed, her eyes glazing over as she looked at the distant woman. But she moved her hips, and, when the feathers stroked her again, she began to moan, knowing full well that this woman watched her.

"Come out," Beauty wanted to say. "Do not be shy." The woman attracted her. She moved her hips ever more rapidly, the broad peacock feather lingering in its strokes. She felt other feathers tickling her between the legs. The delicate sensations were multiplied and became stronger.

Then a shadow passed before her eyes. She felt lips kissing her again. She could no longer see the strange watching one.

It was twilight when Beauty awoke. Azure shadows and the flicker of the lamps. Smell of cedar, roses. The wives caressed her as they lifted her and took her to the passage. She didn't want to leave, her body awakening again, but then she thought of Lexius. And surely they would send word to Lexius that she had pleased them. She went down on her knees obediently.

But just before she entered the passage, she glanced back at the shadowy room and she saw the watcher standing in the corner. This time there was no screen to hide her. She wore violet silk, violet like her eyes, and her high gold-plated girdle was like a piece of armor encasing her narrow waist. And the rose-colored veil hovered about her as if it were a living thing, an aura.

"How do you open the girdle—take it off," Beauty wondered. The woman's head was a little to the side, as though she was trying to disguise her fascination with Beauty, and her breasts seemed to visibly swell beneath the tight bodice of embroidered cloth, that too somewhat like a piece of armor. The oval rings dangling from her ears appeared to shiver, as if they marked the secret excitement the woman felt, which she would not otherwise reveal to anyone.

Maybe it was the flattery of the light—Beauty couldn't know—but this woman seemed infinitely more alluring than the others, like a great, purple tropical bloom set among tiger lilies.

The women were urging Beauty on, though they kissed her as they did so. She must go. She bowed her head and went into the passage, her flesh still tingling from their touch, and she came quickly to the other side, where the two male servants waited for her.

It was evening, and all the torches were lighted in the bath. And after Beauty had been oiled and perfumed and her hair brushed, she was led by three of the grooms to the broadest corridor that she had yet seen, a passage so splendidly decorated with bound slaves and mosaicwork that it gave the impression of tremendous importance.

Yet Beauty became more and more frightened. Where was Lexius? Where was she being taken? The grooms carried with them a casket. She feared she knew what was inside it.

At last, they came to a chamber with a pair of massive doors to the right, a sort of vestibule with the ceiling open to the sky. Beauty could see the stars, feel the warm air.

But when she saw the niche in the wall, the only niche in the chamber, placed directly opposite the doors, she became terrified. The grooms set down the casket and hurriedly removed from it a gold collar and a mass of silk wrapping.

They only smiled at her fear. They stood her in the niche, folded her arms behind her back, and quickly snapped the high, fur-lined gold collar round her neck, its broad rim cradling her jaw, tipping her chin up slightly. She couldn't turn her head, look down. The collar was hooked to the wall behind her. Even if she lifted her feet off the floor, the thing would have held her.

But they were lifting her feet for her, winding each tightly with the long silk strips. They worked up her legs, leaving her sex bare, the wrapping getting tighter and tighter. In a moment, the wrappings were binding her stomach and her waist, sealing her arms to her back, and crisscrossing her breasts to leave them naked.

With each pull of the silk, she was bound more snugly. She had plenty of room to breathe, yet she was utterly rigid, utterly enclosed, and she felt hot and compact and weightless again. She seemed to float in the niche, a tight and helpless thing unable to shield her naked sex or breasts or the patch of naked flesh where her buttocks were pressed together.

Her feet were now positioned well apart, straps binding them to the floor. The high metal collar and its hook were given a last adjustment.

Beauty shivered all over, whimpered. The grooms paid scant attention. They hurried. They brushed her hair down over her shoulders, gave a final touch of wax to her lips. They combed her pubic hair, ignoring her moans. And then she was given a last round of kisses on the lips, a last round of admonitions to be utterly silent.

And off they went down the corridor, leaving her in

this torchlit alcove, a mere fixture like a hundred others she had seen earlier in the passageways.

She stood still, her body seeming to grow under the wrappings, seeming to fill them, to push out at them over every inch of her snugly held body. The silence rang in her ears.

The torches flaring across from her on either side of the doors seemed like living things to her.

She tried to be still, quiet, but suddenly she lost the battle. And her entire body struggled for freedom. She tossed her hair, tried to free her limbs. She effected not the slightest change in the little sculpture that had been made of her.

And then, as the tears spilled down her face, she felt a marvelous, sad abandon. She belonged to the Sultan, to the palace, to this quiet and inevitable moment.

And it was a great honor really that she had been given this special place, that she was not in a row with others. She looked at the doors. She was thankful they held no pinioned slaves in decoration. And she knew, if and when they were opened, that she could cast her eyes down and try to be utterly subservient, as was expected of her.

She luxuriated in the bonds, though she knew the frustration that the night would bring, her sex already remembering the touch of the women of the harem. And she began to dream, though she was still awake, of Lexius and that strange woman, the Sultana perhaps, who had been watching her—the one who hadn't touched her.

Her eyes were closed when she heard a faint sound. Someone coming. Someone to pass her in the shadows. Not to notice her. The steps drew closer, and she breathed anxiously in the tight constriction of the wrappings.

At last, the figures came into view: two beautifully dressed desert Lords in shimmering white headdresses, their foreheads bound with plaited gold, the linen forming neat folds around their faces and over their shoulders. They were talking to each other. They did not even glance at her. And after them a servant came on silent feet, with his hands clasped behind his back and his head down. He seemed frightened, timid.

The hall was once again quiet, and her heart slowed its pace, her breathing returning to normal. Little sounds came to her but they were from far away—laughter, music, too faint to annoy her or soothe her.

She was almost dozing when a sharp clicking sound awoke her. She stared forward and saw that the double doors had moved. Someone had opened them just a little. Someone was watching her from behind the doors. Why didn't the person show himself?

She tried to remain calm. After all, she was helpless, was she not? But the tears sprang to her eyes, and her body grew feverish in the wrappings. Whoever it was, he might come out, torment her. Her naked sex was simple enough to touch, to tease in any way he might choose. Her naked breasts shivered. Why did he remain there? She could almost hear his breathing. And it crossed her mind that it might be one of the servants, who might spend an hour unobserved as he toyed with her.

When nothing happened, when the door merely remained ajar, she cried softly, the light dazzling her, the prospect of the long night ahead far worse than any whipping she had ever received, her tears dripping down her cheeks silently.

LAURENT:
A
LESSON
IN
SUBMISSION

We WERE back in the pal-
ace, in the cool darkness of the corridors, with the smell
of burning oil and burning resin from the torches and no
sound but Lexius's pounding feet and my hands and knees
on the marble.

I knew when he slammed the door and bolted it that
we were back in his chamber. I could feel his anger. I
took a deep breath, staring at the pattern of stars in the
marble. I hadn't remembered them. Lovely red and green
stars with circles inside them. And the sunlight made the
marble warm. The whole room was warm and quiet. I
saw the bed in the corner of my eye—I hadn't remem-

bered that either. Red silk, piled with cushions, lamps on chains hanging on either side of it.

He had crossed the room, taken down a long leather strap from the wall. Good. Now we had something. Not those stupid thongs. I knelt back on my heels again, my cock pumping under the tight circle of the cock strap.

He turned and held the strap in his hands. It was heavy. It would hurt nicely. I might even be sorry before it was done, very sorry. I looked at him levelly. "You're going to cover me or I'm going to cover you before we leave here," I thought. "I make you that wager, young and elegant and silver-tongued Master."

But I just smiled at him. And he stopped, staring at me, his face suddenly blank, as if he didn't believe I was smiling at him.

"You cannot speak in this palace!" he said between his clenched teeth. "You will never dare to do that again!"

"Are you a gelding or not?" I asked. I raised my eyebrows. "Come, Master." I smiled again slowly. "You can tell me. I won't tell anyone."

He appeared to be trying to regain his composure. He took a deep breath. Maybe he was thinking of something worse than whipping, and I wasn't being clever enough. I wanted the whipping!

Around him the little room seemed to glow in the slanting sun—the patterned floor, the red silk bed, the heap of cushions. The windows were covered with enameled and filigreed screens making them into thousands of little windows. And he seemed very much a part of it in his narrow velvet robe, his black hair swept back behind his ears, the little earrings glittering.

"You think you can provoke me into taking you?" he whispered. His lips quivered slightly, revealing the tension in him. His eyes were glittering with anger. Or with excitement. Hard to tell which. But what is the difference, really, whether the source of the light is burning oil or burning wood? It's the light that matters.

I didn't speak. My body was speaking, however. I looked

him up and down, the slender reed of a man that he was, the way his fine, supple skin wrinkled delicately at the edges of his mouth.

His hand moved. It went to his girdle and unfastened it. The thing dropped and his robe opened, the fabric very heavy, the two sides of the robe standing open, and underneath I saw his naked chest, the black curly hair between his legs, and his cock rising like a spike, curving slightly. And the scrotum, quite large, swathed in fine, lacy, dark curls.

"Come here," he said. "On your hands and knees."

I waited a heartbeat or two before I responded. Then I went down on all fours again, my eyes still on him, and I crossed the distance between us. I sat back again without his telling me that I could, and I smelled the cedar and spice perfume rising from his robes, I smelled his dark male smell, and looked up to see the wine-colored nipples under the flap of the robe. I thought about the clamps the grooms had put on me, the way the leashes had pulled them.

"Now we'll see if your tongue can do anything except spout impertinence," he said. He couldn't keep his chest from heaving, couldn't keep his body from giving him away, though the voice was flinty. "Lick it," he said softly.

I gave a secretive laugh. And I knelt up again, careful not to touch his clothes, and I drew in close and licked not the cock, but the scrotum. I licked it closely underneath, pushing the balls up a little with my tongue, stabbing at them with my tongue, then I licked under them to the flesh right behind them. I felt him push forward a little. I felt him sigh. I knew he wanted me to take the balls in my mouth, or to go at them with more pressure, but I did exactly what he had told me to do. If he wanted more, he would have to ask for it.

"Mouth them," he said.

I laughed to myself again.

"Gladly, Master," I said. He tensed at the impertinence. But I had my open mouth against his scrotum and

I was sucking at the balls, one and then the other, trying to get both of them into my mouth, but they were too big. And my own cock was on the edge of agony. I twisted my hips, rotated them, and the pleasure pumped through me, thudding into pain. I opened my mouth wider and pulled at the scrotum.

"The cock," he whispered.

And then I had what I wanted. He pushed it against the roof of my mouth, then down deep into my throat, and I sucked it in long powerful strokes, running my tongue along it, and letting my teeth scrape it lightly. My head swam. My own pelvis was stiff, and the muscles in my legs were so tense they would ache after. He moved forward pressing his crotch into my face, and I felt his hand on the back of my head. He was going to come any second. I backed off, and licked at the tip of the cock, deliberately teasing him. His hand tightened, but he didn't say anything. I licked his cock slowly, playing with the tip. I moved my hands into his robe. The fabric was cool and soft, but the real silk was the flesh of his backside. I closed my hands on it, pinching the flesh, and let my little fingers curl towards his anus.

He reached down to pull my arms out of his robe. He dropped the strap.

And I stood up and flung him back towards the bed, tripping him so that he lost his balance. I jerked him around by the right arm so that he fell on his face, and I started to tear the robe off him.

He was strong, very strong, and he struggled violently. But I was much stronger and considerably bigger. And he had his arms caught in the robe, and, in a moment, I had it torn off him and thrown aside.

"Damn you! Stop this. Damn you!" he said and then came a nice string of threats or curses in his own tongue, but he didn't dare to shout aloud. And the door was bolted. How would anyone get in to help him?

I was laughing. I shoved him down into the silk mattress and held him with my hands and my bent knee and looked at him, his long smooth back, the purest skin, and this backside, this muscular unpunished backside, just waiting for me.

He was struggling like mad. I almost went right into him. But I wanted to do it differently.

"You'll be punished for this, you mad and stupid Prince," he said. And it had conviction, and I liked the sound of it. But I said:

"Keep your mouth still!" And he went silent with amazing ease. He gathered his forces again and pushed at the bed.

I rose up just enough to fling him over on his back. I was straddling him and, when he tried to rise, I smacked him as he had smacked me. And in that second, while he lay stunned, I picked up one of the pillows and ripped the silk covering off it.

It was a nice long piece of red silk, enough to tie his hands. I caught them, slapping him twice again, and tied his wrists, the silk so sheer that it made powerful little knots that all his struggling only strengthened.

Another ripped cover and I had a gag for him. He opened his mouth in another volley of curses trying to hit me with his bound hands, and I flung his hands back and ran the silk gag right across his open mouth before I tied it behind his head. The open mouth made it easier to tighten, keep in place, and when he tried to hit me again I slapped him over and over slowly until he stopped.

Of course, none of these were terribly hard slaps. They wouldn't have affected me much at all. But they were working on him exquisitely. I knew how his head was swimming from them. After all, he had whipped me only moments before in the garden.

He lay still, his bound hands up above his head. His face was dark red, and the silk gag was a slash of brighter red, with his lips closing on it. But the truly exquisite part was his eyes, his immense black eyes staring at me.

"You are a beautiful creature, you know," I said. I could feel his cock nudging my balls. I was still straddling him.

I reached down and felt its hard hot length, the wetness at the tip. "You're almost too beautiful," I said. "Makes me want to sneak out of this place, with you naked, strapped over my saddle, the way your Sultan's soldiers stole me. I'd take you out to the desert, make you my servant, beat you with that thick belt of yours, as you watered the horse, fed the fire, made my supper."

His body quivered all over. His cheeks teemed with color, despite his dark skin. I could almost hear his heart.

I moved down and knelt between his legs. He was not moving a muscle now to resist me. His cock was bobbing. But I was finished playing with him. I had to have him now. Then the other spices might be mine—punishing his buttocks.

I lifted his thighs, hooking my arms under them, and then forced his legs up over my shoulders, lifting his pelvis off the bed.

He moaned, and his eyes flickered like two fires as he glared at me. I felt the little anus, nice and dry, and I touched my cock, touched it for the first time in all these days of torture, and smeared the moisture seeping from it all over the tip until it was very wet, and then I went into him.

He was tight but not too tight. He couldn't lock me out. He moaned again and I went deeper, through the ring of muscle that scraped me and maddened me, until I was well into him. Then I pressed down on him, forcing his legs back against him until he bent his knees over my shoulders, and then I started driving in him, hard. I let my cock slide almost out, then plunge forward, then almost out again, and he sighed against the gag, the silk becoming wet, his eyes glazing over, his beautifully drawn eyebrows contracting. My hand groped for his cock, found it, started stroking it in time with my thrusts.

"This is what you deserve," I said through my teeth. "This is what you really deserve. You are my slave here and now, and damn the rest of them, damn the Sultan, the entire palace."

He was breathing faster and faster, and then I came,

deep inside of him, my fingers closing tight on his cock and feeling the liquid squeeze out, bubble out in spurts as he moaned loudly. It seemed to go on, all the misery of the nights at sea emptied into him. I pressed my thumb into the head of his cock. I squeezed it harder and harder, until all the pleasure had leaked out of me, until I was truly spent, and then I pulled out of him.

I rolled over and lay back, and closed my eyes for a long moment. I wasn't finished with him.

The room was wonderfully warm. No fire can do what the afternoon sun can do in a closed place. And he lay with his eyes shut, his hands above his head still, breathing deeply and quietly.

He had relaxed his leg and his thigh was against mine. After a long moment I said:

"Yes, what a good slave you'd make." I gave a little laugh.

He opened his eyes and looked at the ceiling. Then he went to move, all at once, and I was on top of him again, pinioning his hands.

He didn't try to fight. I got up and stood beside the bed and told him to turn over on his face. He hesitated for a moment. Then he obeyed.

I picked up the long strap. I looked at his buttocks, and the muscles tightened hard, as if he knew I was looking at him. He shifted his hips slightly on the silk. His head was turned towards me, and he was staring straight past me.

"Get up on your hands and knees," I said.

He obeyed with a certain deliberate grace, and he knelt with his head up and his hands still bound, his body quite a lovely picture. Much leaner than mine. But the grace was marvelous. He was like a fine horse for running, not the steed that could carry a knight, but the more high-strung animal for carrying a courier. The red silk gag seemed such a gorgeous insult to him. Yet he knelt quietly, not resisting. Not trying to tear it loose, which he could have done even with his wrists tied.

I doubled up the strap and walloped his buttocks. He

tensed. I walloped him again. He closed his legs together tightly. That was permissible I thought. As long as he was obedient to all the rest.

I whipped him hard over and over again, marveling at the way the lovely olive-toned flesh still managed to show the color. He didn't make a sound. And I went to the foot of the bed so I could swing the strap harder. In a moment, I had nice crisscrosses of dark pink on his flesh. And I swung harder and harder. I was remembering my first whipping at the castle, how it had smarted, how I had struggled and whimpered without ever really moving. How I had tried to divine the meaning of the pain, that I must remain in a lowly position to be whipped for the pleasure of another.

There was an ecstatic freedom in whipping him, not for revenge or anything so foolish or thoughtful. It was merely the completion of a cycle. I loved the sound of the strap smacking him, loved the way his buttocks had begun to dance a little in spite of his efforts to still himself.

He was beginning to change all over. With another series of smacks, his head went down and his back arched as though he was trying to draw his buttocks in. Absolutely useless. And then they danced out again, swayed. He moaned. He couldn't help it any longer. His whole body was swaying, dancing, an overall undulating in response to the strap.

I knew I must have done that when I was whipped, a thousand times without realizing I was doing it. I'd always been lost in the sound, the sweet, hot explosions of pain, the sudden itching right before the strap hit. I gave him a quick volley of really hard licks, and he moaned in time with each of them. In fact, he wasn't even trying to rein himself in. His body was glistening with moisture, the redness alive on the surface of his skin, and he was in constant elegant movement.

I heard a sob against the gag. Good enough. I stopped and went round to the head of the bed and looked at his face. Nice show of tears. But there was no impertinence. I untied his hands.

"Get off onto the floor with your hands down in front of you and straighten your legs," I said.

Slowly, with head bowed, he obeyed. I loved the way his hair fell down in his eyes, the way the gag bound the rest of it. He was thoroughly chastised now. And his backside was nice and hot, burning hot.

I lifted it high with both hands and I made him walk on all fours that way, buttocks up to my pelvis as I walked behind him. I stepped back and whipped him hard in a good circle around the room, made him go quickly. The sweat poured down his arms. His reddened backside would have gotten compliments at the castle.

"Come here, stand still." I said. And I went between his legs again and entered him, startling him, so that he cried out behind the gag.

I reached out and untied the knot behind his head, but I held the two pieces of silk like horses's reins, pulling his head up, and I pumped into him, shoving him forward, his head nice and high, the reins holding him. He was sobbing, but I couldn't tell whether it was from humiliation or pain or both. His backside felt so hot against me, so delicious, and he was so tight.

I came again, spurting into him in violent jerks. And he bore it, not daring to lower his head, the silk taut in my hands.

When it was done, I reached under his belly and felt his cock. Hard. He was a good slave.

I laughed softly. I let the gag drop away. And I went round in front of him.

"Stand up," I said. "I've finished with you."

He obeyed. He was glistening all over. Even his jet-black hair gave off a shimmer. The look in his eyes was mellow and profound, and his mouth looked luscious. We stared into each other's eyes.

"You may do what you like with me now," I said. "I suppose you've earned the privilege." But the mouth—

why hadn't I kissed him? I bent forward—we were the same height—and I did kiss him. I kissed him very tenderly, and he didn't move to resist me. He opened his mouth to me.

My cock came up again. In fact, the pleasure washed through me. It started grinding in me. But it didn't hurt anymore. It was sweet, getting harder and harder and kissing him, this silken giant.

I let him go. I reached up and felt the line of his jaw where the well-shaven hair was just coming out as it does late in the day. I felt the bristle over his lip, on his chin.

His eyes had an indescribable luster. It was the soul but the soul through a veil of beauty that was distracting.

I folded my arms, and I walked over close to the door, and I knelt down there.

So let all hell break loose, I thought. I heard him moving about, saw out of the corner of my eye that he was dressing, running a comb through his hair, straightening his clothes with quick, angry gestures.

I knew he was confused. But so was I. I had never done such things before to anyone, and I had never dreamed how much I would love it, how much I had wanted to do it. I wanted suddenly to cry. And I felt terrified and sad; and half in love with him; and I hated him because he had shown all this to me; and I felt triumphant—all at the same time.

BEAUTY:
MYSTERIOUS
CUSTOMS

I T SEEMED a quarter of an
hour had passed, and still the double doors had not closed.
Now and then they had moved, creaked on their hinges
a little, the opening narrowing, then widening. Beauty,
shivering and weeping in the tight gold wrappings, knew
that someone was watching her. She tried to still the
tumult in her mind, but she could not. And, when panic
swept over her again, she struggled violently and uselessly, the bonds holding her quite firmly.

The door opened wider. And it seemed her heart stopped
altogether. She lowered her gaze as best she could with
her chin thrust up by the collar. And her tears melted

everything into a golden glow through which she saw a richly dressed Lord approaching her. His head was covered by an emerald-green velvet hood embroidered in gold, and his cloak covered him to the floor, his face completely veiled in shadow.

Quite suddenly Beauty felt a hand on her wet sex, and she swallowed a sob as the hand pulled at her pubic hair and pinched her lips, and then parted them with two fingers. She gasped, biting into her lip, trying to be quiet. The fingers pinched her clitoris and pulled on it, as if to stretch it. She moaned aloud, forgetting to close her lips, and the tears slid down her cheeks faster than before, as a gasp caught in her throat with a low, strangled sound.

The hand withdrew. She shut her eyes, waiting for the man to move on, to go down the corridor as the others had towards the distant sound of the music. But he remained there, right in front of her, looking at her. And her soft cries echoed abominably in the marble alcove.

Never before had she been so tightly bound, so helpless. And never had she known such silent tension, as the figure stood before her doing nothing.

But quite suddenly she heard a small voice, a timid voice, speak to her. It said words she couldn't understand and the name "Inanna." With a shock, Beauty realized this was a woman's voice. It was a woman saying her own name, and Beauty saw that this was no Lord at all, this creature in the emerald cloak. Rather it was the violet-eyed woman from the harem.

"Inanna," the woman said again. And she lifted her finger to her lips, gesturing for silence. Her expression wasn't fearful, however. It was determined.

And the sight of the woman covered in the splendid green robe subdued Beauty and strangely aroused her. "Inanna," she thought. "What a lovely name. But what does this creature, Inanna, want of me?" She stared back unabashedly as Inanna looked up at her. Ferocious eyes, they seemed now, and the mouth bittersweet, and the blood dancing underneath the olive skin as it must have danced in Beauty's face. The silence between them was charged with emotion.

Then Inanna moved her hand inside her robes and she drew out a large pair of golden scissors. At once, she opened the scissors and slipped them under the silk wrappings that crossed over Beauty's belly, and she cut the cloth in big slow strokes, easing the cold metal up Beauty's flesh as the cloth fell away quickly.

Beauty could not see this happening because of the high collar. But she felt it keenly, felt the scissors's blade crawling down her left leg and then her right and the tight cloth falling away without a sound to release her. In an instant, she was free of all covering and she could move her arms; and only the collar held her. But Inanna stepped up into the niche and released the hook, and, freeing Beauty from the collar, she took her down out of the niche and towards the doorway.

Beauty glanced back at the open collar and the abandoned silk. Surely others would discover this. But what could she do? This woman was her Mistress, wasn't she? She hesitated, but Inanna opened her cloak and covered Beauty with it and took her through the doors and into a large chamber.

Through a wall of filigree, Beauty saw a bed and a bath, but Inanna pulled her past this, and through another door, and down a narrow passage, one perhaps that only servants used. And as Beauty hurried, the cloak draping her but not covering her, she could feel the body of Inanna next to her, the thick fabric over her breasts, her hips, her arm. Beauty was excited and afraid and half amused by what was happening.

When they reached another door, Inanna opened it and immediately bolted it behind them. They came to another screen, and beyond it was another bedchamber. All the doors were bolted.

The room seemed royal to Beauty because it was immense, its walls covered in delicate flower mosaics, its windows screened and draped in sheer gold cloth, its great white bed strewn with gold satin pillows. Thick white candles burned in their high stands. The light was even and the air warm, the entire room, in spite of its grandeur, soothing and inviting.

Inanna left Beauty and advanced to the bed. With her back to Beauty she took off the emerald robe and hood, and she knelt and hid them beneath the bed, smoothing the white drapery carefully.

She turned around, and the two women looked at each other. Beauty was stunned by Inanna's loveliness, the deep violet of her eyes flaming now on account of her violet garments, the tight thick bodice perfectly revealing the outlines of her nipples. The girdle was gilded metal and higher, tighter than the one she had worn before, coming to a point beneath her breasts and descending in another point almost to her sex, which was covered in tight little pants of fabric as thick as that of the bodice. Her loose pantaloons shimmered as they veiled her naked legs to the cuffs at her ankles.

Beauty took in all of it, took in Inanna's dark hair and the jewels that studded it, and the way that Inanna's eyes fixed upon her, considering her. But Beauty's eyes returned again and again to the girdle. She wanted to open the long row of tiny metal hooks and release the body within. How terrible it was that the wives of the Sultan were like slaves, that they wore this ornate instrument of binding and punishment.

She thought of the women of the harem who had played with her, given her pleasure, worked her as if she were a jointed doll, yet never revealed anything of themselves. Were they denied pleasure?

She looked at Inanna and said silently, with all her being:

"What is it you want of me?" Her own body was full of craving and curiosity and renewed vigor.

Inanna came forward and looked at Beauty, looked at her nakedness. Beauty felt natural, suddenly, and free. And she reached out tentatively, and felt the hard metallic bands of the girdle. Why, the thing was actually hinged at the sides, she realized, and the fabric binding Inanna's breasts and sex looked unbearably hot, confining.

"You took me out of my wrappings," Beauty thought. "Should I take you out of yours?" She lifted her hand, and with her first and second fingers made a gesture that mimicked the cutting of the scissors. She pointed to Inanna's garments. She raised her eyebrows inquiringly, repeating the motion as if she were snipping.

Inanna understood, and her face radiated delight. She even laughed. But then her face went dark. Bittersweet again. "What a terrible thing to be so pretty when you are sad," Beauty thought. "Sadness shouldn't be pretty."

But Inanna took Beauty's hand suddenly and led her to the bed. They sat down together. Inanna stared at Beauty's breasts, and slowly Beauty lifted them with her hands as if offering them. Her body shivered with sensuous feeling as she cupped the flesh and turned it towards Inanna, and Inanna flushed darkly and her lips quivered, her tongue appearing between her teeth for an instant. As she looked at Beauty's breasts, her hair fell down in her face, and the sight of her bent slightly forward, the hair cascading over her shoulders and the tight metal girdle binding her, made Beauty simmer with desire inexplicably.

Beauty reached out and touched the metal girdle. Inanna drew back just a little, but she kept her hands still as if she were powerless. And Beauty closed her hands on the hard cold thing, and this too inexplicably excited her. She opened the clasps one after another. Each made a tiny clicking sound. But now the girdle was ready to come off. She had only to slide her fingers under it and pull it apart.

She did so suddenly, gritting her teeth, and the metal shell released Inanna's waist and the fine wrinkled cloth gathered around it. Inanna shuddered, and her cheeks went crimson. Beauty drew nearer and tore the violet cloth of the bodice, all the way down into the tight pants under the pantaloons. Not a finger lifted to stop her. And then the breasts were free, magnificent breasts, very firm and high, with nipples of a dark rose color, and slightly tipped upward.

Inanna was blushing and shivering uncontrollably. Beauty could feel her heat, yet it seemed unaccountably innocent. She touched the back of her curled hand to Inanna's cheek. And Inanna inclined her head gently to receive the touch. She was clearly in a paroxysm of passion and did not seem to understand it.

Beauty reached for the breasts, but then changed her mind, and she ripped at the cloth again, revealing the smooth curve of Inanna's belly. Then the woman stood up, and she too pushed at the cloth until her pants and pantaloons fell down around her ankles. Shuddering still, her hands trembling, she pulled the tangled garments away from her feet, and she stared at Beauty, her face on the verge of some terrible outburst.

Beauty reached to take her hand. But Inanna backed away. The act of showing herself naked had overwhelmed her. She reached as if to cover her enormous breasts, or the triangle of her pubic hair, but then, sensing the foolishness of it, she clasped her hands behind her back, then in front, helplessly. She implored Beauty with her eyes.

Beauty rose and came towards her. She took her by the shoulders, and Inanna bowed her head. "Why, you are like a frightened virgin," Beauty thought. And she kissed Inanna's burning cheek, their breasts touching. Inanna suddenly opened her arms to Beauty, and her lips found Beauty's neck and covered it with kisses as Beauty sighed and let the sensation pass through her in delicious silvery ripples, like a sound echoing through a long passage. The fact was Inanna boiled with heat. She was hotter than anyone Beauty had ever touched. The passion was spilling out of her even hotter than it did from the Master, Lexius.

Beauty could stand it no longer. She clasped Inanna's head and forced her mouth onto Inanna's mouth and when the woman stiffened, Beauty refused to let her go,

Inanna's mouth opening suddenly. "That's it," Beauty thought, "kiss me, truly kiss me." And she drew the breath out of Inanna, their breasts crushed against each other now. Beauty's arms went round Inanna, and she pressed her pubis against Inanna's pubis and twisted her hips, the small region of her body exploding with a sensation that quickly enveloped her. Inanna was all softness and fire, an absolutely enthralling combination.

"Dear, innocent little thing," Beauty whispered into her ear. Inanna moaned and tossed her hair back and closed her eyes, her mouth fallen open as Beauty kissed her throat, their bodies grinding against each other, the thick nest of Inanna's hair prickling and scratching Beauty, the pressure forcing the sensations to such a pitch that Beauty thought she could no longer remain standing.

Inanna began to cry. It was a hoarse, low cry on the verge of release, the sobs coming like little coughs, her shoulders shivering. But she broke free and scrambled onto the bed, and suddenly let her hair cover her face as she sobbed into the coverlet.

"No, you mustn't be afraid," Beauty said. She lay down beside her and gently turned her over. The breasts were absolutely luscious. Even Princess Elena didn't have such gorgeous breasts, Beauty thought. She forced one of the pillows under Inanna's head and she kissed her, climbing on top of her, their pelvises rubbing slowly against each other again until Inanna's face went red once more and she sighed deeply.

"Yes, that's much better, my sweet darling," Beauty said. She lifted the left breast in her fingers, studying it, her thumb and forefinger imprisoning the small nipple. How tender it was. She bent down and stroked it with her teeth, feeling it grow taller, harder, and hearing Inanna groan painfully. Then Beauty closed her mouth on it and sucked hard and lovingly, her left arm slipping under Inanna to lift her, her right hand fighting Inanna's hand, pushing it away when Inanna tried to defend herself.

Inanna's hips rose off the bed, and she tossed under

Beauty, but Beauty would not let go of the breast, feasting on it, licking it, kissing it.

But suddenly Inanna shoved her away with both hands and turned over, gesturing frantically that they must stop, that it couldn't continue.

"But why?" Beauty whispered. "Do you think it's bad to feel this?" Beauty asked. "Listen to me!" She took Inanna by the shoulders and made her look up.

Inanna's eyes were large and glossy, and the tears clung to her long black eyelashes. Her face was rent with pain, genuine pain.

"It isn't wrong," Beauty said. And she bent to kiss Inanna, but the woman wouldn't allow it.

Beauty waited. She sat back on her heels with her hands on her thighs, and she looked at Inanna. She remembered how forceful her first Master, the Crown Prince, had been with her when he first claimed her. She remembered how she had been overpowered, whipped, made to yield to her feelings. She had no leave to do such things to this voluptuous darling, and she did not want to do them. But something was very wrong here. Inanna was desperate, miserable.

And now, as if to answer Beauty, Inanna sat up and brushed her hair back from her wet face, and then, shaking her head with the saddest expression, she parted her legs and reached down to her own sex and covered it with her hands. Her whole attitude was one of shame, and it hurt Beauty to see it.

She took Inanna's hands away. "But it is nothing to be ashamed of," she said. She wished Inanna could understand her words. She pushed Inanna's hands to the side and parted her legs before Inanna could stop her. And Inanna rested her hands on the bed to steady herself.

"Divine sex," Beauty whispered, and she stroked the place between Inanna's legs reverently. Inanna cried softly, brokenheartedly.

And then Beauty spread the legs wider and looked into the sex, and she saw something that startled her so completely that for the moment she could not recover, could not say what she meant to say, could not reassure Inanna.

She tried to hide her shock. Perhaps it was a trick of light and shadow. And Inanna was sobbing. She would not hold steady. But as Beauty bent closer, as she forced the beautifully shaped thighs wider apart, she saw that she had not been wrong. The sex was mutilated!

The clitoris had been cut out, and there was nothing there but a tiny smooth pad of scar tissue. And the pubic lips had been sheared to half their size, and they too were thickened with scar tissue.

Beauty felt such horror that for a moment she could do nothing to conceal her feelings but stare at this dreadful evidence in front of her. But then she swallowed her revulsion for the act itself, and looked at the enticing creature before her. And then impulsively she kissed Inanna's trembling breasts again, and she kissed her mouth, not letting Inanna shy away. And she licked at the tears that spilled over Inanna's cheeks, locking her in a long kiss that finally subjugated her.

"Yes, yes, darling," Beauty said. "Yes, my precious one." And when Inanna had calmed somewhat, Beauty looked at the multilated sex again and studied it more completely. The little kernel of pleasure excised, yes. And the lips too. And nothing left but the portal that the man might enjoy. The filthy, selfish beast, the animal.

Inanna was watching her. Beauty sat back and lifted her hands to ask a question in gestures. She indicated herself, her hair, her body, to mean "women," then made sweeping gestures all around to mean "all women here" and pointed to the scarred sex inquiringly.

Inanna nodded. She confirmed it with another sweeping gesture of her own: "Yes," she said in Beauty's own tongue, "All . . . all. . . ."

"All women here?"

"Yes," Inanna answered.

Beauty was silent. She knew now why the women of the harem had found her such a curiosity, why they had delighted in her feeling. And her hatred of the Sultan and of all the Lords of the palace became something dark and full of anguish.

Inanna wiped at her tears with the back of her hand. She was staring at Beauty's sex, and her face had lapsed into quiet, childish curiosity.

"But something strange is happening here," Beauty murmured. "This woman does feel! She is as hot as I am hot." She touched her lips as she thought of the kisses. "It was desire that impelled her to come to me, free me from the bindings, bring me here. But has this desire never been consummated?" She looked at Inanna's breasts, at her exquisitely rounded arms, and her long curling brown hair that hung down over her shoulders.

"No, surely she can be made to feel it to the pinnacle," Beauty thought. "It is more than these external parts. It must be." And she gathered Inanna into her arms and again forced her mouth open with kisses.

At first Inanna was puzzled, and with her little moans she questioned Beauty. But Beauty squeezed her breasts as she put her tongue between Inanna's lips. She brought the passion up slowly until Inanna's heart was again pounding. Inanna pressed her legs together, then knelt up as Beauty knelt up, and once again their bodies were wedded, mouths locked, all Beauty's flesh awakened by Inanna's flesh, her pubis electrified as she danced against Inanna. Beauty fed upon the breasts again, greedily and hard, holding tight to Inanna's arms and not letting her go even when the feeling made her frantic.

Finally, Beauty felt Inanna was ready, and roughly she pushed her back on the pillows and parted her legs, and spread apart the little sex that had been so butchered. The vital wetness was there, the delicious smoky-tasting fluids that Beauty could lap with her tongue as Inanna's hips rose in snapping spasms. "Yes, darling," Beauty thought, and her tongue drove deep into the sex, licking at the top of the vagina until Inanna's cries became hoarse and unmodulated. "Yes, yes, darling," she thought, and she closed her mouth on the stunted lips, her tongue seeking the deeper, tougher muscles of the little cavity and pumping against them furiously.

Inanna turned and struggled under her. Her hands pushed at Beauty's hair but not with enough will to dislodge Beauty's head, and Beauty, intent upon her task, forced Inanna's thighs up and tilted her sex back and sucked at it even more savagely. "Yes, come, feel it, my little one," she thought, "feel it deeply inside," and she buried her face in the wet swollen flesh, digging faster and deeper with her tongue, her teeth scraping at the tiny pad of scar tissue where the clitoris had been until Inanna lifted her hips with all her strength and cried out, the whole little mouth convulsing violently. Beauty had done it. She had triumphed. And she sucked the throbbing flesh harder and harder until Inanna's cries went almost into a scream and the woman pulled away and buried her face in the pillow, her whole body shaking.

Beauty sat up. She rested back on her hips again, her own sex ripe, and full of pulse like a heart. Inanna lay still, her face still hidden, and then she sat up slowly, looking stunned and witless, and she stared at Beauty. She threw her arms around Beauty's neck, and she kissed Beauty all over her face and neck and shoulders.

Beauty accepted all this. Then she lay back on the pillows and she let Inanna lie next to her. She moved her hand between Inanna's legs, and she put her fingers into the sex.

"Well, this one is stronger than the others," she thought. "And there has been no one to satisfy her."

And only then, as she snuggled with Inanna, did she realize that they might both be in danger. It must be forbidden for the wives to do this, forbidden for the wives to be naked except for and with the Sultan.

And Beauty felt a profound hatred for the Sultan and a sudden desire to leave this realm and return to the land of the Queen. But she tried to put this out of her mind, to enjoy the pure excitement of lying next to Inanna, and she began to kiss her breasts again.

In fact, it seemed to her that Inanna's breasts were the

most delectable part of her, and she began to knead them as she nibbled at the nipples. A new sense of abandon came over her. She wasn't trying to please Inanna now so much as she was lost in her own desires, her mouth pulling on the nipple, her mind only dimly aware of Inanna once more moving under her.

She parted her legs over Inanna's thigh and pushed her sex against the smooth skin, her burning clitoris throbbing. Suckling Inanna's breast, she rode the thigh, up and down, her body stiffening, her legs hugging Inanna, until suddenly the orgasms flooded her.

When it was over, it did not leave her in peace. She felt herself in the grip of a fever. The lushness of Inanna's body and the softness of her own created some new sense of limitless ecstasy, some vague and mad dream of a night of unfolding pleasures, desire building upon desire.

She sucked on Inanna's tongue, the sweetness intoxicating her and carrying her up and out of her drowsiness. And, remembering dimly the spectacle of Lexius impaling Laurent on his gloved fist, she made her hand into a tight knot and moved it through the charred mouth between Inanna's legs.

Wet as before, tight, deliciously tight, the opening gripped her fist and the part of her wrist that also entered, and the muscles pulsed against her hungrily, further exciting her. And when she felt Inanna's clenched hand enter her, she knew again the old pleasure of being filled, her body embracing all these sensations with increasing urgency. She worked Inanna with her fist as Inanna worked her, Inanna's arm pumping with almost punishing roughness.

When they came it was together, moaning into each other, their bodies drenched in warmth and unbroken tremors of pure ecstasy.

Finally, Beauty lay back on the pillow and rested, her arm still wound around Inanna's arm, her fingers playing with Inanna's fingers. She did not open her eyes when Inanna sat up. She was only dimly conscious of Inanna examining her again, Inanna taking her time as she touched Beauty's breasts and pubic lips, then embracing Beauty and rocking her in her arms as if Beauty were something precious she must never lose: the key to her new and secret realm. She wept again, her tears flowing onto Beauty's face, but the weeping was soft and full of unmistakable relief and happiness.

LAURENT:
THE
GARDEN OF
MALE
DELIGHTS

I‍T SEEMED a long time passed. I knelt in silence, my head bowed, my hands spread on my thighs, my cock rising again. The light in the small room had darkened. Late afternoon. Lexius, looking quite composed in his robes, merely stood watching me. Whether it was anger that fixed him there, or bewilderment I couldn't be certain.

But, when he finally came striding across the room, I felt the force of his will, his ability once again to command both of us.

He put the cock strap around my cock and yanked hard on the leash as he opened the door. In seconds, I was crawling after him. The blood was racing to my head.

And when I saw the garden through the open doors, I felt the faint hope that maybe I wasn't to be specially punished. It was getting dusk already, and the torches on the walls were just being lighted. The lamps hung in the trees gave off their illumination. And the exquisitely bound slaves, their torsos oiled and gleaming, their heads bowed as before, looked as tantalizing as I had thought they would.

There was one change in the picture, however. All the slaves had been blindfolded. Their eyes were masked by gold leather. And I realized that they were struggling in their bonds, moaning softly—moving with more abandon than they had before, as if the blindfolds released them to do so.

Seldom had I been blindfolded. I didn't know what I thought of it—whether it would be good or bad, whether it would make me more or less fearful.

There were more servants at work in the garden. Bowls of fruit were being set down. I could smell the red wine in the open decanters.

A small group of grooms appeared. The Master, whose face I had not glimpsed since I had kissed him, snapped his fingers, and we proceeded to the center of the grove of fig trees, the place where we had been before, and I saw Dmitri and Tristan, bound on their crosses as we had left them. Tristan looked particularly handsome with the blindfold, his golden hair falling down over it.

A carpet had been spread out right before them. There was the small wine table with its circle of goblets, the scattered cushions. The barren cross was to Tristan's right, directly before the fig tree. The blood thundered in my head when I saw it.

The Master at once gave a series of orders. But his voice was soft. There was no anger in it. I was picked up, turned upside down, and taken to the cross. And immediately, I felt my ankles being tethered to the ends of the crossbar, my head dangling just above the ground, my cock bumping the smooth wood.

I saw the upside-down garden spread before me, servants mere blurs of color moving through the greenery.

As soon as I was secure, my arms were lifted up away from the ground and my wrists tied to the brass hooks that held the thighs of the other slaves. And then I felt my cock being bent back and straight up above my inverted body, and it was tied in place between my legs by leather thongs that went round my thighs, holding it firmly. It did not hurt in this unnaturally bent position. But it was on display, and it could touch nothing.

All the bonds were made doubly secure, leather thongs pulled tight, and then one more good loop of leather was bound round my chest and the cross, to steady me and render me completely immobile.

In sum, I was upside down, bound firmly with legs apart and arms apart and my cock pointing upwards. The blood was roaring in my ears, and thudding in my cock.

I felt the blindfold going round my face—it was fur-lined and very cool—and buckled tight on the back of my head. Pure blackness. And all of the noises of the garden suddenly magnified.

Footsteps in the grass. Then the heightened feel of hands rubbing oil into my backside, massaging it well and deep between my legs. The distant sounds of pots and pans, the smell of cooking fires.

I tried to move. I felt an irresistible urge to test the bonds. I struggled. It produced no effect, except that I realized it had been easier because I was blindfolded. Unable to gauge the visual effect, I let myself tremble all over, and feel the cross vibrate slightly under me, as the Punishment Cross had done in the village.

But there was a terrible ignominy to being upside down, a terrible ignominy to the blindfold.

Then I felt the first lash of the strap across my bottom. It came again very quicky, and then again, with a loud cracking noise, more leather than flesh being smacked, and then again, stinging this time remarkably. I felt myself wriggling all over. I felt grateful that it was happening at last, yet afraid of what I would feel moments from now.

And it was bitter to me that I didn't know whether or not Lexius was doing the whipping. Was it he or one of those little grooms?

Whatever the case, it was good, the whipping. It was the thick leather strap that I had craved ever since we left the village, the sound, punishing strap that I needed. It was the beating I had dreamed of every time those delicate thongs teased my cock or the soles of my feet. And the walloping was splendid, coming fast as it did. And with a rush of sublime relief, I lost all resistance.

Even on the village Punishment Cross I had not been so totally given over. That had come only with the increase of pain. Now, as I hung blindfolded and helpless, it happened instantly. My cock was thumping and moving under its tight binding, and the strap was lashing me hard across both buttocks at the same time, and coming so fast that there seemed little or no interval between blows, just unbroken punishment with a sound that seemed nearly deafening to me.

I wondered what the other slaves thought as they heard it—whether they craved it as I might have, or feared it. Whether they knew it was a disgrace to be whipped like this, the sound disrupting the peace and the quiet of the garden.

But the thrashing was going on. The strap was being swung harder and harder. And when a cry broke from me, I realized for the first time that I wasn't gagged. I was bound and blindfolded but not gagged.

Well, that little oversight was immediately remedied. A roll of soft leather was shoved well between my teeth, as the blows from the strap continued. And the gag was pulled well back into my mouth by ties that were then knotted behind my head, holding the gag firmly.

I don't know why it so thoroughly undid me. It was perhaps the last restraint needed, and under all these restraints I went wild, bucking and struggling under the pounding strap and crying aloud against the gag as I hung in darkness. The inside of the soft fur-lined blindfold was moist and hot with my tears. And my cries were muffled, but loud. And I began to struggle in rhythmic motions. I could raise my entire body a few inches, then drop down. And I realized I was rising to reach the blazing hot wallops of the strap, and then dropping away from them and coming up again.

"Yes," I thought, "do it. Do it harder. Whip me soundly for what I've done. Let the blaze of pain grow brighter, hotter." But it was not this coherent, what I thought. It was like a song in my head, made up of the rhythms— the strap, my cries, the creak of the wood.

And at some point as it continued, I realized it was going on longer than any beating I'd ever received before. The blows weren't all that hard now. But I was so sore it scarcely mattered. Nice, lazy loud smacks from the strap had me writhing and crying.

And the garden was filling with voices. Men's voices. I could heard them coming in, laughing, talking. I could even hear, if I listened very carefully, the wine being poured into the goblets. I could smell it again. And smell the green grass right under my head, and smell the fruit, and the strong aroma of roasted meat and sweet aromatic spices. Cinnamon and fowl, cardamom, beef.

So the banquet was in progress. And the beating still went on, but the blows were coming more and more slowly.

Music had commenced. I heard the thumping of strings, the beat of small drums, and then the ring of harps and shrill, unfamiliar sounds from horns I couldn't name. It was dissonant and foreign and delightfully strange, the music.

My rump was burning with pain. And the strap played with it. There would be a long moment in which I would feel every inch on my backside glowing, and then the crack of the strap, the white-hot flair, for an instant. I wept. I realized it might go on like that all the evening long. And there was nothing I could do but cry helplessly.

"But better this," I thought, "than to be one of the

others. Better this, to draw their eyes to it as they dine and drink and laugh together, whoever they are . . . than to be a mere decoration. Yes, the disgraced one again, the punished one. The one with the will."

And I struggled violently on the cross, loving the strength of it, that I couldn't bring it down, and feeling the strap come down harder and faster again, my cries growing louder and more miserable.

Finally, the blows slacked off again. They became teasing. The strap was playing with various little marks, welts, scrapes that it had made in my flesh. I knew this little piece of music.

And it blended with the other music, the music of those who held power, which flooded my senses. Mentally I reached out from the moment, exquisite as it was, and gathered other moments to me, welding the immediate past to the dizzying present. The feel of Lexius's lips— why hadn't I called him Lexius, made him call me Master? I would next time—the feel of his tight little anus when I'd raped him. I savored all this as the strap lazily revived my simmering flesh, and the banquet went on noisily.

I didn't know how much time had passed. I only knew, as I had in the hold of the ship, that something had changed. The men were rising, moving about. The strap was startling me now. I'd be left in peace, then it would lick at me. I was so sore that the scratch of a fingernail would have made me moan. I felt the blood teeming under the welts, and my cock dancing in its leather bindings. The voices in the garden were getting louder, more drunken, more abandoned.

Cloth brushed my back, my head, as men passed me. Then suddenly my head was lifted, and the blindfold was pulled off, and I felt the bonds being loosened from my ankles and wrists and my chest simultaneously. I tensed all over, afraid of falling, of being dropped.

But the grooms quickly had me right side up, and I found myself standing in the grass, a desert Lord before me. Naturally, I hadn't the common sense or self-discipline not to look at him. He wore a full Arab headdress of white linen, and dark wine-colored robes, and his eyes glittered from a dark sunbaked face as he smiled at me. My stunned look seemed only to amuse him. But other such Lords pressed in. I was suddenly turned roughly. And a powerful hand squeezed my sore buttocks. There was laughter. My cock was slapped, my chin lifted, my face examined.

And all around me I could see slaves were being taken down. Dmitri, still blindfolded, was on all fours on the grass, being well raped by a young Lord. And Tristan knelt before another Master, taking the man's cock into his mouth with vigorous motions.

But even more interesting was the sight of Lexius, standing back under the fig tree, watching. Our eyes met for one split second before I was roughly turned around again.

I almost smiled, but it would have been foolish to do so. My reddened buttocks were really delighting these new Masters. They had all to squeeze them, feel the heat, see me wince. I wondered why they didn't whip all the other slaves, too. But no sooner had that little thought come to my head than I heard the straps at work on the others.

The Lord with the sunburnt face pushed me down on my knees and with both his hands kneaded my punished flesh, while another man caught my arms and wound them around his hips. He opened his robe. The cock was ready for my mouth, and I took it, thinking of Lexius when I did so. And in back of me a cock pushed at my buttocks, parted them, and entered.

I felt speared at both ends, and all the more excited by the thought that Lexius witnessed it. And I worked my lips hard on the delicious cock in my mouth, falling into rhythm with the one that was driving into me. The cock pushed deeper into my mouth, deeper into my throat, and the man behind me spanked against my aching backside with each thrust, until finally he spurted into me. I locked my arms tighter around the man I suckled. I nursed him harder and harder, while again my buttocks were pulled apart, kneaded and pinched, and another, bigger cock slipped into me.

At last, I felt the hot salty fluid fill my mouth, and the cock, after a last few licks of my tongue, withdrew through my tight wet lips, as if savoring the motion as much as I did. At once, another took its place as the man in back continued to grind his hips against me.

It seems I took another in front and in back before I was stood upright again and thrown back, my shoulders caught by two men who pushed my head down so that I could see nothing but their robes, my legs spread apart by another man who entered me immediately. My body was rocked by his thrusts, my own cock pumping vainly. A cool mass of cloth suddenly veiled my chest. Another man had straddled me. My head was lifted and cradled to receive his cock. I tried to free my arms to hold to his hips, but those who held me wouldn't allow it.

I was still sucking the cock, greedily, hungrily, my own hunger critical and painful now, when the man who had been raping me withdrew, quite satisfied I think, and I felt the strap licking at my buttocks as the men held my legs apart and up. I was whipped hard, the old welts blazing again, until I was moaning and twisting as I sucked the cock and I could hear laughter around me. I cried bitterly as the pain grew worse. The hands that held my legs tightened. And I clung to the cock, working it feverishly until it came, and then letting the fluid fill my mouth before I slowly, deliberately swallowed it.

I was turned over again, and I glimpsed the grass beneath me, the sandals of those who held me suspended. My buttocks were steaming from the strap. And, as a new cock entered my mouth and another entered my anus, I was whipped from the side, the strap curling over the same punished flesh, and then licking at my back and underneath, at my cock and my nipples. I went into a frenzy as the leather licked my cock again. I pumped my backside against the man who raped me, and drew the other cock into me deeply.

I had no real thoughts now. I had no dreams of other moments or even of Lexius. I was simmering with just the proper mixture of pain and excitement, hoping desperately that my Lords and Masters might at some point want to see my cock perform.

But what need did they have for that?

When they were at last satisfied, I was allowed down on all fours and sent to remain motionless in the center of the nearby carpet. I might as well have been an animal for which they had no more need. And the Lords settled back into their circle. They sat crossed-legged on their cushions and lifted their goblets again—ate, drank, murmured to one another.

I knelt there with my head low, as I had been taught, trying not to see them surrounding me. I wanted to look for Lexius, see that familiar figure again in the trees, know he was watching. But all I could see were the dark shadows surrounding me. I saw the glint of splendid robes, the sharp gleam of the men's eyes, heard the rise and fall of voices.

I was panting, and my cock was humiliatingly alive, moving without my will. But what was that in the Sultan's garden? Now and then one of the men reached out and slapped my cock, or pulled at my nipples. A mercy and a penance. A little laughter from the group, some observation. The situation was unbearably subdued and intimate. I tensed, unable to shield myself. And when my welts were pinched I cried softly, keeping my mouth closed.

The garden was quieter now. But there still came the sound of punishing straps and hoarse, triumphant cries of pleasure.

Finally, two of the grooms appeared with another slave and they took me by the hair, and pulled me out of the circle as they pushed the new slave into it. They snapped their fingers for me to follow them.

LAURENT:
THE GREAT
ROYAL
PRESENCE

I MOVED AFTER them across the grass, glad for the moment to be out of the glare of attention. Yet it was enervating, the manner in which they whispered to each another and only occasionally coaxed me on with a pat on the head or a tug of my hair.

The garden itself was full of those who still feasted, and panting slaves on display as I had been. Some I saw were still on the crosses or had been put back, and many twisted and struggled violently.

I didn't see Lexius.

But we soon came to a brightly lighted room opening off the garden. There were grooms busy with hundreds of slaves. Scattered tables were covered with manacles, straps, caskets of jewels, and other playthings.

I was made to stand up, and a good-sized bronze phallus was obviously chosen for me and I stood numbly watching as it was oiled, marveling at the detailed carving of the thing, the way the circumcised tip and even the surface of the skin was beautifully realized. It had a round loop of metal, a hook, on the wide, round base end of it.

The grooms never even glanced up as they worked. They expected quiet and total compliance. They inserted the phallus, pushing it well up into me, and then put long leather cuffs on my arms and brought my arms back, forcing me to thrust out my chest, and they bound these bracelets tight to the hook on the base of the phallus.

My arms are rather long even for a man of my height and, had they bound my wrists, it would have been more comfortable. But the bracelet was above my wrists, and so my shoulders were held well back and my head up, when this was finished.

I could see other moist, well-muscled slaves in the room being manacled in the same fashion. In fact, there were only big, powerfully built slaves here, none of the smaller, more delicate ones. And the cocks were large, too. And some of the slaves had been soundly thrashed. They had very red backsides.

I tried to yield to this position, to accept the way it forced my chest out, but it was hard for me. The metal phallus felt amazingly hard and punishing, not at all like something made of wood and covered with leather. Next, a large stiff collar was buckled to my neck, one that had several long, narrow, delicate straps dangling from it. It was loose but very strong and rigid, and it forced my chin up high as it rested firmly on my shoulders. Immediately, the long strap that hung down in back—I could feel this—was buckled tight to the phallus hook. Two more straps running from a single hook on the front of the collar were drawn down over my chest and under me, past my organs on either side, and they too were buckled tight to the phallus.

All this was done perfunctorily and with efficient, hard little pulls by the grooms, who then patted my buttocks and made me turn around for a quick inspection. I found it infinitely worse than the easy passivity of the cross. And their eyes moving over me, impersonally yet not indifferently, further intensified the feeling of apprehension.

I was patted again on the buttocks, the mere touch bringing the tears to my eyes, though it felt oddly good. And the groom gave me a little comforting smile and patted the tip of my cock quickly also. The phallus seemed to rock inside me with every breath I took. In fact, every breath moved the straps that ran down my chest, and this moved the phallus slightly. I thought of all the cocks that had been inside me, their heat, the slippery sound of them passing in and out, and the phallus seemed to expand, to grow even harder and heavier, as if to remind me of it all, to punish me for it, to protract the pleasure.

I thought of Lexius again, wondered where he was. Had the long whipping during the banquet been his only revenge? I flexed my buttocks, feeling the cold round rim of the phallus, feeling the smarting flesh tingle around it.

The grooms oiled my cock very fast, as if they did not want to overstimulate it or reward it. When it was gleaming, they oiled my scrotum, massaging it with great gentleness. Then, the handsomer of the two, the one who smiled more often, pressed on my thighs until I bent my legs slightly in a fairly awkward squat. He nodded, and patted me approvingly. I glanced around and saw the others were standing in that way also. Every slave I saw had a very red backside. Some had been beaten on the thighs as well.

It came over me with debilitating clarity that I looked as these others looked, the very posture exemplifying discipline and subservience. And for a moment I was weak all over.

Then I saw Lexius in the doorway, watching me. He had his hands clasped in front of him, and his eyes were narrow and serious. The excitement in me, the confusion, doubled, tripled.

My face burned as he approached. Yet I stood in the

squatting position, eyes lowered, though I couldn't lower my head, marveling at how difficult this was. Punished on the cross, easy. I did not have to cooperate. Now I cooperated. And he was here.

His hand moved towards me, and I thought surely it was to slap me again, but it touched my hair, gently moving it back from my ear. The grooms then gave something to him. One glance and I saw: a pair of pretty jeweled nipple clamps with three very fine chains connecting them.

My chest seemed more vulnerable, thrust out as it was, my shoulders painfully pulled back. The clamps went on fast, and I was panic-stricken because I couldn't see them. The collar kept my chin too high. I couldn't see the three little chains that must have shivered between the clamps, a humiliating decoration that would register each anxious breath I took like a banner registers the breeze even when it is too soft for you to feel it. The thing glowed in my imagination—the clamps, the chains. The pinching sensation was tantalizing.

And Lexius was here, and I was again his personal prisoner. He touched my arm with maddening tenderness and guided me towards the door. I saw the other manacled slaves at a squat in the line. Their faces, held high by the stiff collars, wore an interesting dignity. Even with tears spilling and lips quivering, they had a new complexity. Tristan was there, his cock as hard as mine, and the clamps and chains stood out on his chest as I knew they did on mine, the obvious power of his body magnified by the style of the manacling.

Lexius pushed me into the line behind Tristan, his left hand stroking Tristan's hair affectionately. When he turned his full attention to me, giving my hair a more thorough combing now with the same comb he had used earlier for himself, I remembered the chamber, the heat of us together, the baffling exhilaration of being Master.

Through my teeth I whispered:

"Wouldn't you rather be in line with us?"

His eyes were only a few inches from mine, but he

was looking at my hair. He went on with the comb as if I hadn't spoken.

"It is my destiny to be what I am," he answered, his lips so still it seemed to come direct from his thoughts. "And I cannot change that any more than you can change yours!" He looked directly at me.

"But I already have changed mine," I said with a faint smile.

"Not enough, I would say!" He gritted his teeth. "See that you please me and the Sultan, or you'll pine on the garden walls for a year, I promise you."

"You won't do that to me," I said confidently. But his threat struck my heart.

He stepped back before I could say anything else, and the line moved forward and I followed. When any slave forgot to bend his legs in the squat, he was rapped with the thong. It was the most degrading way to walk, and each step required conscious compliance.

We moved to a central garden path, and down it single file, and all those in the garden were rising and coming towards the same walkway. Many were looking at us, pointing, gesturing. I found it as bad as being carried into the city from the boat earlier, this being on display, being paraded.

Many other slaves were mounted again on the crosses. Some had been polished with gold, others with silver. I wondered if we had been chosen for our size or for the degree of punishment we'd received.

But what did it matter?

In this humiliating position, we moved on up the path as the crowd gathered on the edges of it. We came to a stop and were then divided to line both sides of the path facing each other. I took my position, with Tristan across from me. I could see and hear the crowd all around, but no one touched us or tormented us. Then the grooms came down the path, tapping our thighs and making us squat much lower. The crowd seemed to enjoy the change.

The grooms made us squat as low as we could without

losing our balance. My thighs were smacked over and over with the thong as I struggled to obey. I found it worse even than the little parade. And I felt the nipple clamps pinch me with each shudder that ran through me.

But the air of anticipation suddenly sharpened. The crowd, towering over us and pressing in close so that their robes brushed us, looked towards the doors of the palace to my left. We stared at the path before us.

Suddenly, a gong was sounded. All the Lords bowed from the waist. I knew someone was approaching on the path. I heard moans, soft muted sounds obviously coming from the slaves. I heard such sounds coming from the deepest parts of the garden. And those on my left began to moan, to twist their bodies supplicatingly.

I felt I could not do this. But I remembered Lexius's commands to us, how we must demonstrate our passion. And I had only to think of the words to be suddenly at the mercy of what I truly felt—the desire throbbing in my cock, throbbing in my whole soul, and a sense of my hopelessness and abject position. It was the Sultan who was coming, surely, the Lord who had ordained all this, taught our Queen to keep pleasure slaves, created this great scheme in which we were firmly held as powerless victims of our own desires as well as the pleasure of others. And the scheme was so much more fully realized here, so much more dramatically and efficiently executed.

An eerie pride overcame me, a pride in my own beauty and strength and obvious subjugation. The moaning rose from me with genuine passion, and the tears flooded my eyes. I felt the bracelets holding my arms as I let the feeling move my limbs, let my chest expand, felt the heavy bronze phallus inside me. I wanted my humiliation and obedience to be recognized, if even for an instant. And I had been obedient, despite my little conquest of Lexius. I had been obedient in all other things. And I was overcome with delicious shame and desperation to please, moaning and undulating without resistance.

He was coming nearer. There materialized in the corner of my swimming vision two figures carrying the poles of a high, fringed canopy. Then I saw the figure walking slowly under the canopy.

A young man, perhaps a few years younger than Lexius, and of the same delicate-boned and narrow-limbed race, his body very straight under his heavy robes, his long scarlet cloak, his short dark hair free of any headdress.

He was looking from right to left as he passed. The slaves were crying softly but loudly without moving their lips. I saw him pause, reach out, and examine a slave, but I could not see the slave himself. This was all in luridly colored outline. He moved on now to the next slave, and this one I could see a little better—a black-haired slave with an immense cock who was weeping bitterly. Again he moved on, and this time his eyes passed over our side of the path, and I felt my sobs catching in my throat. What if he did not notice us?

His robes were tightly fitted, I could see that now, and his hair, much shorter than that of the others, was like a dark halo around his head, and he had a quick and lively expression. Beyond that I couldn't study him. No one had to tell me that it would have been unforgivable to look up at him.

He turned to the other side of the path, though he was almost in front of me. And I wept unstintingly. But I saw he was looking at Tristan. And now he spoke, though I couldn't see whom he addressed. I heard Lexius answer him. Lexius was behind him. He came forward, and together they conversed. And then Lexius snapped his fingers. And Tristan, still in the miserable squatting position, was made to walk off behind Lexius.

So at least Tristan had been singled out. That was good. Or so it seemed, until I thought again that I might not be. And the tears slipped down my face as the Sultan turned back to us. Immediately, I saw him approach. I felt his hand on my hair. And the touch itself seemed to ignite to a blaze my smoldering anxiety and longing.

And a strange thought came to me even in the midst

of this terrible moment. All the aching in my thighs, the shuddering in my sore muscles, even the itching soreness of my backside—all of it belonged to this man, the Master. It belonged to him and would have its fullest meaning only if it pleased him. Lexius did not have to tell me so. The crowd, still at a bow, the row of helpless, manacled slaves, the rich canopy and those who held it, and all the rituals of the palace itself—all this told me so. And my nakedness in this moment seemed something quite beyond humiliation. My awkward position seemed perfect for the proper display, and the throbbing in my nipples and cock quite appropriate.

The hand lingered. The fingers burned my cheek, caught the tears, grazed my lips. A sob broke from me, though I kept my lips shut. The fingers were right against them. Dare I kiss the fingers? All I saw was the purple of his robe. The gleam of his red slipper. Then I gave the kiss, and the fingers remained, curled, still, hot against my mouth.

And, when I heard his voice, it was as if in a dream, Lexius's soft answer following like an echo. The thong tapped my thighs. A hand cupped my head, turned me. I moved, keeping the low squat, and saw the whole garden again in a blaze of light. Saw the canopy moving on, saw those who carried the poles behind, saw Lexius following at the elbow of the Lord, and the figure of Tristan following with frightening dignity. I was put at Tristan's side. We continued, part of the procession, together.

LAURENT:
THE
ROYAL
BEDCHAMBER

Iᴛ ꜱᴇᴇᴍᴇᴅ an hour that we were in the garden. But it could not have been a quarter of that time. And, when we reached the doors of the palace again, I was astonished because no other slaves had been chosen. Of course, we were new to the palace. Perhaps it was inevitable that we be observed. I didn't know. I was only relieved that it had happened.

And as we followed the Lord down the corridor, the canopy still over his head, a score of attendants coming behind, I felt the relief more profoundly than fear of what would now be asked of us.

My thighs were aching and the muscles twitching uncontrollably from the squatting position as we came into a large and grandly decorated bedchamber. And at once, the subdued moans of the slaves who decorated the room rose to greet the Master. They were in niches in the walls. And bound to the posts of the bed. And, in the distant bath, their bodies circled the stone jet of a high fountain.

We were made to stop and remain in the center of the room. Lexius moved to the far wall and stood with his hands behind his back and his head bowed.

The grooms of the Sultan removed his cloak and his slippers, and he visibly relaxed, sending his servants away with an off-hand gesture. He turned and walked about as though taking a deep breath after the weight of the ceremonial procession. And he took not the slightest notice of the slaves whose moans grew softer, more unobtrusive, as though there were an etiquette to it.

The bed behind him stood upon a dais and was draped in white and purple veils and covered with thickly tapestried covers. And those bound to the pillars were standing with arms tied high above them, some facing out, others facing in where obviously they might see the Master as he slept. In my dim vision, they looked as they had in the corridors—like statues. As I didn't dare to turn my head or to look at any one particular thing, I could not even tell whether or not these slaves were men or women.

As for the bath, all I could see was an immense pool of water beyond a row of thin, enameled columns, and the circle of slaves standing in the pool, the water spurting upwards and coming down quietly over their shoulders and bellies. Men and women there were in that circle, I could see, their wet bodies reflecting the torchlight becomingly.

Beyond, the arched windows were open to the moon and to soft breezes and quiet night sounds.

I felt hot all over and taut as a bowstring. In fact, I gradually realized I was terrified. And I knew that all such intimate scenes as this had always terrified me. I preferred the garden, the cross, even the procession with its horrid scrutiny. Not this silence in the bedroom which precursed the rawest and most heartfelt disasters of the soul, the most thorough subjugation.

What if I did not understand the Lord's commands, his obvious wishes? Waves of excitement passed over me, further heating me, and confusing me.

The Lord meantime spoke to Lexius. And his voice sounded familiar and pleasant. Lexius answered with obvious respect but the same air of pleasantness. He pointed to us, but which of us I couldn't know, and seemed to be explaining something.

The Lord was amused and he drew near again, and put out his hands, touching our heads simultaneously. He rubbed my hair hard and affectionately, as if I was a good little animal that pleased him. The pain in my thighs worsened. And my heart seemed to open. I held steady, smelling the perfume that rose from his robes and knowing exquisitely that Lexius was pleased, Lexius was here, it was as he wanted. Our other games seemed embarrassingly insignificant. He was right about my destiny, right about destiny itself. And I was fortunate I had not ruined it.

Lexius had come round behind me, and at the Lord's command he gripped my collar and lifted me until I was in a straight standing position. Lovely relief to my legs, though Tristan was left as he was, but I felt suddenly more vulnerable and visible.

I was turned around and I heard the Sultan laugh as he spoke, and I felt a hand touch my sore bottom. It played with the round rim of the wide phallus. And a sense of shame surprised me and inundated me. Lexius whipped the front of my knees as he bent my head down. I kept my legs ramrod straight and lowered my head and chest as far as I could. But having my arms bound to the phallus made it impossible for me to bend low. I was merely bent over.

The hands examined the welts. My sense of shame deepened. But it didn't mean I had been disobedient, did it, the redness, the evidence of the whipping? Other slaves had been whipped just for pleasure. And it pleased him obviously. Why else would he touch, comment? Nevertheless, I felt small and miserable, and my tears came again, and when I felt a little sob inside me, my chest tensed and all the straps pulled tight and my manacled arms pulled at the phallus. It made me sob a little harder, silently, feeling all of it, and his fingers dividing my buttocks as if to see my anus and then touching the hair there, smoothing it.

He talked rapidly and pleasantly still to Lexius. I realized that at the palace at least the slave would have known what was said. This foreign tongue utterly dismissed us. I might have been the subject of their discourse. Or maybe it was about something else altogether.

Whatever the case, Lexius whipped my chin teasingly with the thong. I straightened. He turned me by the hook in the phallus until I was facing the bath. I saw the Sultan to my right, though I didn't look at him.

Lexius whipped my calves sharply and quickly with four or five strokes, and I started to march, hoping this was correct, and then I saw him point the thong to the far row of columns, and I marched quickly towards the columns, feeling again a weird mixture of dignity and humiliation due to the straps and manacles.

I heard the snap of his fingers when I had reached the columns, and I turned around, my face coloring, and I marched back, seeing the dim, blurred outline of the two robed figures watching me.

I stepped high and fast, and the whole little procedure had its predictable effect. I felt more the slave than I had even moments ago, more than I had on the path. Lexius whipped me and pointed for me to turn again and repeat the march. And as I did so, weeping heavily and silently, I hoped that pleased them. It occurred to me as I came back across the room that it would be terrible if my tears were construed as impertinence, as a lack of submission. And this thought so frightened me that I was crying worse than before as I stopped before them. I stared forward, seeing nothing but the carvings on the far walls, the spirals, the leaves, tracery of pattern and color.

The Sultan's hand went up to my face and felt the tears as it had on the path. My throat was moving under the high collar with repeated sobs. And I felt I could hardly endure the sweetness of it, the maddening increase of tension, as he touched my naked chest, as he moved his hand away from my stinging nipples and down to touch my naval. If he touched my cock, I knew I might lose control. And this produced helpless moans.

But the thong quickly pushed me to the side. I was directed to squat again, and now Tristan was made to rise, to bend over.

And I was slightly amazed to realize I might look right at the Sultan without his noticing it. I couldn't lower my head because of the collar. And there he was, standing to my left and quite absorbed with Tristan. I decided, or rather couldn't resist the temptation, to study him.

I saw a youthful face, just as I had suspected I would, and one that was nothing as formidable or mysterious as that of Lexius. His power did not represent itself in obvious pride or haughtiness. This was for lesser men. Rather, he exuded an extraordinary presence, a radiance. He was smiling as he kneaded Tristan's buttocks and played with the bronze phallus, obviously rocking it with the hook as Tristan bent over.

Then Tristan was made to stand up, and the Sultan's face took on a charming air of appreciation of Tristan's beauty. In sum, he seemed a pleasant, handsome man, quick-witted, and enjoying his slaves casually. His short, full hair was beautiful, more lustrous than that of most of the men here, and it grew back from his temples in thick, lovely waves. His eyes were brown and, for all their quickness, just a little thoughtful.

He was a being I might have liked instantly in some harmless place. But now, this cheerfulness, this obvious good nature, made me feel weaker, more abandoned. I didn't fully understand it. But I knew it had to do with his expression, that he so thoroughly enjoyed us, and it seemed so natural.

At the castle, there had been a deliberate quality to everything that was done. We were royalty. We were to be enhanced by our service. Here, we were nameless and nothing.

The Sultan's face brightened as Tristan was made to march, and it seemed that Tristan did so infinitely better than I did. He had more dignity, more spirit. His shoulders were more cruelly bent back, it seemed, because his arms were a little shorter than mine and laced more tightly to the phallus.

I tried not to see. He was doing it all too well. And my desire rose and fell in awesome and tormenting rhythm.

Tristan was soon enough made to squat beside me. And now we were turned to face the distant row of columns and the bath and then made to kneel together.

My heart shrank when Lexius showed us a gilded ball. I understood the game. But how would we ever manage to retrieve it when we could not use our hands? I shuddered at the thought of our awkwardness. The game was precisely the kind of intimacy I had dreaded when we entered the bedchamber. It was bad enough to be scrutinized; now we must strive to give amusement.

Instantly, Lexius sent the ball rolling across the floor, and, on our knees, Tristan and I struggled after it. Tristan pulled ahead of me and dipped to catch it in his teeth. He managed it without falling. And I realized suddenly that I had failed. Tristan had won. There was nothing to do but struggle back to our Masters, where Lexius was already taking the ball from Tristan's mouth as he stroked Tristan's hair approvingly.

He glared at me, and his thong whipped my bare belly as I knelt before him. I could hear the Sultan's laughter, though I looked down and saw nothing but the floor gleaming before me. Lexius whipped my chest, my legs. I winced, the tears spilling again. He forced us around, in position to compete with each other again, and once more the ball was thrown. And this time I really went after it.

Tristan and I struggled against each other, trying to push each other to the side as the ball came to rest before us. I managed to get hold of it, but he confounded me by snatching it right from my mouth and turning at once to take it back to the Master.

I was in a silent rage. Both of us had been commanded to please the Sultan, and now we had to fight each other to do so, and one would win and one would lose. It seemed beastly unfair.

But all I could do was return to our Lords and be whipped again by that hated little thong, the thing finding the sore flesh in back this time as I knelt still, weeping.

The third time I got the ball and shoved Tristan over when he tried to take it. And the fourth time Tristan got it again, and I was frantic. By the fifth race, we were both out of breath and had forgotten all about grace of any sort, and I could hear the Sultan laughing lightly as he watched Tristan steal the ball from me, and me stumble after him. I dreaded the thong this time as it cut at my welts, and I wept miserably as it came whistling down through the air, the strokes long and hard and fast as Tristan knelt receiving approval.

But the Sultan shocked me suddenly because he drew near and he touched my face again. The thong stopped. And, in a moment of exquisite stillness, his silken fingers wiped my tears once more, as if he liked the feel of them. And there came the lovely warm feeling of my heart opening again, as it had on the garden path, the feeling that I belonged to him. I felt I had tried to please. I was simply slower, less agile, than Tristan. His fingers lingered. And when his voice rose, speaking rapidly to Lexius, I felt that it was touching me too, stroking me, possessing me and tormenting me with perfect authority.

In a blur I saw Lexius's thong tapping Tristan, directing him to turn and approach the bed on his knees. I was ordered to follow, but the Sultan walked along beside me, and I felt his hand playing with my hair still, lifting it above the collar.

I was in a low ache of desire. My faculties were drowning in it. I saw the bodies tethered to the four posts of the bed—beauties all, women turned in to face the Lord as he slept, men turned out, and all of them moving under their bonds as if to acknowledge the Master's approach—and my vision seemed to dim even more, so that the bed looked not like a bed but rather like an altar. The tapestried covers blazed with tiny configurations.

We knelt at the foot of the dais. And Lexius and the Sultan were behind us. There was the soft sound of cloth falling, of fabric untied, bits of metal unclasped.

Then the naked figure of the Sultan moved into my vision. He stepped up on the dais, his body shimmering in its cleanliness and smoothness, its lack of any mark, and he sat down on the side of the bed, facing us.

I tried not to look into his face. But I could see he was smiling. His organ was erect, and it seemed a momentous thing to see it, in this world where so many underlings were naked. The thong tapped Tristan, directed him to stand and to go up on the dais, and then to stretch out on the bed. The Sultan turned to watch him, and I burned with envy, with terror. But, immediately, the thong summoned me too, and I rose from my knees and made the step and then looked down on the covers where Tristan lay, still manacled, as if he were a gorgeous victim to be slaughtered in blood offering. My heart was beating hard and loud in my ears. I looked at his cock and let my eyes move timidly to the right until I could see the naked lap of the Master, and his organ rising from its shadow of black hair, a fine enough endowment.

The thong tapped my shoulder. It tapped my chin and pointed to the bed, to the spot before Tristan's cock. I moved slowly, tentatively, but the directions were clear. I was to lie beside him, facing him, but with my head at his cock, and my cock at his head. My heart was racing now.

The cover felt rough beneath me, the thick embroidery

oddly like sand under my skin. And I felt the manacles cruelly. I had to struggle like an armless thing to assume the correct position, and lying on my side was awkward, and I felt like the bound victim now. And there was Tristan's cock right near my lips. And I knew that his lips were near my organ as well. I twisted against the manacles, against the abrasive cover, and I felt my cock touch Tristan, but, before I could move away, a hand on the back of my head urged me forward. I took the gleaming cock into my mouth and felt Tristan's mouth close on me in the same moment.

The pleasure engulfed me completely. I moved down on the cock, my lips tight, my tongue playing with the length of it, my mouth savoring it, and felt the hard sucking on my own cock carry me up and out of the divine penance of the last few hours.

I knew that I was undulating, straining against the manacles, that each motion of my head on the cock made me look all the more like a lost soul struggling vainly on the altar of the bed, but it did not matter. What mattered was to suck the cock and to be suckled by Tristan's firm, delicious mouth, to have all my spirit dragged out of me. And when at last I came, thrusting uncontrollably into him, I felt his fluids feeding me as if I had been starving forever for them. It seemed we rocked each other's bodies with our strength, our muffled moans.

And then I felt the hands separating us. I was made to lie on my back, my bound arms under me, forcing my chest up as my head fell back, my eyes half closing. I couldn't see the nipple clamps, of course. But I could feel them, and feel the chains against my chest, and it seemed these were mountain peaks of exposure.

Then I realized that the Sultan was smiling down on me. Brown eyes, smooth lips, drawing closer and closer. It seemed a deity descending, who only accidentally bore a resemblance to an ordinary man. He knelt on all fours above me.

And his lips touched mine. Or, to be more truthful, they touched the wetness on my lips. Then he opened my mouth and his tongue dipped deep inside and lapped at Tristan's semen, which was still on my tongue, still in my throat. And realizing what he wanted, I opened my mouth to him, kissing and being kissed, and wishing I could feel his whole weight, even if it did hurt my clamped nipples. But that he denied me as he hovered over me.

I knew that Tristan was being moved. That Lexius was near. But I could think of nothing but this kissing, the desire ebbing as it had to do after the climax, and then coming back painfully and exquisitely soon.

And now it was not really kissing. My mouth was pushed open wider by his tongue, and he lapped the semen out of my mouth, cleaning my mouth with his tongue, as it were, as each prod of it aroused me.

And slowly, through the haze of rekindled feeling, I saw that Tristan was behind him, above him. I felt him press down against me. His body felt like Lexius's body had felt, pampered and silken, strong but lean. His fingers moved over my chest, released the nipple clamps. They slipped to the side with their chains, were taken away. And his chest rested against my sore skin, making it throb deliciously.

Tristan was above him, looking down into my face. Radiant blue eyes. And, when the Sultan groaned, I realized that Tristan had entered him. I felt the weight.

But the Sultan went on searching my mouth with his tongue, forcing my jaws wider. Tristan thudded against him, pushing him against me, and my cock rose between the Sultan's thighs, feeling the sweet, hairless, protected flesh there.

When Tristan came I bucked, stroking the tight thighs with my thrusts, pushing again to climax, and I felt the thighs press together to take me. I came, moaning, even as the Sultan's tongue went on with its work, lapping at my teeth, lapping under my tongue, licking my lips slowly.

He rested then for a little while, his arm under my neck. I lay bound and helpless beneath him and let the pleasure die away slowly.

Then he stirred. He rose up, refreshed, ready for more, and then straddled me. His face was almost boyish as we looked at each other, a bit of dark hair fallen in his eyes. I saw Tristan sitting on the left, looking at us. The Sultan pushed me firmly to mean I must turn over on my face. And I struggled to move myself.

He rose up to give me space to do it, and I felt Lexius's hands assisting me. Then I was on my chest, and I felt the leather bracelets being taken off. My shoulders relaxed. My whole body softened against the cover. The hard, bronze phallus was drawn out, and as I lay still, my anus burning like a ring of fire, his all too human cock slipped inside, stoking the fire and increasing it. How good that felt after the cold bronze, that human thing inside me. I kept my hands at my sides. I closed my eyes. My own cock was pressed to the rough tapestry cover. And my sore backside rose to feel his weight, feel his rocking cadence.

I was in a daze more pure than any that I'd known earlier. And it was a gratuitous sweetness that he was using me, would empty into me, and I knew something about him now, something interesting, though it did not really matter. He wanted the fluids of other men. That was why those Lords in the garden had been allowed to use us, why the grooms had not washed us before they put in the phalluses.

It amused me. We'd been purged, then filled with masculine juices. And now he had eaten from my mouth and he reamed out my backside slowly as he worked towards the pinnacle, his body sealed to the abraded, welted flesh. He took his time, and I saw in lovely blurred images the garden again, the procession, his smiling face, all the bits and pieces of this mosaic that was life in the palace of the Sultan.

Before he was finished with me, Tristan had mounted him again. I felt the added weight and heard the Sultan moan with a slight, supplicating sound.

LAURENT:
MORE
SECRET
LESSONS

Tristan and the Sultan lay in an embrace on the bed, both of them naked, and they were kissing, their mouths feeding slowly upon each other.

In silence, Lexius motioned for me to withdraw. I watched him pull the curtains round the bed and lower the lamps.

Then I proceeded on hands and knees out of the room, wondering why I so much feared Lexius's disappointment that I had not been chosen to remain instead of Tristan.

It seemed an impossible thing. Tristan and I had both been ordered to please, and then pitted against each other. Could there have been two chosen to remain?

In the shadowy corridor, Lexius snapped his fingers for me to move quickly ahead. All the way back to the bath, he whipped me hard and in silence. At every turn in the corridors, I hoped he might slack off. But he did not. And, by the time I was given over to the grooms, I was throbbing with pain again and weeping softly.

But then it was all gentleness, except for the purge itself, which was quite thorough. And as the oil was being rubbed in, as the massage soothed my aching arms and legs, I slipped into a deep sleep away from all dreams and thoughts of the future.

When I awoke, I was lying on a pallet on the floor. Lamps were lighted in the room. I knew I was in Lexius's chamber. I rolled over and rested my head in my hands, looking about me. Lexius was standing at the window, looking out into the darkened garden. He wore his robe, but I could see it was loose, ungirdled, probably open in front. It seemed he was whispering with his thoughts, or murmuring. I couldn't make out the words he said. He might as well have been singing.

He turned and was startled when he saw me looking at him. I was resting my head on my right elbow. His robe was open, and he was naked under it. He came closer, his back to the pale illumination seeping through the window.

"No one has ever done to me what you did," he whispered.

I laughed softly. Here I was in his rooms, unmanacled, and he naked, and he was saying this to me.

"How unfortunate for you," I said. "Beg me and I might do it again." I didn't wait for him to answer. I stood up. "But tell me first—did we please the Sultan? Are you satisfied?"

He took a step backwards. I realized I could drive him right to the wall merely by advancing towards him. It was too amusing.

"You pleased him!" he said a little breathlessly.

And he was so handsome in a fragile sort of way, a feline man, something like the sword with which the desert people fight—gracefully shaped and light yet deadly.

"And you, were you pleased?" I stepped a little closer, and again he backed away.

"You ask foolish questions," he said. "There were a hundred new slaves on the garden path. He might have passed us over completely. As it was, he chose both of you."

"And now I choose you," I said. "Aren't you flattered?" I reached out and took a lock of his hair.

He shuddered.

"Please . . ." he said softly. He looked down, rather irresistibly, I thought.

"Please what?" I asked. I kissed the hollow of his cheek, and then his eyes, forcing them closed with my kisses. It was as if he were bound and manacled and couldn't move.

"Please be gentle," he answered. Then he opened his eyes, and his arms wound round me as if he couldn't control himself. He embraced me and held me tightly as if he were a lost child. I kissed his neck, his lips. I ran my hands under his robe and along his narrow back, loving the feel of his skin, his smell, the floss of his hair against me.

"Of course, I'll be gentle," I purred into his ear. "I will be very gentle . . . when it suits me."

He broke away and dropped down on his knees, and took my cock in his mouth, his whole body hungry for it, starving for it. I stood motionless, letting him move up and down on it, letting his tongue and his teeth do their work, my hand on his shoulders.

"Not so quickly, young one," I said softly. It was excruciating to move his mouth away. He kissed the tip. I pushed off his robe and lifted him up. "Put your arms around my neck and hold tight," I said. I lifted his legs as he obeyed, and I wound them around my waist. My cock was bumping under his spread backside, and then I shoved into him, my hands cupping his buttocks, his arms grasping tighter to me, his head bent on my shoulder. I stood with legs apart and thrust into him with all my strength, and his body rode the thrusts, my fingers pinching, clawing at the flesh I'd whipped earlier.

"After I come," I whispered in his ear, squeezing his backside, "I am going to take that strap of yours and whip you again, whip you so hard that all day long under your beautiful robes you'll feel the marks I put on you, you'll know you're as much a slave as those beings you command, and you'll know who your Master is."

The only answer was another lingering kiss as I spent into him.

I didn't whip him so hard. After all, he was a mere fledgling. But I made him crawl about the room, I made him bathe my feet with his tongue, and I made him arrange the pillows for me on the bed. Then I seated myself and made him kneel beside me, with his hands behind his neck as slaves at the castle had been trained to do.

I inspected what I had done, and I played with his cock a little, wondering how he liked the teasing, the hunger. I whipped his cock with the strap. It was so blood dark that it was almost purple in the lamplight. His face was beautifully tormented, eyes full of suffering and absorption in what was happening to him. I felt a peculiar stirring inside me when I looked at his eyes, something rare, and strong, and unlike the overall weakness I had felt when I looked at the Sultan.

"Now we will talk," I said. "And you will tell me first, where is Tristan?"

This startled him, naturally.

"Sleeping," he answered. "The Sultan released him an hour or so ago."

"I want you to send for him. I want to talk to him, and I want to see him take you."

"O, please, no . . ." he said. He went down to kiss my feet.

I doubled up the strap and smacked his face with it.

"Do you want marks on your face, Lexius?" I asked. "Put your hands behind your neck, and keep your form when I'm talking to you."

"Why do you do this to me?" he whispered. "Why must the revenge be taken out on me?" His eyes were so large, so beautiful. I couldn't keep myself from leaning over and kissing him, feeling his hot mouth suck at my mouth.

It was unlike kissing any other man, kissing him. He pumped a molten spirit into his kisses. He said things with them—more than he knew, I suspected. I could have kissed him for a long time, that alone giving him surges of pleasure.

"I don't do it for revenge," I said. "I do it because I like to do these things to you, and you need it. You positively require it. You wish you were on your hands and knees with us. You know you do."

He burst into tears, silently, biting his lip. "If I could serve you always. . . ."

"Yes, I know. But you can't pick whom you serve. That's the trick. You must give yourself over to the idea of service. You must surrender to that. . . . And each true Master or Mistress becomes all Masters and Mistresses."

"No, I cannot believe that."

I laughed softly. "I should run away and take you with me. I should put on your handsome robes, darken my face and hair, and take you with me, naked over my saddle, as I said before."

He was shuddering, eating the language, and being intoxicated by it. He knew everything about training and punishing and disciplining, and absolutely nothing about being on the other end of it.

I lifted his chin. He wanted me to kiss him again, and I did, taking my time with it, wishing it didn't make me feel so much his slave suddenly. I ran my tongue down along the inside of his lower lip.

"Get Tristan," I said. "Bring him here. And, if you speak another word in protest, I'll let Tristan whip you also."

If he didn't see through that little ploy, he was not only beautiful but brainless.

After he rang the bell, he went to the door and waited. Without opening it, he gave the order. And he stood with his arms folded and head bowed, looking lost, as if he needed some fine, strong Prince to fight the dragons of his passion and rescue him from destruction. How touching. I sat on the bed, devouring him with my eyes. I loved the curve of his cheekbones, the fine line of his jaw, the way that he passed through the attitudes of man, boy, woman, and angel with varying gestures and little changes in his expression.

A knock on the door startled him. Again he spoke. He listened. Then he unbolted the door and beckoned, and Tristan came in on his knees, eyes down demurely. Lexius bolted the door behind him.

"Now I have two slaves," I said, sitting up. "Or you have two Masters, Lexius. It's difficult to judge the situation one way or the other."

Tristan looked up at me, saw me naked on the bed, and then glanced in perfect bewilderment at Lexius.

"Come here, come sit with me. I want to talk to you," I said to Tristan. "And you, Lexius, kneel here as you were before and be quiet."

That summed it up, I thought. Tristan took a moment to absorb it, however. He took in the naked body of our Master, and then he looked at me. He rose and came over to the bed, and sat down beside me.

"Kiss me," I said. I put my hand up to guide his face. Nice kiss, more robust but less intense than the kisses of Lexius, who was kneeling right behind Tristan. "Now turn and kiss our forlorn Master there," I said.

Tristan obeyed, slipping his arm around Lexius, and Lexius gave himself to the kiss a little too completely to suit me. And maybe to spite me.

When Tristan turned back, his eyes questioned me directly.

I ignored the question.

"Tell me what happened after I was dismissed. Did you continue to please the Sultan?"

"Yes," Tristan answered. "It was rather like a dream—being chosen, lying with him finally. There was something so tender in him. He isn't our Master really. He's our Sovereign. There's quite a difference."

"True," I said, smiling.

He wanted to say more, but again he glanced at Lexius.

"Let him alone," I said. "He's my slave, and he awaits my will, and I'll let you have him in a moment. But talk to me first. Are you content, or are you still grieving for your old Master in the village?"

"Not grieving anymore," he said, then he broke off. "Laurent, I was sorry that I had to win over you—"

"Don't be foolish, Tristan. It was what we were made to do, and I lost because I couldn't win. It's as simple as that."

He looked again at Lexius.

"Why are you tormenting him, Laurent?" he asked, his tone slightly accusatory.

"I'm glad you're content," I said. "I couldn't tell. But what if the Sultan never asks for you again?"

"That doesn't matter, really," he answered. "Unless, of course, it matters to Lexius. But Lexius won't ask the impossible of us. We've been noticed, that's what Lexius wanted."

"And you'll be just as happy?" I asked.

Tristan thought for a moment before he answered.

"There's something very different here," he said, finally. "The atmosphere is charged with a different sense of things. I'm not lost as I was so long ago at the castle when I served a timid Master who didn't know how to discipline me. And I am not condemned in shame to the village where I need my Master, Nicolas to retrieve me from chaos and shape my suffering for me. I am a part of a finer, more sacrosanct order." He studied me. "Do you see my meaning?"

I nodded and gestured for him to continue. It was clear

he had more to say, and his expression let me know that he was telling the truth. The misery I'd seen in his face all the time we were at sea was truly gone now.

"The palace is engulfing," he said, "as the village was. In fact, it is infinitely more so. But we are not bad slaves here. We are merely part of an immense world in which our suffering is offered up to our Lord and his Court whether or not he ever deigns to acknowledge it. I find something sublime in this. It is as if I have advanced to another stage of understanding."

Again, I nodded. I remembered my feelings in the garden when the Sultan had picked me from the ranks. But this was only part of the many things I could and did feel about this place and what had happened to us. In this room, with Lexius, something different was occurring.

"I began to understand it," Tristan said, "when we were first taken from the ship and carried through the streets to be viewed by the common people. And it came fully clear to me when I was blindfolded and bound in the garden. In this place we are *nothing* but our bodies, *nothing* but the pleasure we give, *nothing* but our capacity for evincing feeling. All else is gone, and it is quite impossible to think of something as *personal* as whippings on the Public Turntable of the village or the constant education in passivity and submissiveness we knew at the castle."

"True," I said. "But without your old Master, Nicolas, without his love as you described, isn't there a terrible loneliness—"

"No," he said candidly. "Since we are nothing here, we are all connected to each other. In the village and the castle, we were divided by shame, by individual humiliations and punishments. Here we are joined in the indifference of the Master. And we are all cared for in that indifference and used rather well, I think. It is like the designs on the walls here. There are no pictures of men and women, as you find in Europe. There are only flowers, spirals, repetitive designs that suggest a continuum. And we are part of that continuum. To be noticed by the Sultan for a night, to be valued now and then—that is all we can and should hope for. It is as if he paused in the corridor and he touched the mosaic on the wall. He touched the design as the sun hits it. But it is a design like all the other designs, and, when he moves on, it lapses back into the overall pattern."

"You're such a philosopher, Tristan," I whispered. "You overawe me."

"Don't you feel the same? That there is a great order of things here that is in itself rather exciting?"

"Yes, I can feel this," I said.

His face clouded. "Then why do you upset the order, Laurent?" He asked. He looked at Lexius. "Why have you done this to Lexius?"

I smiled. "I don't upset the order," I said. "I merely give it a secret dimension that makes it more interesting to me. Do you think our Lord Lexius couldn't defend himself if he chose to? He could summon his army of grooms, but he doesn't."

I climbed off the bed. I took Lexius's hands from behind his neck and twisted his arms back so his wrists were firmly held right at his backside. In sum, I trussed him much as we had been trussed with the bracelets and the phallus. I stood him up and forced him to bend over. He was absolutely pliant in all this, though he was crying. I kissed his cheek, and he softened gratefully, but his cock didn't soften.

"Now, our Lord needs to be punished," I said to Tristan. "Have you never felt that need? Have a little compassion. He is a mere beginner in this realm. It's hard for him."

The tears streamed down Lexius's face beautifully. The light caught the tears. But another light suffused Tristan's face as he looked up at Lexius. He rose on his knees on the bed and put his hands on the sides of Lexius's face. There was love and understanding in Tristan's expression.

"Look at his body," I said softly. "You've seen stronger slaves, slaves more well muscled, but look at the quality of his skin."

Tristan's eyes moved over him slowly, and Lexius cried softly.

"The nipples," I said. "They're virginal. Never been whipped, clamped."

Tristan examined them. "Very lovely," he said. He watched Lexius carefully. He played with Lexius's nipples just a little roughly.

I could feel the tension shoot through Lexiu , his arms stiffening in my grasp. I pulled them back harder, forcing his chest out.

"And the cock. It's a good size, a good length, wouldn't you say?"

Tristan inspected it with his fingers as he had the nipples. He pinched the tip, scratched at it a little with his nails, ran his hand down the length of it.

"I would say he's as fine a quality as we are," I murmured, drawing near to Lexius's ear.

"True," Tristan said very earnestly. "But he's *too* virginal. When a slave's been used, really well worked, the body is enhanced in some way."

"I know. If we work on him every time there is the opportunity, we can make him perfect. By the time we are sent home, he will be as good a slave as we are."

Tristan smiled. "What a lovely thought. What a lovely secret aspect to things." He kissed Lexius on the cheek. I could see the gratitude in Lexius's manner, and see Tristan drawn to him, see and feel the current that passed between them.

"Yes," I answered. "A lovely secret aspect to things. I have found my lover here, as you did in the village. And my lover is Lexius. And I think I will love him all the more in a little while when he punishes me or trains me as he must, when another day dawns here in which he is again the Master."

Tristan's cock was hard, his eyes a bit feverish as they moved over Lexius.

"I would like to whip him," he said quietly.

"Of course," I said. "Turn around, Lexius." I let his arms go.

"Bend over and put your hands down between your legs," Tristan said. He got off the bed so that he could stand behind Lexius, turning him to just the right position. "Gather your balls and keep them covered with your hands and brought forward."

Lexius obeyed, bending from the waist. I stood beside him. Tristan adjusted the position of his backside, then spread his legs a little wider. He took the strap from me, and then he swung it hard, whipping Lexius right in the crack of his backside.

Lexius winced. I was a little surprised myself at the deliberation of it. But Tristan was clearly not going to waste this opportunity. He seemed the very opposite of the weak Master he had once had who couldn't work him.

He whipped Lexius again in the same manner, and, moving even farther back, he swung the strap up, smacking the anus and the crack and even the fingers with which Lexius protected his scrotum. Lexius couldn't keep still. But the whipping went on, moving into a nice cadence. And Lexius wept, his rear rising and falling with his struggles, the strap cracking again and again on the tender flesh between his anus and his lifted scrotum.

I went round to the front and lifted Lexius's chin.

"Look into my eyes," I said. The whipping continued in very thorough style. This was better than I had hoped it might be. Lexius was biting his lip, gasping. I felt that stirring of feeling again, that fount of affection and love. I was frightened suddenly.

I went down on my knees and kissed him again, and it was just as powerful as before, the strap sending the shudders through him, his tears spilling onto my face.

"Tristan," I said. Kisses, wet sucking kisses. "Don't you want him? Don't you want to show him how it is done properly, give him a good coring?"

Tristan was more than ready.

"Straighten up. I want you standing to take it," I said.

Lexius obeyed, still holding his scrotum. I was still on my knees looking up at him.

Tristan put his arms around Lexius's chest, and his fingers found the little virginal nipples.

"Spread your legs," I said to Lexius. I held his hips as Tristan entered him. And I let my lips touch the hungry, obedient cock, the poor, mastered cock right in front of me.

Then I went down on it to the hairy root, and, just before Tristan came, Lexius came, utterly dissolved in cries and release, so that we both supported him.

When it was finished and every last vibration of it was gone, he moved sluggishly to the bed, not waiting for any command or permission, and he lay there weeping uncontrollably.

I lay down beside him, and Tristan lay on the other side. I was still hard, but I could save it for the morning, save it for the next round of torment. It was nice just to be next to him and to kiss his neck.

"Don't weep so, Lexius," I said. "You know you needed it, you wanted it."

Tristan reached down between his legs and felt the reddened flesh below the anus.

"It's true, Master," he said softly. "How long have you wanted it?"

Lexius quieted a little. He moved his arm around my chest, drawing me even closer to him. He reached out for Tristan in the same way.

"I'm frightened," he whispered. "Desperately frightened."

"Don't be," I said. "You have us to master you, train you. And we will do it lovingly, at every opportunity."

We both kissed him and caressed him until he was still. He turned over. I wiped his tears.

"There are so many things I am going to do to you," I said. "So many things I mean to teach you."

He nodded, lowering his eyes.

"Do you . . . do you feel love for me?" he asked softly,

but his eyes were brilliant and clear as they looked up at me.

I was about to answer, of course, that I did, when my voice caught in my throat. I was looking down at him, and I opened my mouth to speak but nothing came. Then I heard myself answer:

"Yes, I do feel love for you."

And something passed between us, something silent, something locking us together. And this time when I kissed him I claimed him utterly. I shut out Tristan. I shut out the palace. I shut out our distant Lord the Sultan.

And when I drew back I was puzzled. I was the one who was frightened.

Tristan's face was calm and wistful.

A long moment passed.

"It's such an irony," Lexius said under his breath.

"No, it isn't really. There are Lords in the Queen's Court who give themselves over to slavery. It happens. . . ."

"No, I didn't mean that, that I should be so easily mastered," he answered. "The irony is that it should be *you* and that the Sultan should find both of you so pleasing. He's ordered you for the games in his garden tomorrow. You'll fetch the ball and bring it back to his feet. He'll pit you against each other in many games for his amusement and the amusement of his men. He's never chosen my slaves for that before. And he chooses you, and you choose me for this. That is the irony."

I shook my head. "Again, not really." I laughed softly. Tristan and I exchanged glances.

"We should rest now for the games, shouldn't we, Master?" Tristan asked.

"Yes," Lexius said. He sat up. He kissed us both again. "Please the Sultan and try not to be too cruel to me." He stood up and he put on his robe, and wound the girdle around it. I got his slippers for him and put them on his feet. He stood waiting for me to finish and then he gave his comb to me. I combed his hair, moving around him as I did it, and the feeling of possessing him, of owning him, transmuted itself into an awesome pride.

"You're mine," I whispered.

"Yes, that's true," he said. "And now you and Tristan will be bound to the crosses in the garden to sleep."

I winced. My face must have colored. But Tristan only smiled, glancing down bashfully.

"But don't worry about the sunlight," Lexius said. "The blindfold will keep it out. And you can listen to the song of the birds in peace."

The shock diffused.

"Is this your revenge?" I asked.

"No," he said simply, looking at me. "The Sultan's order. And he'll be awake soon. He may walk out into the garden."

"Then I can tell you the truth," I said, despite the catch in my throat. "I love those crosses!"

"Then why did you provoke me yesterday when I tried to mount you? Seems to me you would have done anything to avoid it."

I shrugged. "I wasn't tired then. I'm tired now. The crosses are good for resting."

But my face was still coloring intolerably.

"It makes you quake with fear, and you know it," he said. His voice was icy now, full of command. All the trembling and diffidence gone.

"True," I said. I gave him back his comb. "I suppose that's why I love it."

My courage had begun to fail me a little as we approached the door to the garden. The sharp shift from Master to slave left me giddy and full of a strange new ache that I could not clearly define or contain within myself. As we moved on our hands and knees down the corridor, I felt a profound vulnerability, an overwhelming need to cling to Lexius, to seek shelter in his arms, if only for a moment.

But it would have been folly to ask for this. He was

the Lord and Master again, and, whatever the confusion in his soul, it was now locked against me. Yet he dragged his feet in his own graceful way.

And when we reached the archway, he paused, his eyes moving over the little paradise of trees and flowers, over the slaves already tethered as we would soon be tethered.

"Any second," I thought, "he will call for the grooms. It will be done."

But Lexius merely stood motionless. And then I realized that both he and Tristan were looking down the path at four heavily robed Lords who approached us rapidly, their white linen headdresses pulled up to hide their faces as if they were out in the windblown sand rather than in this sheltered garden of the palace.

They looked like a hundred other such Lords, it seemed to me, save for the fact that they carried with them two rolled-up carpets, as if they were truly heading for a camp in the desert.

"Strange," I thought. "Why don't they have the servants carry these rugs for them?"

On and on they came until suddenly Tristan said "No!" so loudly that Lexius and I were both startled.

"What is it?" Lexius demanded.

But then we all knew. And we were forced back into the corridor and completely surrounded.

BEAUTY:
INTO
THE ARMS
OF
FATE

I T WAS near to morning.
Beauty could feel the fresh air coming through the grill
over the window even before she saw the light. It was
the sound of knocking that roused her.

Inanna lay still in her arms. And the knocking, unan-
swered, went on and on as Beauty sat up in the bed,
staring at the bolted doors. She held her breath until the
knocking stopped. Then she roused Inanna.

Immediately, Inanna was alarmed. She looked about
herself in confusion, eyes blinking uncomfortably in the
morning sun. Then she stared at Beauty, and her alarm
turned to terror.

Beauty wasn't unprepared for this moment. She knew what she had to do—slip out of Inanna's bedroom and somehow get back to the grooms without getting Inanna into trouble. Fighting the desire to embrace and kiss Inanna, she climbed off the bed and went to the door and listened. Then she turned to Inanna and made a gesture of farewell, blowing a kiss to Inanna, who burst into silent tears immediately.

Inanna came fast across the room and threw her arms around Beauty, and for a long moment they kissed again, the long luxurious kisses Beauty so loved. Inanna's tender, hot little sex was pressed against Beauty's legs, her breasts shivering against Beauty. When she bowed her head, her hair falling down to veil her face, Beauty lifted her chin and opened her mouth again, drinking the sweetness from it. Inanna was like a bird in a cage in Beauty's arms, her violet eyes magnified by their tears, her lips moist and beautifully reddened it seemed by her crying.

"Lovely, ripe creature," Beauty whispered, feeling of Inanna's plump little arms, pressing her thumb against Inanna's rounded chin as Inanna's mouth quivered hungrily. But there was no time now for lovemaking.

Beauty made the gesture for Inanna to be quiet and still, and she listened at the door again.

Inanna's face was full of misery. She seemed suddenly frantic, no doubt blaming herself for what might now happen to Beauty. But Beauty smiled again to reassure her and motioned for her to stay where she was. Then she opened the door and slipped into the corridor.

Inanna, her eyes swimming with tears again, crept out after her and pointed to a far door, in the opposite direction from that through which they'd come earlier.

As she removed the bolt, Beauty glanced back one more time, and her heart went out to Inanna. She thought of all the things that had befallen her since her passions had been awakened, and this last night seemed unlike any other. She wished she could tell Inanna that it would not be their last, that somehow they would manage to be together again. And it seemed Inanna did understand. She could see the determination in Inanna's eyes. There would be nights ahead to rival this one, no matter what the danger. And the thought that this inviting body with its luscious endowments belonged to Beauty as it did to no one else absolutely inflamed Beauty. She had many more things to teach Inanna. . . .

Inanna touched her hand to her lips and sent an urgent kiss to Beauty and, as Beauty nodded, Inanna nodded.

Then Beauty opened the door and ran fast and silently through the small empty passageway, rounding corner after corner, until she saw the massive double doors that most certainly would admit her again to the main corridors of the palace.

She paused for a moment to catch her breath. She did not know where to go, how to give herself up to those who must certainly be already searching for her. But it was a comfort to her that they could not question her. Only Lexius could do that. And if she did not lie to him at once, say some brute of a Lord had stolen her from the niche, how Lexius might punish her.

The thought chilled her, and yet it aroused her. She did not know whether she could lie. But she did know she would never betray Inanna. And she had never really been punished for serious wickedness, never been mercilessly questioned about any important or secret disobedience.

Now she was in possession of this wondrous intrigue, and she would know undreamed-of tortures when she heard Lexius's angry voice, when he became maddened by her silence.

Yet silence it must be. Disgrace and punishment it must be. And surely he would never dare to assume. . . .

But no matter. Beauty was ready. And her task now was to get through those doors and as far away from them as quickly as she could, so that no one could guess where she had been during her long absence.

Trembling, she stepped out into the wide marble hall

with its all too familiar torchlight and silent, bound slaves in their niches. Without even glancing to the right or the left, she ran to the very end of the hall and turned into another empty corridor.

On and on she ran, knowing that surely the slaves saw her. But who would question them as to what they had seen? She must get as far as she could from Inanna's quarters. And the silence and emptiness of the early-morning palace were her allies.

Her terror mounting, she turned another corner, and now she slowed her pace, her heart pounding, her nakedness all the more humiliating as she glimpsed for the first time the eyes of those on either side of her.

She bowed her head. If only she knew where to go. She would throw herself on the mercy of the grooms immediately. And surely they would understand she had not freed herself from her bonds. Someone had done it to her. And why wouldn't they assume the obvious: that it had been some masculine brute who had carried her off? Who would ever even suspect Inanna?

O, if only she would come upon the grooms, and then it would be over. She dreaded the sight of anger in their young faces, but let it come to pass if it must. Whatever Lexius did, she would remain silent.

All these thoughts were revolving in her head, her body constantly reminding her of Inanna's warmth, embraces, when suddenly she saw several Lords appear at the end of the corridor ahead of her.

This was her worst fear come true: that she would be discovered by others before the grooms found her. And when she saw the men pause for a moment and then advance towards her with great and deliberate speed, she panicked. She turned and ran as fast as she could, dreading a humiliating encounter, hoping against hope the grooms would appear to restore order.

And to her horror, the men came thudding after her.

"But why?" she thought desperately. "Why do they not merely send for the grooms? Why do they themselves chase me?"

And she almost screamed as she felt herself being picked up, the robes of the men suddenly closing her in, a heavy cloth being thrown around her. She was wound in the cloth as if it were a shroud and to her terror, she was lifted and thrown over a strong shoulder.

"But what is happening!" she screamed, only to have the sound muffled by the tight cloth. Surely this was not the way runaway slaves were apprehended. Something was wrong, very wrong.

And when the men continued to run, her body bouncing helplessly against her captor, she knew real fear as she had the night the Sultan's soldiers had raided the village to bring her here. They were stealing her, as she'd been stolen then. And she kicked and struggled and shrieked, only to have the tight wrapping hold her helpless.

Within moments, they were out of the palace. She heard the crunch of feet on sand, then on stones, echoing as if in a street. And then the unmistakable noises of the city surrounded her. Even the old smells reached her. They were actually moving through the marketplace!

And again, she shrieked and struggled, only to hear her own muffled cries closed inside the tight wrapping with her. Why, probably nobody even noticed these robed men moving through the crowd with a bolt of goods thrown over a shoulder. And, even if they did know there was a helpless being inside, what did they care? Mightn't it be a slave being taken to market?

She was weeping unstintingly when she heard their feet hit hollow wood, when she smelled the salt sea. They were taking her aboard a ship! Her thoughts raced desperately from Inanna to Tristan and Laurent, and Elena, and even the poor, forgotten Dmitri and Rosalynd. They would never even know what had happened to her!

"O, please, help me, help me!" she wailed. But the steps went on. She was being carried down a ladder, yes, she was sure of it. And into the hold of the ship. And the ship was alive with shouts and running feet. It was moving out of the harbor!

LAURENT:
DECISION
FOR
LEXIUS

But what do you mean, you are rescuing us!" Tristan cried out. "I won't go, I tell you! I don't want to be rescued!"

The man's face went white with rage. He had thrown down two carpets on the floor of the corridor. He had ordered us to lie down on these carpets so that we might be rolled up in them and carried out of the palace.

"How dare you!" He spit his words at Tristan now, while Lexius was held helpless by the others, a hand clamped over his mouth so that he couldn't sound an alarm for those unsuspecting servants who moved beyond in the garden.

I did not move to obey or to rebel. In an instant, I had realized it all. The tallest of the Lords was our own Captain of the Guard from the Queen's village. And the man who glared in fury at Tristan now was his former Master in the village, Nicolas, the Queen's Chronicler. They had come to take us home to our sovereign.

Instantly, Nicolas threw a rope around Tristan's arms, binding them tight to his chest, and then he looped the end around Tristan's wrists, forcing him down on his knees near the border of the carpet.

"I tell you I don't want to go!" Tristan said. "You have no right to steal us back. I beg you, beg you, to leave us here!"

"You're a slave, and you will do as I say!" Nicolas hissed in anger. "Lie down at once and be quiet, lest we're all discovered!" And he flung Tristan forward on his face and quickly rolled him over and over in the carpet, until no one could have told a man was hidden there.

"And you, Prince, must I bind you!" he demanded of me, pointing to the other carpet. The Captain of the Guard, who held Lexius in his firm grip, glared at me.

"Get down on that carpet and lie quiet, Laurent!" the Captain said. "We're in danger, all of us!"

"Are we?" I asked. "What will happen if your little plan is discovered?" I stared at Lexius. He was frantic. And he had never looked so charming and beautiful as he did now, with the Captain's hand over his mouth, his black hair tumbled into his enormous eyes, his slender body straining under its sleek robe. So I was never to see him again, and I wondered if he would be blamed for this! Who knew what would happen to him if he was blamed?

"Do as I say at once, Prince!" the Captain said, his face now twisted with the same desperate anger that disfigured Nicolas. Nicolas had the rope ready for me, and the two other men waited to assist him. But they could never have taken me against my will. And I was not as easily over-whelmed as Tristan.

"Hmmm. . . . Leave this place," I said slowly, looking

Lexius up and down, "and go back to the punishment of the village. . . ." I puzzled over it as if I had all the time in the world, seeing them become more anxious, more fearful of discovery by the second.

Behind them the garden lay quiet. Behind me was the corridor where anyone might approach at any moment.

"Very well," I said, "I'll come, but only if this one comes with me!" And I reached out and tore open Lexius's robe, revealing his naked chest down to the waist. I yanked him out of the Captain's grasp and shucked the robe off him completely. He stood trembling, but he did not raise a finger to help himself.

"What are you doing?" the Captain demanded.

"We're taking him with us," I said. "Or I don't go."

I threw Lexius forward onto the carpet. He gasped and lay still, his hair covering his face, his hands pressed against the rug as if he might suddenly rise and run. But he did not. And the welts and marks gleamed on his quivering backside.

I waited one second more, and then I lay down alongside him and placed my arm over his shoulder, bracing myself for the hot, stuffy wool to enclose me.

"Very well, then! Come on!" I heard Nicolas say desperately. "Hurry." He dropped down on his knees and reached for the edges of the rug.

But the Captain of the Guard stepped up and put his foot squarely on my back.

"Get up," he said to Lexius. "Or we'll take you, I swear it."

And I laughed softly as I saw Lexius lie motionless and silent, unable to save himself.

In an instant, they had us both wrapped in the rug, bound tightly together, and they were running with their heavy bundles. I had my arm around Lexius's neck, and he cried softly against my shoulder.

"How could you do this to me!" he pleaded, but it had a low dignified sound to it that I liked.

"Don't play games with me," I said in his ear. "You came of your own free will, my melancholy Lord."

"Laurent, I'm frightened," he whispered.

"Don't be," I said, softening, just a little regretful of my ominous tone. "You were born to be a slave, Lexius. And you know it. But you can forget what you know of Sultans and gilded manacles and jeweled leather and grand palaces."

BEAUTY:
REVELATIONS
AT SEA

BEAUTY SAT sobbing in the middle of the open carpet. The hold of the ship was very small and the lantern creeked on its hook, the ship traveling fast over the open sea, the windows pounded with spray, the whole craft listing slightly.

Now and then, she looked up at the baffled Captain of the Guard and at the angry Nicolas, who stared back at her.

Tristan sat in the corner with his knees drawn up and his head resting on his knees. And Laurent lay, smiling, on the bunk, watching everything as though it were very amusing.

And Lexius, poor beautiful Lexius, lay against the far wall, his face buried in the crook of his arm, his naked body seeming infinitely more vulnerable than her own. She could not understand why he had been recently whipped, why he had been brought with them.

"You can't mean, Princess, that you actually wished to remain in this strange land," Nicolas pleaded with her.

"But my Lord, it was such an elegant place, and so full of new delights and new intrigues. Why did you have to come? Why didn't you rescue Dmitri or Rosalynd or Elena?"

"Because we were not sent to rescue Rosalynd, or Dmitri or Elena," Nicolas replied angrily. "By all reports they are content in the Sultan's land and we were told to leave them there."

"And so was I content in the Sultan's land!" Beauty raged. "Why did you do this to me!"

"I too was content," said Laurent quietly. "Why didn't you leave us with the others?"

"Must I remind you that you are the Queen's slaves?" Nicolas stormed, glaring at Laurent and then at the silent Tristan. "It is Her Majesty who decides where and how her slaves will serve her. Your insolence is intolerable!"

Beauty could only break into helpless sobs again.

"Come," said the Captain of the Guard finally. "We have a long time to spend at sea. And you must not spend it weeping." He helped Beauty to her feet.

And unable to resist the urge to lean upon him, she pressed her face against his leather jerkin.

"There, there, my sweet," he said. "You haven't forgotten your Master, have you?" He led her out of the room and into a small adjacent cabin. The low wooden roof sloped down over the shelf bed. A bit of sun shone bright through the wet little porthole.

The Captain sat down on the side of the bed, and he put Beauty on his lap, his fingers inspecting her body— her breasts, her sex, her thighs.

She had to admit to herself that she was soothed by his touch. She leaned against his shoulder, and the feel of his rough beard delighted her, the smell of his leather clothes delighted her. It seemed in his hair she could smell the fresh country winds of Europe, and even the smell of the fresh cut grass in the fields of the village manor houses.

But still she cried. She would never see her beloved Inanna again. And would Inanna remember the lessons Beauty had taught her? Would she find some shared passion with the other women of the harem? Beauty could only hope so. What Beauty herself had learned, of the sweetness and intensity of such love, would always be with her.

Yet even now, in the Captain's arms, she thought of other kinds of love, of Mistress Lockley's rough wooden paddle that had punished her so well in the village, of the Captain's leather strap, and his hard cock which was pushing against her naked thigh now, the rough cloth of his breeches cruelly imprisoning it. She let her fingers touch it through the cloth. She felt it move, like a being unto itself.

And her nipples became two stiff little points as she sighed, her mouth opening as she looked up at the Captain. He was smiling and studying her. And he let her kiss the crust of beard on his chin and chew on his lower lip. She squirmed on his lap, pressing her breasts to his jerkin. His hand moved under her bottom, squeezing the flesh.

"No marks, no welts," he whispered in her ear.

"No, My Lord," she said. Just those delicate little thongs lashing at her. How she hated them. She slipped her arms tightly around his neck, her mouth covering his. She pushed her tongue between his lips.

"And we have become so forward," he said.

"Do you dislike it, My Lord?" she whispered, feeding on his lower lip, licking at his tongue and his teeth as she had done with Inanna.

"No, I can't say that I do," he said. "You don't know how I've missed you." He kissed her hard in response, his large roughened hand rising to squeeze her breast, to pull it towards him.

The sheer size of him aroused her.

"But I want your little bottom nicely pink and warm when I take you," he said.

"Anything to please you, My Lord," she said. "It's been so long. I'm . . . I'm a little afraid. I want so to please you."

"Of course you do," he said. He slid his hand between her legs and lifted her by her sex. And her legs felt weak, as if they could not actually support her. Returning to the village was like returning to a dream she could not shake off, could not wake from. She would cry again if she thought too much about it. Lovely Inanna.

But her Captain looked like a golden god to her in the sunlight from the tiny window, his crude-shaven beard glittering in the shadows, his eyes burning in the deep, tanned creases of his handsome face.

As he flung her over his lap, something snapped inside her head, some last little bit of resistance. As his enormous hand closed on her bottom, she rose up to fit herself into it, moaning with the hard pinch that came, the fingers stroking her flesh.

"Too smooth, too fine," he whispered above her. "Don't these little Arabs know how to punish properly?"

And with the first hard wallops, her sex pumped with juices against the Captain's thigh, her heart racing. The spanks echoed loudly in the tiny cabin, her flesh tingling, then burning, then flooded with delicious pain, her tears rising and quickly spilling.

"I am yours, my Lord," she whispered, half in love, half in supplication, the blows coming faster and harder on her bottom. He gathered her chin in his left hand and lifted her head. But he did not stop the punishment. "O, My Lord, I belong to you," she whimpered and cried, and it seemed all the memories of the village came back to her. "I will be yours again, won't I? I beg you!" she cried out.

"Shh, stop your impertinence," he said softly. And she was quickly rewarded with a new volley of hard spanks as she rocked and undulated under them without shame or modulation.

As it went on and on, it seemed the hardest punishment she had ever received. And she bit down on her lip not to beg for mercy. Yet she felt it was what she needed, what she deserved, what was wanted to clear away her doubts and fears.

And when the Captain flung her back on the bed, she was ready for his cock and lifted her hips to receive it. The small shelf bed seemed to shake under his thrusts. She bounced on the coverlet, her sore bottom slamming against the rough cloth, his weight riding her, crushing her, the cock stretching her and filling her divinely. Finally she climaxed, screaming against her sealed lips, and in the white-hot flashes of pleasure she saw both the Captain and Inanna. She thought of Inanna's gorgeous breasts, her wet little vagina; she thought of the Captain's thick organ and his semen spilling into her with his most violent thrusts; and she was crying for joy and for pain, the Captain's hand over her mouth, muffling her cries, which gave her the freedom to let them go from her whole being.

She lay still under him when it was done, her whole body gasping. And she was slightly dismayed when he lifted her. He was taking off his belt.

"But what have I done, My Lord?" she whispered.

"Nothing, my love. I want that bottom and those legs in good color, as they used to be." He stood her before him as he sat again on the side of the bed, his breeches still open, his cock still erect.

"O, My Lord," she begged, dissolving in weakness, the aftershocks of the pleasure growing stronger instead of fainter. He was doubling the strap.

"Now, every morning at sea, we will begin with a nice whipping, do you hear me, Princess?"

"Yes, My Lord," she whispered. So it was all as it should be again. So simple. She placed her hands on the back of her neck. And what had she dreamed in the ship before, about finding love? Well, there had been that heavenly taste. And it would come again. For now she had her Captain.

"Spread your legs," he said. "And now I want you to dance as you're whipped. Move those hips!" And the strap came down as she moaned and swung her bottom from side to side, the movement seeming to ease the pain, her sex throbbing. Her heart was gripped with fear and happiness.

It was almost dark. Beauty was lying on the carpet beside Laurent, their heads together on a pillow. The Captain and Nicolas and the others who had helped in the "rescue" had gone to take their evening meal together. The slaves had been fed, and Tristan was asleep in the corner. And so was Lexius. The ship was small and ill-equipped. No cages, no shackles.

It still puzzled Beauty that only she and Laurent and Tristan had been rescued. Had the Queen some new and special use for them? It was an agony not to know, and to suffer such envy of Dmitri, Elena, and Rosalynd.

And Beauty was also worried about Tristan. Nicolas, his former Master, had not spoken a word to Tristan since they had put to sea. He could not forgive Tristan for not wanting to be rescued.

"O, why can't he just punish Tristan and be done with it," Beauty thought. All through the evening meal, she had admired Laurent's strictness with Lexius. Laurent had forced him to eat his supper and to drink some wine, though Lexius insisted he wanted none, and then Laurent had made love to him slowly and deliberately, in spite of Lexius's obvious shame at being taken in front of others. Lexius was the most polite and demure slave Beauty had ever seen.

"He is almost too fine for you," she whispered to Laurent now as they rested together, the cabin warm and silent around them. "He's more of a Lady's slave, I think."

"You may use him if you like," Laurent said. "You may whip him, too, if you think he needs it."

Beauty laughed. She had never whipped another slave and did not really want—o, well, maybe. . . .

"How did you manage it," she asked, "the transformation from slave to Master, so easily?" She was glad of a chance to talk to Laurent. Laurent had always fascinated her. She could not get rid of the image in her memory of Laurent in the village strapped to the Punishment Cross. There was something insolent and wondrous about Laurent. She could not fully define it. He seemed to have an understanding of things which others did not possess.

"It has never been one or the other for me," Laurent said. "In my dreams, I liked both parts of the drama. And when I saw the opportunity I became the Master. Moving back and forth only sharpens the whole experience somewhat."

Beauty felt a little tumult in her loins at the confident sound of his voice, the soft ironic tone it had—ever on the edge of laughter. She turned to look at him in the shadows. His body was so large, so full of dormant power even as he lay there. He was taller even than her Captain. And his cock was still a little stiff, ready enough to be awakened. She looked into his dark brown eyes and saw he was watching her, smiling at her. Probably knowing her thoughts.

She blushed with sudden shyness. She couldn't fall in love with Laurent. No, that was impossible, quite.

But she didn't move when she felt his lips against her cheek. "Divine little brat," he growled in her ear. "You know, this might be our only chance. . . ." And his voice died away into a lower growl, the purr of a lion, his lips grazing her shoulder hotly.

"But the Captain—"

"Yes, he'll be so angry," Laurent said. He laughed. He rolled over and mounted her. Beauty ran her arms up and around his back. His sheer size astonished her and weakened her. If he kissed her again, she would not, could not, resist.

"He'll punish us," she said.

"Well, I should hope so!" Laurent said, eyebrows raised in mock indignation, and he kissed her, his mouth harsher and more demanding than that of the Captain.

His kiss seemed to open her soul more profoundly, more deliberately. She yielded, her breasts like two beating hearts against his chest. And she felt the massive cock moving into her wet cleft, almost bruising her with its careless speed, its necessity.

It lifted her hips off the bare floor and plunged them back down again, its width so punishing that she was overcome with the heat of her spasms, her climax rendering her perfectly without will, her arms and legs flopping beneath Laurent. And when he came in her, she felt her body battered by him, ridden by him and his tempestuous and enigmatic spirit.

They lay quiet and undisturbed afterwards. She half-wished she had not done it. Why could she never love her Masters? Why was this strange and ironic slave so interesting to her? She could have wept inwardly. Would she never have anyone to love? She had loved Inanna, and now Inanna was beyond reach; and, of course, the Captain was her precious darling, the big brute, but. . . . She did weep, her eyes now and then moving to Laurent's sleeping form beside her. But she was very quiet.

When the Captain came to take her to bed, Beauty gave Laurent's hand a little squeeze, which Laurent silently answered.

As she lay beside the Captain, she wondered what would happen to her when they reached the Queen's shores. Surely she would have to work out her time in the village; it was only fair. They couldn't make her go back to the castle. And Laurent and Tristan would be in the village, surely. But if she were made to return to the Queen, she could always run away as Laurent had. And she saw him again in her memory, tethered to the Punishment Cross.

The days at sea passed in a swoon for Beauty. The Captain was strict with her and worked her constantly. But still she found opportunities to couple with Laurent again. And each time it was quiet and furtive and wrenched her soul.

Tristan, meantime, insisted he did not care that Nicolas was angry with him. It was to the village he would give himself when he returned, as he had given himself to the Sultan's palace. He said his brief time in this alien land had taught him new things.

"You were right, Beauty," he said, "when you asked only for harsh punishments."

But Beauty couldn't help but know that Laurent had been busily mastering both Tristan and Lexius, taking either when he chose, and that Tristan worshiped Laurent in a way that was clearly individual and personal.

Laurent even borrowed the Captain's belt to whip his two slaves, to which both of them responded beautifully. Beauty wondered how on earth Laurent would ever manage to be a slave again when they reached the village. The sound of him whipping the other two penetrated the bedchamber where she slept with the Captain. It would not let her sleep.

It was a wonder Laurent didn't somehow master the Captain, she thought. In truth, the Captain admired Laurent—they were good friends—though the Captain frequently reminded Laurent that he was a punished runaway and might expect the worst in the village.

"This trip is so different from the last one," Beauty thought with a smile. She felt the welts the Captain had given her, her fingers pushing at them and making them pulse. "It can go on and on, for all I care."

But this wasn't really the complete expression of her feelings. She longed for the engulfing world of the village. She needed to see its whole small society working and struggling around her. She needed to find her place in the scheme of things, give herself over to it, as Tristan said that he would do. And only then would the immensity and artifice of the Sultan's palace be forgotten, would the remembered scent and feel of Inanna leave her in peace.

Around the twelfth day, the Captain told Beauty that they were almost home. They would put into port at a neighboring kingdom and then reach the Queen's harbor the following morning.

Beauty was filled with longing and apprehension. While Nicolas and the Captain were ashore meeting with the Queen's ambassadors, she sat with Tristan and Laurent talking softly.

They all hoped to be kept in the village. Tristan said again that he no longer loved Nicolas.

"I love the one who punishes me well," he added bashfully, his eyes gleaming as he glanced at Laurent.

"Nicolas should have whipped you soundly when we first came on board," Laurent said. "And then you would be his again."

"Yes, but he didn't. And he is the Master, not I. I will love a Master again someday, but he must be a powerful Lord who is capable of taking all decisions upon himself, forgiving all weakness in the slave as he guides him."

Laurent nodded. "If I were ever reprieved," he said softly, looking at Tristan, "ever given the chance to become one of the Queen's Court, I would choose you for my slave and bring you to heights of experience you've never dreamed of."

Tristan smiled at this, blushing again, eyes flashing as he looked down and then back up at Laurent.

Only Lexius was quiet. But he had been so well trained by Laurent that Beauty was convinced he could bear anything that lay before him. It frightened her a little to picture him on the auction block. He was so graceful, so dignified, and his eyes were filled with such innocence.

How they would strip it away from him. But then, she and Tristan had endured it. . . .

It was very late at night before the ship put out to sea for the last leg of the voyage. The Captain came down the steps, his face dark and pensive. He lugged with him a finely made wooden casket, which he set down before Beauty in the little cabin.

"This is what I feared," he said. His whole manner was different. It seemed he did not even want to look at Beauty. Beauty sat on the bed, staring at him.

"What is it, My Lord?" she asked.

She watched him unlock the casket and throw back the lid. She saw dresses inside, veils, a long pointed cone of a hat, bracelets, and other finery.

"Your Majesty," he said softly, averting his eyes. "We will be in port before daylight. And you must be dressed again and ready to meet the emissaries from your father's kingdom. You are to be released from your servitude and sent home to your family."

"What!" Beauty shrieked, leaping up from the bed. "You can't mean this! Captain!"

"Princess, please, this is difficult enough," he said, his face red as he looked away. "We have received word from our Queen. It can't be prevented."

"I won't go!" Beauty gasped. "I won't go! First the rescue and now this! This!" She was beside herself. She stood up and kicked the casket with her naked foot. "Take these clothes away, dump them in the sea. I won't wear them, do you hear!" She would lose her mind if all this didn't stop.

"Beauty, please!" the Captain whispered, as if he feared to raise his voice. "Don't you understand? It was you we were sent to rescue from the Sultan. Your father and mother are the Queen's closest allies. They heard at once of your kidnap and were outraged that the Queen let you be taken across the sea. And they demanded that you be brought back. We only brought Tristan as well because

Nicolas wanted it. And as for Laurent, we took him because we had the opportunity and the Queen said he ought to be brought back to serve out his punishment as a runaway. But you were the true object of the mission. And now your father and mother are demanding you be reprieved from all service on account of your misfortune."

"What misfortune!" Beauty screamed.

"And the Queen has no choice but to comply because she is ashamed that you were ever kidnapped and taken away." He hung his head. "You're to be married immediately," he stammered. "This is what I have heard."

"No!" Beauty shrieked. "I won't go!" she sobbed and clenched her fists. "I won't go, I tell you!" But the Captain only turned and sadly left the cabin.

"Please, Princess. Dress yourself," he said through the closed door. "We have no maids to help you."

It was almost light. Beauty lay naked and crying still as she had all night. She could not look at the casket of clothes.

When she heard the door she did not look up. Laurent came silently into the cabin and bent over her. She had never seen him before in this little room, and he looked like a giant under the low ceiling. She couldn't bear to look at him, to see the strong limbs she would never be able to touch again or his strangely wise and patient face.

He reached down and gathered her up from the pillow.

"Come, you have to dress," he said. "I'll help you." And he took the silver-handled brush from the casket and ran it through her long hair as she wept. And with a clean handkerchief he wiped her eyes and her cheeks.

Then he chose a dark violet gown for her, a color that was only worn by Princesses. And Beauty thought of Inanna when she saw the fabric, and she wept even more miserably. Palace, village, castle—they all passed before her, her sorrow overflowing.

The cloth felt hot to her, confining. And, as Laurent laced up the gown in back, she felt as if she were being put into a new kind of bondage. The slippers pinched her feet as he put them on. She could not bear the weight of the cone-shaped hat on her head, and the veils around her confused her, tickled her, annoyed her.

"O, this is beastly!" she growled finally.

"I'm sorry, Beauty," he said, his voice taking on a tenderness she had never heard in it before. She looked into his dark brown eyes, and it seemed to her she would never know heat and pleasure again, sweet pain and true abandon.

"Kiss me, Laurent, please," she asked as she rose from the side of the bed and put out her arms to him.

"I can't, Beauty. It's morning. If you look out the window you'll see your father's men on the dock waiting for you. Be brave, my love. You'll be married in no time and you'll forget—"

"O, don't say it!"

He looked sad, genuinely sad. As he brushed his brown hair out of his eyes, they glazed silently with tears.

"My darling Beauty," he said. "Believe me, I understand."

And it broke her heart when he knelt and kissed her slipper.

"Laurent!" she whispered, desperately.

But he was gone immediately, leaving the cabin door open for her.

She turned and stared into an empty room. And there was the stairway leading to the sunlight.

Gathering her voluminous velvet skirts, she made her way up the steps, her tears flowing copiously.

LAURENT:
JUDGMENT OF
THE
QUEEN

FOR A LONG time, I stood
watching through the little window as Princess Beauty
rode away with her father's men. Up the hill they went
and into the forest. And my heart died a little inside me,
though I did not completely understand why. Many slaves
I had seen released, and many had shed tears, as she had.
But she had been unlike any other, shining so magnifi-
cently in her slavery that for me she seemed to rival the
sun. And now she had been taken so brutally from us;
how could it not scar her sensuous and savage soul?

I was thankful that there was no time to brood upon
it. The voyage was over, and Tristan and Lexius and I
now faced the worst.

We were but a few miles from the dreaded village and the great castle, and my friendly shipboard comrade, the Captain of the Guard, was now once again the commander of Her Majesty's soldiers. And in command of us.

Even the sky looked different here, closer, more ominous. And I could see the dark woods encroaching, feel the low, vibrant proximity of the old ways that had made of me a slave who loved both subservience and dominance.

Beauty and her escorts were gone from view. I heard steps on the ladder leading down to the cabin where we had gone to watch her, unseen, through the portholes. I braced myself for what was to come.

Yet I was still unprepared for the cold, authoritative manner with which the Captain of the Guard addressed us as he opened the door, ordering his soldiers to bind us so that we might be taken to the castle for the Queen's personal judgment.

No one dared to question him. Nicolas, the Queen's Chronicler, had already gone ashore without so much as a farewell glance at Tristan. The Captain was our Master now, and his soldiers went to work immediately.

We were made to lie facedown on the floor, and then our arms were pulled back and our legs bent at the knees so that our wrists might be bound tightly to our ankles, one firm loop of leather binding all four limbs together. And there were no gilded and jeweled fetters here. This was done with coarse rawhide strips that held us quite well, our bodies slightly bowed by the trussing. Then we were gagged by a long belt of leather, passed through our open lips, its two ends then extended to the knot that bound our ankles and wrists and there secured also. It held our mouths open, though covered, and our heads up off the ground and looking forward.

As for our cocks, they were left free and hard to dangle beneath us when we were lifted.

And lifted we were, first by the soldiers who carried us onto the dock. And then each of us was hung from a long, smooth pole of wood, the pole being passed under our bound ankles and wrists, a soldier at each end to carry it.

It seemed more appropriate to runaways than to us, I thought, confused by the roughness. But then I realized, as we were carried up the hill towards the village, that we *were* rebels. We had rebelled at the rescue. And now this must be accounted for.

And it hit me with full force that we really had left behind all the soft elegance of the Sultan's world. We were in for the crudest punishment. The bells of the village clanged, apparently in honor of the men who had managed to bring us back. And, as I was jogged along, swinging from the pole, I could see far ahead the crowds that lined the high ramparts.

The soldier who walked in front of me glanced back every now and then. He must have liked the spectacle of a trussed slave swinging from the pole. I could not see Lexius and Tristan because they were being carried behind me. But I wondered if they felt the same new fear that I felt. How much harsher it would all seem after the refinement we had known so briefly. And we were Princes again, Tristan and I. There was no sweet anonymity that we had enjoyed so much in the Sultan's palace.

Of course, I feared most for Lexius. But there was always the hope that the Queen would send him back. Or keep him at the castle. I would lose him, whatever happened. I wouldn't feel that silky skin again. But I was prepared for this.

Our ignominious procession entered the village just as I was afraid it would. Crowds met us at the south gates, common people pushing and shoving to get a close look at us. And the slow beat of the drum preceded us again as we were carried through the narrow, crooked streets towards the marketplace.

I saw the familiar cobblestones beneath me, the high gables, the crude leather shoes of the people who lined the walls, laughing and pointing and enjoying the fairly unusual sight of slaves bound like game to the spit as we moved slowly onward.

The wide leather belt pressed against my teeth, but there was plenty of room for air, though I knew that with every deep breath, my chest heaved most noticeably. And though my vision was blurred, I nevertheless stared back at those who looked at me, seeing the same predictable superiority in their faces that I hadn't seen enough when I was a captured runaway on the Punishment Cross.

How strange it all was: We were home and yet it was utterly new, the variations of the Sultan's palace having given the village an alarming gleam, my mind keenly aware of each step the soldiers took, though I saw the garden of the Sultan in strange, warm flashes.

In due time, we were carried through the marketplace and out of the north gates. The high, pointed towers of the castle loomed above us. The cries of the villagers were soon left behind, and we were carried uphill at a fairly brisk pace through the hot morning sun, the banners of the castle flapping in the breeze ahead as if in greeting.

I was calm for a little while. After all, I knew what to expect, did I not?

But, when we crossed the drawbridge, my heart started to race again. The soldiers lined the yard on either side to salute the Captain of the Guard. The doors of the castle were opened. All the accoutrements of the Queen's power surrounded us.

And there were the Lords and Ladies of the Court, come out to watch us being brought in—all the old royal finery that we were accustomed to. I felt the sting of familiar voices, glimpsed familiar faces. And I felt a catch in my throat as I heard the old language, laughter. The ambience of the Court came back. Bored Masters and Mistresses inspected us out of the corner of the eye— men and women who might find us quite amusing if we weren't in such disgrace. In an hour they would be back to their old occupations.

The procession moved into the Great Hall. I cursed

the strap that held my mouth open and my head up. I wished I could bow my head. But I couldn't. And I couldn't force myself to look down. I saw the Court assembling in all its glory—heavy velvet gowns with long dagged sleeves; the fine jerkins of the Lords; the throne itself and upon it Her Majesty, already seated, her hands on the armrests, her shoulders covered with an ermine-edged cloak, her hair long and black and twisting, like serpents, beneath her white veil, her face hard as porcelain.

In silence, we were set down on the stone floor at her feet, the poles withdrawn, the soldiers receding, until we were alone there—three bound slaves, resting on our chests, our heads raised, waiting for judgment.

"I see you've done well. You've accomplished the mission," said the Queen, obviously addressing the Captain of the Guard.

I didn't dare to look at her. But I couldn't keep myself from glancing to the left and the right, and with a sudden shock I saw Lady Elvera, standing near the throne, staring at me. As it always did, her beauty frightened me. It seemed part and parcel of her coldness. And, as I stared at her composed figure in its tight-fitting gown of apricot velvet, a sense of her luxurious and undisturbed life came over me—a life from which I had been cast out. I felt my heart beating in my throat. I moaned, though I hadn't meant to. I felt the stone pressing on my belly and my cock, and the old shame quickened in me, quickened as it had after I'd run away. I was not fit to kiss My Lady's slippers anymore or be her garden plaything.

"Yes, Your Majesty," the Captain of the Guard was saying, "and Princess Beauty has been sent home to her Kingdom with the proper rewards, as you decreed. Her party has probably already crossed the border."

"Good," said the Queen.

I knew secretly that her tone was probably amusing many in the Hall. The Queen had always been jealous of the Crown Prince's love for Princess Beauty. Princess Beauty. . . . Ah, so much confusion. Was she really sorry not to be bound here with us, not to be naked and helpless before the scornful Court of men and women who would someday be our equals?

But the Captain was continuing. And slowly, I picked up the thread:

". . . all showed the most ferocious ingratitude, begging to remain in the Sultan's Land, furious that they had been rescued."

"This is absolute impertinence!" the Queen said. She rose from the chair. "For this they will pay dearly. But this one, this dark-haired one who cries so piteously—who is he?"

"Lexius, the chief of all the grooms for the Sultan," the Captain said. "It was Laurent who stripped him naked and forced him to come with us. But the man could have saved himself. He chose to come and be thrown upon Her Majesty's mercy."

"That's very interesting, Captain," said the Queen. I saw her take several steps down from the dais. In the corner of my eye, her figure moved towards the bound figure of Lexius that rested to the right of me. I saw her bend to touch his hair.

How did it all seem to him? This clumsy stone edifice, its gaping, unadorned hall, this powerful woman, so different from the shuddering darlings of the Sultan's harem. I could hear Lexius moaning, see the motion of his struggling. Was he pleading for release or to serve?

"Unbind him," the Queen said. "And we will see what he is made of."

The leather bonds were quickly cut. Lexius gathered his knees under him and pressed his forehead to the floor. I had told him on shipboard the various ways he could show his respect here, very much the same as we had shown it in his Land. And a dark pride rose in me as I saw him crawl forward and press his lips to the Queen's slipper.

"Very nice manners, Captain," the Queen observed. "Lift your head, Lexius." He obeyed. "And now, tell me that you wish to serve me."

"Yes, Your Majesty," came his soft, resonant voice. "I beg to serve you."

"I choose my slaves, Lexius," she said. "They do not choose to come to me. But I shall see if you can be effectively used. The first thing we will do is strip away the vanity and softness and dignity bred into you in your native Land."

"Yes, Your Majesty," he answered anxiously.

"Take him down to the kitchen. He will serve there as punished slaves do, the plaything of the servants, scouring pots and pans on his knees, bearing their needs when they see fit. And, after a good two weeks of that, have him thoroughly bathed and oiled and brought to my chamber."

I gasped behind the gag. This would be so difficult for him. The kitchen slaves laughing and prodding him with their wooden spoons, paddling him for nothing, oiling him with the cooking grease before they whipped him back and forth across the floor for nothing more than an afternoon's diversion. But it would do just what the Queen wanted it to do. It would make a gorgeous slave out of him. After all, everyone knew she had trained her own Prince Alexi this way, and he was incomparable.

Lexius was taken away. We did not even look at each other to say farewell. But I had more important things to think of.

"And now for these two, these ungrateful rebels," the Queen said, turning her attention to Tristan and me. "When will I not hear discouraging reports of Tristan and Laurent?" Her voice showed genuine irritation. "Bad slaves, disobedient slaves, and ungrateful when freed from the Sultan's bondage!"

The blood pounded in my face. I could feel the eyes of the Court on me, the eyes of those I knew, had spoken with, had served in the past. How much safer the Sultan's garden seemed, with its preordained roles, than this deliberately temporary servitude. Yet there was no escape from this! It was as absolute as the garden had been.

The Queen drew near, and I saw her skirts before my

eyes. I couldn't move to kiss her slipper or I would have done it.

"Tristan is a young slave," she said, "but you, Laurent, you served Lady Elvera for a year. You are well trained and yet you disobey, you rebel!" Her voice was caustic. "You even bring back the Sultan's servant on a whim. You are determined to distinguish yourself."

I heard myself whimpering in response, my tongue touching the leather belt over my mouth, my cheeks burning against it.

She moved closer. The velvet of her skirt touched my face, and I felt her slipper against my nipple. I began to weep. I couldn't contain it. All my ideas about the things that had happened to me left me. The fierce Master who had trained Lexius on the ship was vanquished again, wouldn't come to my aid. I felt only the tension of the Queen's disapproval, and my own unworthiness. And yet I knew I would rebel again, given half the chance! I was truly incorrigible. Nothing but punishment was right for me.

"There is but one place for you both," she said. "The place that will strengthen Tristan's uncertain soul and quell your strong spirit thoroughly. You will be sent back to the village, but you will not be sold from the auction block. You will be delivered over to the Public Pony Stables."

My crying increased. I couldn't stop it. It seemed the leather belt did little to muffle the sound of it.

"And there you will serve night and day all year," she continued. "And strictly as ponies—to be rented out for the pulling of carriages and carts and other draught work. You will spend your waking hours harnessed and bitted with the proper horsetail phalluses fitted into place, and you will know no reprieve from this to enjoy the attention or affection of any Master or Mistress."

I closed my eyes. My mind traveled back to the time so long ago, it seemed, when I had been brought through the village on the Punishment Cross, and the human ponies had pulled the cart, Tristan among them. The image of the black horsetails streaking from their backsides, their heads held high by the bits, obliterated all other thoughts in an instant. It seemed infinitely worse than marching with my hands tied to the bronze phallus in the Sultan's garden. And it would be done not for the Sultan and the royal guests but for the common and thrifty people of the village.

"Only when that year is passed will your names be brought again to my attention," said the Queen, "and I give you my word that you are more likely to find yourself on the village auction block than at my feet when your service as ponies is ended."

"An excellent punishment, Your Majesty," said the Captain of the Guard softly. "And these are such strong slaves, well muscled. Tristan has already tasted the bit. For Laurent it will do wonders."

"I wish to hear no more of it," said the Queen. "These are not Princes fit for my service. They are horses to be well worked and well whipped in the village. Get them out of my sight immediately."

Tristan's face was red and streaked with tears when I finally saw it. We were both lifted again on poles, as we had been before, and hurriedly carried out of the Great Hall, leaving the Court behind us.

In the yard before the drawbridge, crude little signs were put around our necks, both bearing the single word: PONY.

And after that we were rushed across the drawbridge and downhill, once more, towards the dreaded village.

I tried not to envision the pony shackles. It was something absolutely unknown to me. And my only hope was that my bonds would be tight, and my position of servitude rigidly maintained by stern disciplinarians who would show me how to bear it.

One year . . . phalluses . . . bits. . . . It rang in my ears as we were carried back through the gates into the swarming noontime marketplace.

We caused quite a stir, the crowds gathering as the trumpet was blown before the auction block. The villagers moved in closely this time, though the soldiers ordered them back, and hands pushed at my naked arms and legs, making my body swing from the pole. I was choking on my tears, marveling that my understanding of what was happening did not lessen the degradation of it.

"What does understanding mean?" I wondered. To know that I had brought it all on myself, that humiliation and yielding are inevitable at any stage of the game—somehow it produces no calm, no defense. The hands that pulled at my exposed nipples, lifted my hair from around my face—these hands reached through all my carefully pondered defenses.

The ship, the Sultan, the secret mastering of Lexius, all swept away most certainly.

"Two fine ponies," cried the herald, "to be added at once to the village livery stables. Two fine steeds for hire at the regular rate to pull the finest coach or the heaviest farm wagon."

The soldiers hoisted the poles high. We were swinging above a sea of faces, hands slapping at my cock, slipping between my legs to squeeze my buttocks. And the sun glared on the many windows that surrounded the square, on the weathervanes turning on the gabled roofs, on the hot dusty panorama of village life—into which we had passed again.

The herald's voice went on recounting that for one year we would serve, that all should thank Her Gracious Majesty for the beautiful steeds maintained in the town and the reasonable prices asked for their service. And then the trumpet was sounded again, and off we were taken, the poles lowered, our bodies swinging close to the cobblestones again, the villagers turning back to their work, the houses of the quiet street suddenly rising on either side of us, as the soldiers carried us on towards the mystery of the new existence.

LAURENT:
FIRST
DAY AMONG
THE
PONIES

IT WAS a giant stable like many another, I think, except that real horses had never been in it. The mud floor was strewn with sawdust and hay merely to make it soft and keep the dust down. Its rafters were hung with harnesses of the light and delicate sort fit only for men. And the bits and reins streamed from hooks along the rough wooden walls, while in a large open area drenched with sun from the open doors to the street stood a circle of empty wooden pillories. They were high enough for a man on his knees, with holes for the neck and the hands. And I thought as I glanced at them that I would know what they were for, perhaps, sooner than I wanted to know.

What interested me more were the stalls to the far right. And the naked men inside them, two and three to a stall, their backsides well striped from the belt, their very sturdy legs firmly planted on the floor, their torsos bent over a thick wooden beam, their arms bound in the small of their backs as they merely stood there. With few exceptions, all wore leather boots to which horseshoes had been attached, and in two of the stalls grooms worked—true stable boys in leather and homespun—scrubbing down their charges or rubbing them with oil, their attitude one of casualness and busyness.

The sight took my breath away. It was strangely beautiful and absolutely devastating. It made me realize in a flash what was to befall us. Words alone had not been enough.

After the white marble and golden-threaded fabrics of the Sultan's palace, the tinted flesh and perfumed hair, this was shockingly real, the *world* itself, to which I'd been returned at last to pick up the thread of an existence for which I'd been bound before the raiders ever came.

Tristan and I were set down on the floor. Our bonds were cut. And I saw a tall stable boy approaching, a strongly built blond-haired young man, no more than twenty, with light freckles on his sun-darkened face and bright, cheerful green eyes. He smiled as he walked around us, his hands on his hips. Tristan and I stretched out our limbs, but we didn't dare move any more than that.

I heard one of the soldiers say:

"Two more, Gareth. And you'll have them the full year. Scrub them, feed them, and harness them up right away. Captain's orders."

"Beauties, sir, beauties," said the boy cheerfully. "All right, you two. Up on your feet. Ever been ponies before? I want a nod or a shake of the head, not a verbal answer." He gave my bottom a slap as I rose. "Arms behind your back, folded, that's it!" I saw his hand squeeze Tristan's backside. Tristan was still badly shaken, and he bowed his head, looking oddly regal as well as defeated, a sight that was heartrending even to me.

"And what's all this?" said the boy, taking out a clean linen handkerchief and wiping Tristan's tears, and then mine. He had a stunning face, the boy, big handsome smile. "Tears from a pair of good ponies?" he said. "We can't have that now, can we? Ponies are proud creatures. They cry when they're punished. Otherwise they march with their heads high. That's it." He gave me a good slap under the chin, snapping my head up. Tristan had already lifted his head properly.

The boy went round us again in a circle. My cock was pumping more madly than ever. A new form of debasement was being visited upon us. No Court and villagers to watch now. We were in the charge of this rough-hewn young servant, and even glancing at his high brown boots and his powerful hands, still on his hips, excited me.

But a shadow suddenly fell over the stable, and I realized that my old friend, the Captain of the Guard, had come in.

"Good afternoon, Captain," said the boy. "Congratulations on the mission. The whole village is afire with the gossip."

"Gareth, I'm glad you're here," said the Captain. "I want these two to be your special charge. You're the best groom in the village."

"You flatter me, Captain." The boy laughed. "But I don't think you'll find anyone here who loves his work more than I do. And these two, gorgeous steeds! Look at the way they stand. They have pony blood. I can see it already."

"Harness them together whenever it's possible," said the Captain. I saw his hand go up to stroke Tristan's head. He took the white handkerchief from the boy and wiped Tristan's face again.

"You know, this is the best punishment you could have drawn, Tristan," the Captain said under his breath. "You know you need it."

"Yes, Captain," Tristan whispered. "But I'm frightened."

"Don't be. You and Laurent will be the pride of the

stables in no time. There'll be a list on the door out there of the villagers who want to hire you."

Tristan shuddered. "I need courage, Captain," he said.

"No, Tristan," he said seriously, "you need the harness and the bit and stern discipline, as you needed it before. You must understand something about being a pony. It is not merely another part of your slavery. It is a way of life unto itself."

A way of life unto itself.

He stepped over to me, and I felt my cock stiffen as if it were possible for it to get any stiffer. The stable boy stood back with his arms folded, watching all this, his yellow hair falling down on his forehead a little, freckles very pretty in the sunshine. Such nice white teeth.

"And you, Laurent? Tears from you?" the Captain said soothingly to me. He wiped my face again. "Don't tell me you're frightened?"

"I don't know, Captain," I said. I wanted to say that I wouldn't know until the bit and harness and the phallus were in place. But that would have been asking for it. I didn't have the courage to ask for it. It would come soon enough.

"Chances are," he said, "that this is where you would have been placed if the Sultan's soldiers hadn't raided the village." He put his arm around my shoulder, and it seemed suddenly real, the time we had spent at sea, when we had both whipped and played with Lexius and Tristan. "It's the perfect thing for you," he assured me. "You have more will and strength pumping in your veins than most slaves. That is what Gareth calls pony blood. And the pony life will simplify everything for you; it will quite literally and symbolically harness your strength."

"Yes, Captain," I said. I stared in a daze at the long row of stalls, the backsides of the pony slaves, their horseshoed boots on the hay-strewn earth. "But will you . . . will you . . . ?"

"Yes, Laurent?"

"Will you let me know now and then how it goes with

Lexius?" My dear and elegant Lexius, who would soon enough be gathered into the Queen's arms. "And Princess Beauty . . . if you hear any word."

"We don't speak of those who leave the Kingdom," he said. "But I'll let you know if there is any gossip." I could see the sadness, the longing for Beauty, in his face. "As for Lexius, I'll tell you how he fares. And you can be sure, both of you, that I'll see you often. If I don't see you trotting every day in the streets, I'll come looking for you."

He turned my face towards him and kissed me, rather hard, on the mouth. Then he kissed Tristan in the same fashion, and I studied the two rough-shaven faces together, the mingling of the blond hair, the half-lidded eyes. Men kissing. Such a lovely sight. "Be strict with them, Gareth," he said as he let go of Tristan. "Train them well. When in doubt, whip."

And then he was gone. And we were alone with this robust young stable-boy Master who was already making my heart trip.

"All right, my young steeds," he said in the same cheerful voice as before. "Keep your chins high and move down the row to the last stall. And do it as ponies always do, at a brisk march, arms tightly folded against your backs, knees high. I don't want to have to remind you of this ever again. You march with spirit at all times, whether shoed or not, whether in the streets or in the stables, with pride in the strength of your bodies."

We obeyed, moving down the long line of stalls, and came to the last one, which was empty. I saw the feeding trough beneath the window, with its bowls of clean water and of meal, and the two broad, flat beams crossing the stall, over which we had to bend at the waist, one beam to suport our chests, the other our bellies. Gareth pushed us to the far sides of the stall so that he could stand between us, and he ordered us to bend over and we obeyed, resting our torsos on the beams, our heads right above the feeding bowls.

"Now lap that water, and do it with enthusiasm," he said. "I won't have any vanity here, any holding back. You're ponies now."

No soft, silken fingers here; no perfumed ointments; no tender voices talking in that impenetrable Arabic tongue that seemed so suited to sensuality.

The wet scrub brush hit my backside and started its vigorous work immediately, the water trickling down my naked legs. I felt a rush of shame as I lapped the water, hating the wetness against my face, but I was thirsty and I did as he said, amazingly eager to please him, liking the smell of his rawhide jerkin, his suntanned skin.

He scrubbed me well, ducking under the beams and coming up between them or in front of them when he had to, his movements firm and brusque, as he did his chores, his voice reassuring. And then he turned to Tristan, just as our food was brought to us, a good serving of thick meat soup, which he told us to finish off completely.

But I had taken only a few morsels when he stopped me.

"No. I can see we need some training immediately. I told you to eat it, and I mean for you to devour it and fast. I'll have none of those dainty manners here. Now let me see you go at it."

Again, I was blushing with shame to have to pick up the meat and vegetables with my tongue, to have the stew on my face, but I didn't dare disobey him. I felt an extraordinary affection for him.

"Now, that's better," he said. I saw him patting Tristan's shoulder. "I'll tell you right now what it means to be a pony. It means pride in what you are, and a loss of all false pride in what you are no longer. You march briskly, you keep your heads high, your cocks hard, and you show your gratitude for the slightest kindness. You obey all commands, even the simplest, with enthusiasm."

We had finished our food, and we remained bent over the bar as our boots were put on, the laces pulled tight over my calves, the heavy horseshoes weighing my feet, so that the tears came to my eyes again. I had known these horseshoe boots on the Bridle Path at the castle, when Lady Elvera had whipped me alongside her horse. But that was nothing to this. This was a world of austere punishments, and, overwhelmed with confusion, I began to weep, making no effort to stop it. I knew what was coming.

As I remained in place, the phallus was pushed inside me, and I felt the soft brush of the horse's tail, and I swallowed, wishing I was bitted already so that my crying would be less noticeable and might not make Gareth angry.

Tristan too was having a difficult time, and that further confused me. When I turned my head and glanced back to see the bushy horsetail in him, the sight of it enthralled me.

Meantime, the harnesses were being buckled on, fine straps that ran down over our shoulders, under our legs, through a circular hook on the back of the phallus and up to a strap around our waists, where they were buckled securely. It was a good and thorough job, though I didn't feel the true panic, the true defenselessness, until my folded arms were strapped tight and connected to the rest of the harness.

With relief, I knew that my will wasn't so important now. And a sob did break from me when the stiff rolled-leather bit was forced back between my teeth and I felt the reins against the sides of my face.

"Up, Laurent," Gareth said, with a firm tug of the reins. And, as I stood up straight and moved backwards in the heavy horseshoed boots, I felt him attaching weighted clamps to my nipples, the weights brushing the skin of my chest as they pulled down on the nipples. The tears were a flood coming down my face. And we were not even out of the stables.

Tristan moaned as he received the same treatment, and I felt that doubling confusion again when I turned to glance at him. But this time, Gareth pulled hard on my reins and told me to look ahead if I didn't want a nice collar to keep my head straight.

"Ponies don't look around like that, my boy!" he said and swatted me hard with his open hand, jolting the phallus inside me. "If they do, they're soundly whipped and fitted with blinders."

When his fingers touched my cock, binding my balls against it with a tight cock ring, I could hardly stand the gentleness of the touch, the heat of the sensation.

"Now, that's nice," he said, walking back and forth in front of us. His white sleeves were rolled up to show the gold fleece on his sun-bronzed arms, and his hips moved enticingly under the leather tunic to suggest a comfortable swagger.

"And if I have to put up with those tears," he said, "I want your faces held high for the world to see them. If you must cry, then your Masters and Mistresses should enjoy the sight of it. But you don't fool me, either of you. You're perfect ponies. And your tears will only make me whip both of you harder. Now march to the front of the stables!"

We both obeyed. I felt him gather the reins behind me, the phallus like a club forced into my anus, hard and unyielding as the bronze phallus had been, thick, and firmly held there by the harness. The weights pulled at my nipples. In fact, there seemed no part of my body that was left in peace, the cock ring tightening on my cock, the glove-soft fit of the boots rendering the rest of me shamefully naked. The harness seemed to govern me, contain me, to unify a thousand sensations and torments.

And as I felt myself dissolving in these sensations, there came the loud crashing smack of Gareth's strap on my backside. Another blow rang out, and I heard Tristan wince behind his bit. We were marched past the pillories and through another pair of doors into a big stable yard where carts and carriages stood in their stalls, and a gate stood open to the east road of the village.

I felt panic again, panic that we were to be driven out

there, panic that we were to be seen in this new livery of shame, and the more I shook with sobs and anxious breaths the more the harness constricted me and the weights danced as they hung from my nipples.

Gareth came up beside me and ran a quick comb through my hair.

"Now, Laurent," he said, scoldingly. "What is there to be afraid of?" He patted my bottom where he had whipped it only moments ago. "No, I'm not tormenting you," he said. "I'm quite serious. Let me tell you something about fear: Fear is only good when you have a choice in things."

He jerked the phallus to make sure it was in well. It seemed to grind me harder, more deeply, my anus itching and throbbing around it. I couldn't stop crying.

"But do you have a choice in things?" he asked honestly. "Think on it. Do you?"

I shook my head to admit that I didn't.

"No, that isn't how a pony answers," he said gently. "I want a good shake of the head. That's it. Again. That's it."

I obeyed, and each toss of my head tightened the harnessing, moved the weights, jarred the phallus. He touched my neck with maddening gentleness. I wanted to turn to him, weep against his shoulder.

"Now, as I was saying," he said. "And you listen to this, too, Tristan. Fear is only important when you have a choice. Or some control. You have none. In a few moments, the Lord Mayor will be here with his farm cart. He'll be returning the old team, and you'll be part of the new team to take the cart back out to the manor house for the afternoon load, and you've no choice in this whatsoever. You're going to be marched out there and tethered to the cart, and you'll pull it all afternoon and be whipped soundly as you do it. And there is absolutely nothing you can do to prevent it. So when you think about it, what is there to be afraid of? For a year you will do this, and nothing can change it. You understand me, you know you do. I want a nod now."

Tristan and I both nodded. And to my surprise, I was

a little calmer, the fear seeming to darken, become something else, something nameless. Hard to explain it—perhaps impossible—the feel of this new life beginning, just
beginning. . . . All the roads I had followed had led me
to this place, this gate, this beginning.

Gareth took a little oil in his hands from a nearby jug,
and he rubbed it onto my balls, murmuring that it would
make them "glisten," and then he gave the tip of my cock
the same polishing. I could hardly endure the stimulation,
the chills crawling over my skin, and I shied away from
his hand as he laughed and pinched my rump.

"When are those tears going to stop?" he said as he
kissed my ear. "Chew hard on the bit when you cry. Chew
hard. Doesn't that feel good, the soft leather in your
teeth? Ponies like it."

It did feel good. He was right. It helped to chew on
it, to work it between my jaws, the stiff roll of leather
tasting good and feeling strong enough to take the clamp-
ing down, the chewing.

Out of the corner of my eye, I watched him polishing
Tristan, thinking, "Any moment we will be out on the
road; we will be marching and hundreds will see us—if
they bother to look up, bother to take notice."

Gareth turned to me again. A small loop of black leather
was fixed just under the tip of my cock and this was
adorned with a small bell that gave a low, brassy jangling
noise with every movement. Unendurably degrading. Such
a little thing.

Memories of the exquisite adornments in the Sultan's
world inundated me—jewels, gold, the multicolored carpets strewn on the soft, green, garden grass, the fine
leather manacles—and the tears streamed down my face,
but it was not that I wanted to be there! It was only that
the dramatic change intensified everything!

Tristan, too, was being made to wear the bell, and every
movement of our cocks brought some appalling sound
from the things. And we would become accustomed to
all this, I knew. In a month, it would seem natural!

I watched Gareth take from a hook on the wall a long-handled thrash I'd never seen before. It was a bundle of stiff but flexible leather strips, a sort of cat-o'-nine-tails, and with this he thrashed both of us soundly.

It did not hurt like the wallop of the strap, but the strips were heavy and they covered all of the flesh in each sweeping blow easily. Almost caressing they were, enveloping the naked skin in countless stings and prickles and scratches.

Gareth took our reins again and marched us to the gate. My heart came up in my mouth. I looked out over the broad road to the far wall of the village. On the top of the wall, the soldiers passed back and forth lazily, mere silhouettes against the sunny sky. One of them stopped and waved to Gareth, and Gareth waved back. A carriage appeared to the south, and it came on fast, pulled by eight human steeds, all harnessed and bitted as we were. I stared at it, stupefied.

"Do you see that?" Gareth asked. I gave as vigorous a nod as I could. "Now remember, as you march, that that is what you look like. And you belong to those who see you. Step high, step proud. I can forgive some faults, but lack of spirit isn't one of them."

Two more coaches went thundering past, slaves prancing, horseshoes ringing on the stones, leaving me all the more breathless, petrified.

For a year we would do this, this would be our lives. And, within seconds, the first excruciating test would begin in earnest.

My tears poured down, as freely as ever, but I swallowed the sobs, chewing on the leather bit, liking the feel of it as Gareth said I would, and when I flexed my muscles I liked the pull of the harness, the knowledge that I was bound too well for rebellion to make much difference.

In moments, the Mayor's cart appeared, lumbering up to the gate and blocking everything beyond it. It was piled with linens, furniture, other merchandise, apparently to be taken out to the manor house from the market. And other stable boys quickly unharnessed the six dusty and windblown pony slaves who had been pulling it. Four fresh ponies were driven out from the stables and harnessed in the front places as we waited.

I wondered if I had ever known such tension, such a feeling of dread and weakness. Of course I had a thousand times, but what did it matter? The past did not come to my aid. I was on the cutting edge of the present. Gareth's hand closed on my shoulder. The other stable boys moved in to help. And Tristan and I were ushered into place behind the first two pairs of steeds rather roughly.

I felt straps looped under and over my bound arms and through the ring attached to the phallus. The reins were lifted behind me.

And, before I could resign myself, or prepare my spirit for it, the reins and harness were pulled, the phallus lifting me off my feet, and the team was suddenly galloping.

Not a moment to beg for mercy, for time, for some last touch of comfort from Gareth. No. We were lifting our knees, moving fast on the cobblestones of the road, passing into the stream of traffic that we had studied in mingled apprehension and horror.

And I realized in these harrowing moments that the harness and bit, the boots and the phallus, were unlike any devices to which I'd ever been subjected. They had a clear and useful purpose! They weren't merely to torture us, humiliate us, make us malleable for the amusement of others. They were for the simple and efficient pulling of this cart along the road. We were, as the Queen had said, workhorses.

Was it less debasing or more so, that we had been so cleverly put to work, our tendencies as slaves so expertly channeled? I didn't know. I knew only, as we pounded suddenly into the middle of the road, that I was drenched in shame, each marching step intensifying it, and yet I felt as I always did at the core of punishment: the coming of a tranquility, a quiet place in the very center of frenzy, in which I could surrender all the parts of my being.

The driver's strap licked down with a loud popping noise at my legs. The sight of the ponies in front of me stunned me. The bushy black tails swayed and danced in their reddened rumps. Their legs pumped at the ground, their hair shimmered against their shoulders.

And we made the same picture, except that the driver's long strap smacked us hard over and over again. And it wasn't the maddening little sting of the Sultan's thongs. It was a good smack each time the leather whipped us. And down the road we went in a loud clatter of horseshoes, the sky shining overhead as it had done on a thousand warm summer days, other carriages passing us.

I can't say the country road was easier than the village road. If anything, there was more traffic. Slaves at work in the fields, small carts rattling by, a string of slaves bound to a fence, their bottoms being soundly whipped by an angry Master.

And when we pulled into the farm road, our brief rest in harness was hardly an escape from our new station. The naked and dusty farm slaves pushed indifferently past us, unloading the cart, then piling it high with fruit and vegetables for market. At the kitchen door, a scullery maid watched us idly.

The experienced ponies pawed the ground with their horseshoe boots; they shook their heads now and then when the flies came near; they stretched their muscles as though loving their own nakedness.

But Tristan and I were rather still, and it seemed each tiny variation of the country scene took more of the mental skin off me, deepening the sense of my lowliness. Even the geese pecking near our feet seemed part of a world that had condemned us to be rude beasts and would keep us there.

If anyone enjoyed the sight of our hard cocks, our tortured nipples, this wasn't revealed to us. The driver of the cart, pacing up and down, whacked us with his doubled strap more out of boredom than inclination.

And when two of the other ponies rubbed against each other, the driver punished them with hard and cold annoyance.

"No touching there," he declared. And the scullery maid slowly roused herself to fetch a wooden paddle for him. Stepping in front of us, he found plenty of room to punish the offenders, switching back and forth between the two rumps, jerking up the phallus by its hook with his left hand as he soundly whacked at the bottom and thighs with the paddle.

Tristan and I watched, petrified, the ponies groaning under the hard smacks, the muscles of their reddened buttocks contracting and releasing helplessly. I knew I must never make this mistake of rubbing against another harnessed body. Yet I felt certain that someday I would make it.

Finally, we were again driven out. We trotted fast, muscles tingling, backsides smarting under the strap, the bits pulled harshly back, the pace just a little too quick for us so that it soon had us crying.

Driven into the marketplace, we were again allowed to rest, the noonday crowd taking only a little more notice of us than the farm servants had, someone stopping to pat a rump here or slap a cock there, the ponies who were touched tossing their heads and stamping their feet as if they liked it! I knew when some passerby finally touched me I would do the same. And then suddenly I was doing it, tossing my hair and chewing hard on the bit, as a young boy with a sack slung over his shoulder stopped to call us fine steeds and play with the weights that hung from my nipples.

"It will take us over," I thought. "It will become second nature."

And as the afternoon passed in a succession of such trips, I grew not accustomed to it so much as profoundly resigned to it. Yet I knew that true understanding, true appreciation of the pony life, would only come with the passing of days and then weeks. I could not conceive of my frame of mind six months along. It would be an interesting revelation to me.

At nightfall, we made our last trip, no longer tethered to the Mayor's cart but to the refuse wagon that traveled about the deserted market to receive the sweepings. Sluggishly we moved, as the cart was filled, naked slaves driven to the work by their crude and impatient overseers.

The villagers, dressed for the evening now, moved past the deserted shops and stands towards the nearby Place of Public Punishment. And we could hear the paddles and straps at work there, the cheers and screams of the crowd, the general noise of festivity. From that too we were, for better or worse, excluded.

It was the stable world for us, the hearty young grooms unharnessing us with simple words:

"Easy now," and "Steady," and "Head up, that's a good boy," as they whipped us to our stalls, and over the beams for feeding and watering.

It was a good feeling to have the boots slide off, to feel the balls of my feet on the soft, slightly moist floor, to feel the scrub brush sudsing me thoroughly. My arms were unbound and I was allowed to stretch them for a moment before folding them on my back again.

No one had to tell us to eat or drink with enthusiasm this time: We were hungry! But we were also tortured with desire. And, as I lay over the beams, the stable boy lifting my head to clean my face and my teeth, I felt my cock a jutting shaft of pure hunger. It was nowhere near the rough wood that supported me. They were much too clever for that. And I knew what happened to those of us who tried to touch others.

I hoped against hope for some relief. Surely we were given relief. But, when the water and food dishes were cleared away, a large down pillow was laid in the trough and my head was pushed into it for resting. This had a remarkable effect on me. We would sleep in this fashion, I realized, our weight on the beams, head on the pillow.

We could stretch our legs if we wished, or just let our feet rest on the earth. It was a good and completely debasing position. I turned my head towards Tristan. He was looking at me. Who would see if I reached out and touched his cock? I could do it. His eyes were two glittering orbs in the shadows.

In the meantime ponies were marched in and out. I could hear the sounds of the harnessing and unharnessing, the voices of villagers in the yard asking for this or that steed. The stable was darker but no quieter than it had been at morning. The stable boys whistled as they went about their tasks. Now and then they teased a pony with loud affectionate voices.

I continued to gaze at Tristan, unable on account of the crossbeams to see his cock. Bad enough to see his handsome face against the pillow. How soon would they catch me if I mounted him, dug my cock in deep and. . . . But they might have ways to punish us of which I hadn't thought. . . .

Suddenly Gareth appeared. I heard his voice at the same moment that I felt his hand stroking my sore backside.

"Well, the drivers did their work on you two," he said. "And by all reports you're fine ponies. I'm proud of you."

The flush of pleasure I felt was just another extraordinary humiliation.

"Now, up, both of you, arms folded firmly on your backs and heads high, as if you wore the bit. Out there now, move quickly."

He marched us past the doors to the wagon yard, and I saw another pair of open doors in the side of the stable. A beam like a bolt lay across the span of the opening at midpoint. A man would have to duck under it or climb over it to get through, the former being much easier.

"That's the recreation yard, and you'll be there for an hour," Gareth said. "Now, down on your hands and knees, and see you stay down in the yard. No pony walks upright save to march to his Master's commands or to trot in harness. Disobey and I'll chain your elbows to your knees so that you can't stand up. Don't make me do it."

We went down on all fours, and he swatted our rumps with his open hands to drive us through the doorway.

Immediately, we entered a clean-swept dirt yard lighted by torches and lanterns, with several large old trees against the far wall and naked ponies sitting or prowling about on all fours everywhere. There was a peaceful atmosphere until we were seen, and at once the other steeds moved towards us.

I understood what would take place. And I didn't try to fight or run. Everywhere I looked, I saw naked flanks, long unruly locks, smiling faces. Directly in front of me a beautiful young pony, blond-haired and gray-eyed, smiled as he reached up and stroked my face and opened my mouth with his thumb.

I waited, unsure as to how far I would let this go, when I felt another behind me, the cock already pushing into my anus, and yet another had thrown his arm over my shoulder and was pulling at my nipples roughly. I backed up, bucked, only driving the cock in deeper, and I was caught in front by the beautiful one, who laughed as he sat back on his heels and pushed my head down towards his cock forcefully. My arms were pulled out from under me by another pony, and I opened my mouth on the cock even though I wasn't sure I wanted to. I was groaning from the hard grinding I was getting in back. And I was also boiling over with excitement. I liked these steeds if only. . . .

And then I felt a wet, firm mouth on my own organ, sucking at it hard, as another pony's tongue lapped fiercely at my balls, and I didn't care anymore about who made the decisions. I was sucking the pretty boy, and being sucked, and my backside was being ground out hard, and I was happier than I had ever been in the Sultan's garden.

As soon as I came, it seemed, I was thrown over on my back. The pretty one had had enough sucking and wanted to take me. He smiled down at me as he drove in harder even than the first pony had, and my legs went up and over his shoulders as his hands cupped me and lifted me.

"You're a pretty one, Laurent," he whispered between his panting breaths.

"You're not bad yourself," I whispered back. My head was being held by another pony, whose cock danced just above me.

"Not so loud when you talk," whispered the pretty one, and then he came, his face blood-red, his eyes squeezed shut. He was pulled off me by one of the others before he was finished. Again a mouth was on me, arms locked around my hips. And my head was straddled, a cock dancing just above me. I lapped at it with my tongue, made it dance more, then it came down, and I opened my lips to receive it, biting it a little, stabbing the tiny hole with my tongue, then sucking it.

I lost track of how many used me. But I kept an eye out for the pretty blond one. He was on his knees at a trough, washing his cock in the fresh, flowing water. That was the way after it had been in another's backside. You had to clean it before you could put it in another mouth, I could see that. And I decided I'd get into his backside now before he got away.

He laughed loudly when I slipped my arms under his arms and pulled him back away from the trough. I stabbed him hard and lifted him on my pelvis. "Like it, you little devil?" I whispered in his ear.

He was gasping. "Go easy!"

"The hell I will," I said. I ground his nipples between my forefingers and thumbs as I rammed him, bouncing him up and down.

After I came, I threw him forward on all fours and smacked him hard over and over with my open hand until he scrambled away under the trees. I went after him.

"Please, Laurent! Have a little respect for an older steed!" he said. He lay on the soft earth looking up at the night sky, his chest heaving. I lay down on my elbow beside him.

"What's your name, pretty boy?" I asked.

"Jerard," he said. He looked at me, and the smile broke out on his face again. He was quite lovely. "I saw you harnessed up this morning. Saw you several times on the road. You're the finest stock in the place, you and Tristan."

"Don't you forget it." I smiled down at him. "And, next time we meet in this yard, you'll introduce yourself properly to me. You won't take what you want without asking."

I slid my hand under his shoulder and hurled him over on his face. I could still see the mark of my hand on his bottom. And I rested my chest on his back and spanked him as hard as I could over and over again.

He laughed and moaned at the same time, but the laughter died out as his cries got louder and louder. He struggled and twisted in the dirt. His backside was so narrow and lean I could cup the whole span of it in my hand when I wanted to rest. But I didn't want very much to rest. I spanked him harder probably than all the straps of the drivers who had used him.

"Laurent, please, please . . ." he gasped.

"You'll ask for what you want—"

"I'll beg! I swear it. I'll beg!" he cried.

I sat up and rested back against the trunk of the tree. Others were resting in that manner. I could see that only standing upright was forbidden.

Jerard lifted his head, hair all tangled in his eyes, and he smiled, rather bravely, I thought, but good-naturedly. I liked him. His left hand went back timidly to his bottom and massaged the redness. That was something I had never seen before. "Nice to have a period of rest when you can do that sort of thing," I thought. I couldn't recall any opportunity in my castle or village or palace life when I'd been able to rub my bottom after a whipping.

"Does that feel good?" I asked.

He nodded. "You're a devil, Laurent!" he whispered. And he bent forward and kissed my hand as it rested in the grass. "Do you have to be as rough as our Masters?"

"I see a bucket over there by the trough," I said. "Get it in your teeth, and come back here and wash my cock, and then wash it again with your mouth. And hurry."

As I waited for him to carry out the commands, I looked around. Several other ponies were smiling at me as they rested on their haunches. Tristan was wrapped up in the arms of an enormous black-haired steed who was covering his chest with rather tender kisses. Another pony came near them as I watched, and the black-haired steed made the smallest threatening gesture and the intruder was sent running.

I smiled. Jerard was back. He bathed my cock slowly and thoroughly. It was coming up again under the warm water.

I said to myself, as I played with his hair, "This is paradise."

BEAUTY:
COURTLY
LIFE
IN ALL
ITS GLORY

Beauty, PROPERLY gowned
and bejeweled, walked back and forth across the room,
eating an apple, only now and then tossing her long sleek
mane of blond hair over her shoulder and glancing at the
robust and splendidly dressed young Prince who had come
to her father's dreary castle to court her.

Such an innocent face.

In a low, fervent voice he spoke the predictable words—
that he adored Beauty, would be most happy to make
her his Queen, that their families would be overjoyed at
the union.

A half hour ago Beauty had interrupted the nauseating

diatribe to ask if he had ever heard of the strange pleasure customs of Queen Eleanor's kingdom.

He had stared at her with wide eyes.

"No, My Lady," he had said.

"Pity," she had whispered with an acidic smile.

She wondered now why she hadn't sent the Prince away. She had been sending men away since she had returned to her father's house. But her father, though weary and disappointed, only continued to write letters, to receive more guests, to open his doors to more suitors.

At night Beauty lay crying against her pillow, her waking and sleeping dreams the same: of the lost pleasures of the world she had known beyond the border of her parents' land, a subject which no one broached at court, which she herself never mentioned in public or private.

She stopped and looked at this young Prince now. She threw away the half-eaten apple. Something about the young man fascinated her. Of course he was handsome. She had let it be known she would marry only a handsome man. No one thought it unusual of a Princess with such endowments.

But there were other things about him. He had violet-blue eyes, rather like those of Inanna or more truly like those of Tristan. He was blond like Tristan—dark gold hair, thick and bushy around his face, leaving the lower part of his neck bare. "Rather enticing to see the bare neck," Beauty thought. And the young man was big and broad-shouldered like the Captain of the Guard, like Laurent.

Ah, Laurent! It was Laurent she most thought of, remembered. The Captain of the Guard was a dark, faceless sentinel in her dreams. The sound of his strap rose and fell. But it was Laurent's smiling face she saw, Laurent's enormous cock that she longed for. Laurent!

Something had changed in the room.

The Prince had stopped speaking. He was gazing at her. His courtly ardor had melted away into a rare and honest silence. He stood with his hands clasped behind his back, his cloak hanging off one shoulder, and a sadness came over him.

"You will refuse me, too, won't you, my Lady?" he asked quietly. "And you will haunt my nights forever after."

"Is that so?" she asked. Something in her quickened. It was not a sarcastic reply. The moment was suddenly important.

"I want so to please you, Princess," he whispered.

Please you, please you, please you. The words made her smile. How often she had heard them spoken in the far off world of the castle and the village, and in the even more distant fantasy world of the Sultan. How often she had spoken them herself.

"Do you, my dear Prince?" she asked gently. She was aware that her demeanor had changed, and that he realized it. He stood motionless, looking at her across the room, the afternoon sun falling in broad shafts on the stone floor between them. It glinted in his hair, on his eyebrows.

She advanced, and she thought she saw him shrink back, saw a flicker of undefined feeling in his face.

"Answer me, Prince," she said coldly. Yes, she had seen it. The wave of redness rising to his cheeks confirmed it. He was baffled. "Then bolt the doors," she said in a low voice. "All of them."

He hesitated but a moment. How virginal he looked. What was under those breeches? Her eyes passed up and down over him, and she saw it again, the inward shrinking, the vulnerability that made his size and fair countenance suddenly quite irresistible.

"Bolt the doors, Prince," she said threateningly.

And, moving like one in a dream, he went to obey, glancing back at her timidly.

There was a stool in the corner, a broad three-legged thing. Beauty's maid sat upon it when she wasn't needed.

"Set the stool in the center of the room," she said, and she felt a little catch in her chest as she watched him obey her. He glanced up at her before he righted himself, after setting down the stool, and she liked this, his body bent over, his eyes gazing up, the color in his cheeks. Divine color.

She folded her arms and leaned against the carved side of the fireplace. She knew it was not a ladylike position. Her velvet gown annoyed her.

"Take off your clothes," she whispered. "All of them."

For a moment he was too astonished to respond. He stared at her as if he had heard wrong.

"Off with them," she said in a monotone. "I want to see your body, see what you look like."

Again, he hesitated, and then the blush on his face deepened as he bowed his head and began to unlace the jerkin. Lovely, the sight of his flaming cheeks, and the jerkin opening over the wrinkled shirt. He pulled the ties that laced the shirt, and there was his bare chest. Yes, more, and more. Yes, off the arms. Quite naked.

Fine nipples, maybe just a little too pale, and each surrounded with a little blond hair, and the hair moving down the center of the chest to a curling growth on the belly.

And now the breeches were down, and he was stepping out of the boots. Nice cock. And very hard. Of course. When had it gotten hard? When she had ordered him to bolt the doors? Or to remove his clothes? Actually it didn't matter. Her own sex was moist and hot between her legs.

When he looked up at her again, he was stark naked— the only naked man she had seen since she had left the ship moored at Queen Eleanor's dock, and she felt her own face tingling and her lips moving into a smile shamelessly.

But it wasn't good to smile at him so soon. She stiffened slightly. She felt a great warmth in her breasts. She hated the velvet gown that covered her.

"Up on the stool, Prince, so I can have a good look at you."

That was too much, or so it seemed for an instant. He opened his mouth, but then he only swallowed. O, very handsome. He would have been welcomed by Queen Eleanor and her voluptuous Court. And what an ordeal it would have been! And that fair skin, revealing everything, as Tristan's skin did. And he didn't have the cunning of Laurent.

He turned and looked at the stool. He was paralyzed.

"Up on the stool, Prince," she said stepping forward, "and put your hands on the back of your neck. That way I can see you well. Your hands and arms aren't in the way."

He stared at her. She stared back. And then he turned and in a slow, almost somnolent, fashion climbed onto the stool and put his hands behind his neck as she had commanded. He appeared astonished, astonished that he had done it.

And when he looked at her again, his face was redder than any face she had ever seen, making his eyes glitter, his hair look rather like gold, the way Tristan's hair had often looked. He swallowed again, and he looked down, but probably he did not see his erect cock. He looked past it, into his own newly awakened soul, pondering with shame that he was so defenseless.

But that did not really matter to Beauty. She looked at the cock. It would do. It wasn't Laurent's organ, but then there weren't very many that thick, were there? It was a good cock actually, curving upwards a little sharply above the scrotum, and very red now, red as the Prince's face.

As she drew closer, the cock became even redder. She reached out and touched it with her thumb and forefinger. The Prince shrank back.

"Hold still, Prince," she said. "I want to inspect you. And that requires your quiet compliance." How shy he looked as she pinched the flesh, glancing up at him. He couldn't meet her gaze. His lower lip was trembling exquisitely. If she had seen him at the castle, she would have been drawn to him as she'd been to Tristan. Yes—when you stripped away everything, he was a fine young sapling of a Prince who would come into full leaf under the lash quite predictably.

The lash. She looked about. His belt would have to do. But she was not ready for that, and he would have to get off the stool and hand it to her. For now she walked around behind him and looked at his buttocks. She felt the virginal skin, and she smiled as he shivered noticeably, as his hair shivered on the back of his naked neck rather touchingly.

She took his buttocks firmly in hand and spread them. This was almost going too far. He shuddered, and the muscles tightened.

"Open to me. I want to have a look at you."

"Princess!" he gasped.

"You heard me, Prince," she said gently but authoritatively. "Relax these beautiful muscles so that I can examine you." She thought she heard a little gasp as he obeyed. The well-molded flesh went soft, and she parted the cheeks and looked at the hair-ringed anus. It was so small and pink, wrinkled, secretive. Who would have thought it could take a stout phallus, a cock, a fist clad in golden leather?

But for this tender fledgling something smaller would do. Almost anything really. She looked lazily about the room. A candle was the obvious thing, and there were many of them, some only an inch in width.

And as she went to take one from its holder, she remembered how she had pierced Tristan in this way when they had made love together in Nicolas's house in the village. The memory galvanized her. She felt a totally unfamiliar sense of power.

When she turned, she glanced up and saw tears wetting the Prince's face, and this further excited her. In fact, the wetness between her legs surprised her.

"Don't be frightened, my darling," she said. "Look at

your cock. Your cock knows what you need and what you desire, even better than I do. Your cock is grateful that you've found me."

She moved behind him again and, opening him with one hand, her fingers spreading him wide, she slowly inserted the wick end of the candle. Gently, and kindly, she worked it in, a fraction of an inch at a time, ignoring the Prince's deep moans until he held a good six inches of it. It jutted out, a splendidly humiliating sight, and it moved as he contracted his buttocks again, his moans soft but resonant and imploring.

She backed away, heady with the sense of possessing him. Why, she could do anything to him, couldn't she? In time. . . .

"Keep it in," she said. "If you force it out or let it fall out, I'll be very disappointed and angry with you. It's there to remind you that for now you belong to me, you're mine. You're speared by it, and it claims you, holds you powerless."

To her pure and sweet amazement, he nodded slowly. He did not argue with her.

"We're speaking a universal language of pleasure, aren't we, Prince?" she said in a low voice.

Again, he nodded. But it was so difficult for him, he was suffering so much. Her heart went out to him, and mingled with her compassion was a terrible loneliness, a terrible envy. It was strong, this feeling of power, but stronger still were her memories of being overpowered. Best not to think of both simultaneously. . . .

"Now, Prince, I want to whip you. Drop down and take your belt from your clothes and give it to me."

As he moved slowly to obey, his hands shaking uncontrollably, the candle sticking out from his backside, she went on talking in a soothing voice:

"It's not that you've done anything wrong. I will whip you because I wish to," she said. He turned to her and put the belt in her hand, but he didn't move away once she had it. He stood right in front of her, trembling. And she touched his curling chest hair with her fingers, tugging on it, running her fingers around his left nipple.

"Yes, what is it?" she asked.

"Princess . . ." he said haltingly.

"Speak, my dear," she said. "No one has said you may not speak, after all."

"I love you, Princess."

"Of course you do," she said. "Now back on the stool, and after I've whipped you I'll let you know whether or not I'm pleased. Remember, keep the candle tight in place. Now move, my love. We must not waste these private moments."

She moved behind him as he obeyed. She swung the strap hard and watched in fascination as it left a broad pink impression on the side of his right buttock. Again she struck him, marveling that the strength of the blow seemed to be echoed by his whole frame, even the shivering of his hair, his hands still trembling though he clasped his neck obediently.

Now she gave him the third blow, harder than the other two sweeping him under the buttocks, beneath the jutting candle, and she liked the sight of this the best, and so she gave him more and more good smacks there, making the candle move as he moved, making him rise on the balls of his feet as he struggled to keep still, his groans strangely eloquent.

"Anyone ever whipped you before, Prince?" she asked.

"No, Princess," he said in a raw, torn voice. Exquisite.

And in thanks she worked on his thighs and on his calves, on the flesh behind his knees and on his ankles, his legs seeming to move without moving. What control he had. She tried to remember if she had had this control. What did it matter? That was all gone for the present. And she had this instead, and she thought back not to the whippings she had suffered but to the times at sea when she had seen Laurent strapping Lexius and Tristan.

She came round in front of the Prince. His face was more stricken than she had imagined.

"You behave beautifully, my darling," she said. "I am truly impressed with your demeanor."

"Princess, I adore you," he whispered. He was gifted with extraordinary looks. Why hadn't she fully appreciated them before now?

She gathered the length of the strap in her hand, leaving only a good tongue of it free, and with this she whipped his cock hard, clearly frightening him and startling him.

"Princess!" he gasped.

She only smiled. Better to whip his firm little belly, and she did, and then his chest, watching the marks shine out like tracks in water. She whipped his nipples.

"O, Princess, I beg you . . ." he whispered, barely parting his lips.

"Would that I had time to make you sorry that you begged me," she said. "But there isn't time. Get down here, Prince, on your hands and knees. You will now pleasure me."

As he obeyed, she opened the lower hooks of her skirt, her gown falling back below the waist. That was all he needed to see of her, she reasoned. And she felt her own fluids melting down her thighs. She snapped her fingers for him to approach.

"Your tongue, Prince," she said, and she parted her legs, feeling his face against her, and the tongue lapping at her.

It had been so long, so dreadfully long! And his tongue was strong and quick and ravenous. He nuzzled into her, his hair pushing the velvet skirts farther away, tickling her lower belly. She sighed and slipped a few steps back. He reached up and took hold of her.

"Take me, Prince," she said. She couldn't bear the clothes anymore. She tore them open, let them drop off. He pulled her down on the hard stone floor.

"Ah, my darling, my darling," he gasped. He pushed her legs wide apart as he went into her. She reached for the candle and found it with both hands and worked him with it. He gritted his teeth and rode her hard, as she rode him with the candle.

"Harder, my Prince, harder, or I promise you I will whip every inch of you with the strap!" she whispered, biting his ear, his hair covering her face. Then she came in a white explosion of mindless ecstasy, barely conscious of his juices flooding her.

Only a few moments of slumber. She pulled the candle out of his body and kissed his cheek. Had she done that long ago with Tristan? What did it matter?

She rose and put on her gown again, snapping the hooks impatiently. He too struggled to his feet.

"Get dressed," she said, "and go, Prince. Leave the Kingdom. I won't marry you."

"But Princess," he cried. He was on his knees still, and he flung himself at her, catching her skirt.

"No, Prince. I told you. I refuse your suit. Leave me."

"But Princess, I'll be your slave, your secret slave!" he implored her. "In the privacy of our chambers—"

"I know, my dear. And you are a good slave, without question," she answered. "But you see, I don't really want a slave. I want to be one."

For a long moment, he stared at her. She knew the torture he was enduring. But it didn't matter, really, what he thought. He could never master her. She knew it, and whether or not he knew it wasn't important.

"Get dressed!" she said again.

And this time he obeyed. But his face stayed red. He was still trembling even when he was fully garbed again, with his cloak over his shoulders.

For a long moment she studied him. Then she began to speak in a low, rapid voice.

"If you want to be a pleasure slave," she said, "go directly east of here to the Land of Queen Eleanor. Cross the border. And as soon as you are within sight of a village, take off your clothes and put them in your leather traveling bag and bury them. Bury them deep so that no one can find them. Then approach the village, and, when the villagers see you, run from them. They'll think you're a fugitive slave, and they'll catch you quick enough and take you to the Captain of the Guard for punishment. Then tell him the truth, that you beg to serve Queen Eleanor. Now, go, my love, and take my word for it. It's worth it."

He stared at her, more amazed by her words perhaps than by anything else.

"I'd go with you, if I could, but they'd only send me back," she said. "It's no use. Now go. You can reach the border before dark."

He didn't answer. He made some small adjustment to his sword, his belt. Then he came nearer to her and looked down at her.

She let herself be kissed, and then she clasped his hand tight for a moment.

"Will you go?" she whispered. But she didn't wait for an answer. "If you do, and you see the slave Prince Laurent, tell him that I remember him and I love him. Tell Tristan too. . . ."

Futile message, futile link with all that had been taken from her.

But he appeared to weigh her words carefully. And then he was gone, out of the room and down the stairs. And in the soft afternoon sunlight, she was alone again.

"What am I to do?" she cried softly to herself. "What am I to do?" And she wept bitterly. She thought of Laurent, how easily he had risen from slave to Master. She could not do it. She was too jealous of the suffering she inflicted, too eager for the subjugation. She couldn't follow in Laurent's footsteps. She couldn't imitate the example of the fierce Lady Juliana, who had gone from naked slave to Mistress, apparently without batting an eye. Maybe she lacked some dimension of spirit that Laurent and Juliana possessed.

But had Laurent been able to pass back again into the slave ranks as simply? Surely he and Tristan had met with dire punishment. How had Laurent fared? If only she knew. If only she knew a particle of the discipline he suffered now.

As late afternoon came on, she went out of the castle. As her courtiers and ladies-in-waiting trailed behind her, she walked through the village streets. People paused to bow from the waist to her. The wives came to the doors of their cottages to pay their silent respect.

She looked at the faces of those she passed. She looked at the stolid farmers and the milkmaids and the rich burghers, wondering what went on in the depths of their souls. Did none of them dream of sensual realms where passions were flamed to white-hot heat, of exotic and demanding rituals that laid bare the very mystery of erotic love? Did none of these simple people long for Masters or slaves in their secret hearts?

Normal life, ordinary life. She wondered if there were not lies worked into the fabric, lies she could discover if only she took the risk. But, when she studied the serving girl at the door of the Inn or the soldier who dismounted to bow to her, she saw only masks of common attitude and disposition, as she saw them on the faces of her courtiers, her maids. All were bound to show respect for the Princess as she, by custom and law, was bound to her proper and lofty place.

And, suffering silently, she made her way back to her lonely chambers.

And she sat by the window, resting her head on her folded arms on the stone sill, dreaming of Laurent and all those she had left behind, of a rich and priceless education of body and soul interrupted and forever lost.

"Dear young Prince," she sighed, remembering her rejected suitor, "I hope you have made it into the Queen's country. I did not even think to ask you your name."

LAURENT:
LIFE
AMONG THE
PONIES

T**HAT FIRST** day among the
ponies had had its significant revelations, but the true
lessons of the new life came with time, with the constant
day-to-day discipline of the stable and the numerous small
aspects of my prolonged and rigid servitude.

I had known many an ordeal before, but no special test
had been sustained as this existence was. And it took a
while for me to grasp what it meant that Tristan and I
had been condemned for twelve months, that we were
not to be spirited out of the stables for the Public Turntable, or a night with the soldiers at the Inn, or any other
diversion.

We slumbered, worked, ate, drank, dreamed, and made love as ponies. And, as Gareth had said, ponies are proud beasts, and we soon admitted this pride, and a profound addiction to the long gallops in the fresh air, to the firm feel of our harnesses and bits, and to the quick struggle with our fellow steeds in the recreation yard.

But never did the routine make things easy. Never did the discipline soften. Each day was an adventure of accomplishments and failures, of shocks and humiliations, of rewards or severe punishments.

We slept, as I have described, in our stalls, bent over at the waist, our heads resting on pillows. And this position, though quite comfortable, did as much as anything else to strengthen the sense that we had left the world of men behind. At dawn we were hastily fed and oiled, and taken out in the yard for hiring to the waiting populace. And it was no uncommon thing for the villagers to feel our muscles before they chose us or even to test us with a few wallops of the strap to see whether or not we responded with quickness and good form.

Not a day passed that Tristan and I weren't asked for a dozen times, and Jerard, who had asked Gareth for the privilege, was frequently tethered in the same team with us. I grew used to having Jerard near, just as I was used to Tristan, and used to whispering little threats in Jerard's ear.

At the recreation periods, Jerard was mine completely, and no one dared to challange me, least of all Jerard himself. I whipped his backside lustily, and he soon was so well trained that he didn't wait for me to tell him to assume the proper position for the whipping. He came on his hands and knees knowing what was to happen and kissing my hands after. It was the joke of the stables that I whipped him harder than any coachman, that he was twice as red as any other steed.

But these little interludes were brief. It was the daily work that made up our true life. As the months passed, we knew every manner of cart, coach, and wagon. We pulled the fancy gilded carriage of the rich country Lords, who divided their time between the castle and the manor house. We pulled the runaways on their Punishment Crosses to the public display and chastisement. And, just as frequently, we found ourselves drawing plows in the fields or singled out for the lone chore of tugging a little basket cart to market.

These lone treks, though physically easy, were often especially degrading. I found I hated it when I was separated from the other ponies and harnessed by myself to a little cart. And to be driven along by a weary farmer on foot, his strap always busy no matter how hot the day, kept me in steady fear and agitation. Becoming known to the individual farmers made it worse, as they began to ask for me by name, and let me know how much they appreciated my size and strength and what fun it was to whip me to market.

It was always a relief to be back with Tristan, and Jerard, and the others in front of a big coach, even though I never became accustomed to the villagers pointing to the fine equipage and murmuring their approval. The villagers could be quite a torment. There were young men and women who liked nothing better than to discover a team in harness on the side of the road, waiting helplessly and mutely for the coachman or Master or Mistress. We would find ourselves mercilessly teased, our horsetails pulled and pushed as the bushy hair stroked and tickled our legs, our cocks slapped to make the degrading little bells rings.

But the worst moment came when some determined young boy or girl decided to pump a big cock and empty it. No matter how much the ponies loved one another, the others would laugh behind their bits at the plight of the victim, knowing how he struggled not to come as the hands stroked him, played with him. Of course, to come and to be found out was to be severely punished. And the villagers who played with us knew it. During the day a pony's cock was to be hard. Any satisfaction for it was forbidden.

The first time the unfortunate trick was done to me, we were tethered to the coach of the Lord Mayor and had driven him back from the farm to his fine house on the high road. We were waiting outside for him and his wife to appear when the offending boys surrounded me and one began to work my cock mercilessly. I danced back in the harness, trying to escape the hands—I even pleaded behind the bit, another thing that is strictly forbidden—but the friction was too great, and finally I came in the hand of the brat, who then scolded me as if I'd dared to do the unmentionable. Then he had the gall to call the coachman.

Foolishly, I had thought I would be allowed to speak in my defense. But ponies don't speak; they are mute, bitted, creatures.

And when we returned to the stables, I was unharnessed and taken to one of the stable pillories. On my knees in the hay, I bent over to have my hands and head locked into place in the wooden board, and there I remained until Gareth appeared, who scolded me furiously. Gareth was as good at scolding as he was at affection.

I begged through moans and tears to be allowed to explain. I should have known it was not important. Gareth made up a mixture of flour and honey, telling me just what he was doing, and with this he painted my backside and my cock and my nipples and belly. The stuff clung to my skin, a hideous disfigurement compared with the beauty of the harnesses. Gareth finished his work by describing the letter P on my chest with the mixture, which he explained stood for "punishment."

And then I was tethered in a heavy old harness to a street sweeper's cart, the only fit place for a slave who had been so marked, and I soon saw the real meaning of the punishment. Even when I was at a fast trot, a rare thing with a clumsy street sweeper's cart, the flies gathered to taste the honey. They crawled over my private parts and my bottom, deviling me unmercifully.

For hours the punishment went on, and it seemed all

the gains I had made in acceptance and composure were reduced to nothing. When finally I was driven home, I was pilloried again, and the slaves on their way to recreation were allowed to rape my mouth or my backside as they saw fit, while I remained helpless.

It was an odious combination of debasement and discomfort, but the very worst aspect of it was the contrition I felt, the profound disgrace at having been a bad pony. There was little secret humor or gloating in it for me. I was bad. And I vowed never to fail again in any way—a goal that, for all its difficulty, was not entirely impossible.

Of course, I didn't achieve it. There were many times in the passing months when the village boys or girls used me in that way, and I couldn't control myself. At least half the time I was caught and punished for it.

But a more severe punishment was to come when I was caught, of my accord and out of sheer weakness and complacency of spirit, kissing and nuzzling up to Tristan. We were in our stall, and I thought surely no one would know of it. But a stable boy caught a glimpse as he passed, and Gareth was suddenly bitting me, and backing me out of the stall, and walloping me with the belt rather mercilessly.

I was stunned with shame as Gareth demanded to know how I could behave in this way. Didn't I want to please him? I nodded my head, tears flooding down my face. I don't think I had ever in my entire existence wanted to please anyone as much. As he harnessed me, I wondered how he would punish me. Soon enough I had the answer.

The phallus I was to wear was dipped first in a thick amber colored liquid, deliciously scented with spice, which caused my anus to itch miserably as soon as it was inserted. Gareth waited for me to feel it, to begin to twist my hips and to cry.

"We often save that one for a listless pony," he said, smacking me. "It perks them up instantly. All along the road they grind their hips when they can, trying to soothe that itch. You don't need it for spirit, beautiful boy. You need it for disobedience. You won't commit those little sins with Tristan again."

I was rushed into the yard and tethered to a coach that was headed for the manor houses. I shed disgraceful tears as I tried not to undulate my hips. I lost the battle. And, almost immediately, the other ponies began to laugh and whisper behind their bits: "Like that, Laurent?" and "Doesn't that feel good, Laurent!" I didn't answer with the threats that came to mind. There was nobody who could get away from me in the recreation yard, but what kind of a threat was that when most of them didn't want to?

As we marched out, I couldn't stand the strain anymore, and I pumped and rolled my hips, trying to ease the itching, the sensation increasing and decreasing in throbbing waves that passed all through me.

Every moment of every hour was underscored by the sensation. It grew no worse; it grew no better. Twisting helped and did not help. And many a villager laughed as he watched me, knowing full well the cause of my ignominious movements. Never had I known such a searing, draining torture.

And by the time I was returned to the stables, I was exhausted. I was unharnessed with the phallus still tied firmly in place, and I fell down on my hands and knees and whimpered at Gareth's feet, the bit still in my mouth, the reins dragging.

"Are you going to be a good boy?" he demanded, his hands on his hips. I nodded passionately.

"Stand up in the door of that stall," he said, "and grab hold of those hooks hanging from the beam.

I obeyed, reaching out for the two hooks, my arms spread wide. I went up on the balls of my feet as I held the hooks. He stood behind me, and, gathering the reins that hung loose from the bit in my mouth, he tied them tight on the back of my head. Then I felt him loosening the phallus, and just that slight shift of it sent exquisite relief from the itching all through me. When he had it out, he opened the oil jug and quickly covered the phallus with oil. I chewed hard on the bit, moans flowing out of me.

Then I felt the phallus again, riding into me, past the hot itching flesh, and I almost died of sheer ecstasy. In and out, he drove it, soothing the itch, exhausting it, driving me into a frenzy. I cried as before but in gratitude. And as I snapped my hips, the phallus rocked inside me, and suddenly I came with great forceful, uncontrollable jerks into the air.

"That's it," he said, at once dissolving my fear, "that's it."

I leaned my head against my raised arm. I was his devoted and abandoned slave without reserve. I belonged to him and the stables and the village. There was no division in me, and he knew it.

I did not so much as whimper when he put me back into the pillory.

That night as the other ponies took me, I half-slumbered, wordlessly aware of how much I enjoyed their friendly pats, their tousling of my hair, their swatting me on the rump, telling me what a good steed I was, how they'd each had the awful itching phallus themselves, and that I'd borne it well, considering.

There was a rich echo of the maddening itch now and then as I was raped, but apparently there was not enough of the perfumed liquid left in me to discourage the others.

"What would happen if it was put on our cocks?" I wondered. "Best not to think about that," I told myself.

What I thought about day to day was improving my form, marching better than the other ponies, deciding which coachmen I liked best, which coaches I enjoyed most pulling. I grew to love the other ponies, to understand their state of mind.

Ponies felt safe in their harnesses. They could take any manner of abuse as long as they were confined within their appointed role. It was intimacy that terrified them more than anything, the prospect of being taken out of harness and into some village bedroom where a lone man or woman might talk to them and play with them to his or her heart's content. Even the Public Turntable was too intimate for them. They shuddered when they saw the slaves up there being paddled for the crowd. That is why it was such a torment to them when the village boys and girls played with them. Yet they loved nothing more than to pull the chariots in the race on fair day with the whole village watching them. It was what they were "born" to do.

I passed into this state of mind without entirely sharing it. After all, I rather adored the other punishments, too. But I didn't miss them. I was happier in bit and harness than out of them. And, whereas these other punishments of castle and village life tended to isolate the slave, pony existence drew us together. And we amplified each other's pleasure and pain.

I became used to all the stable boys, to their jovial greetings and responses. In fact, they were part of the comradery even when they paddled us or tormented us. And it was no secret that they loved their work.

Tristan all this time seemed just as content as I was, and in the recreation yard he admitted this. Things were harder for him; he was more gentle than me by nature.

But the real test and the real change came for him when his former Master, Nicolas, started to hang about.

At first, we saw Nicolas only occasionally passing the wagon yard. And, though I had not been very interested in him on the voyage from the Sultanate, I began to realize he was quite a charming and aristocratic young man. His white hair gave him a special luster; and he always wore velvet as if he were a Lord; and the expression on his face struck terror in the ponies, especially those who had pulled his coach.

After a few weeks of his quiet comings and goings, we started to see him at the gate every day. He was there in the morning, watching when we trotted off, and there at evening when we came back. And, though he pretended to be watching everything around him, his eyes settled on Tristan again and again.

Finally, one afternoon he sent for Tristan to draw a little market cart for him, just the sort of chore that froze my soul. I was scared for Tristan. Nicolas would walk right by him and torment him. I hated to see Tristan harnessed and rigged to the cart. Nicolas stood by with a long, stiff thrash in his hand, the kind that really marks the legs, just studying Tristan as he was bitted and fitted up well. Then he whipped Tristan's thighs hard to move him out of the yard.

"What a terrible thing for Tristan," I thought. "Tristan is too gentle for these things. If he had a mean streak, as I have, he would know how to handle that imperious wretch. He does not."

Seems I was quite wrong. Not about Tristan's lack of a mean streak, but about its being a terrible thing.

Tristan wasn't back to the stables until near midnight. And, after he was fed and massaged and oiled, he told me in low whispers what had happened:

"You know how frightened of him I was," he said, "of his temper, his disappointment in me."

"Yes, go on."

"And for the first few hours he whipped me mercilessly, all through the market. And I tried to be cold, to think only of being a good pony, to put him in the scheme of things, like a star in a constellation. Not to think on who he really was. But I kept thinking of when we had loved each other, he and I. And by noontime I knew I was grateful just to be near him. How wretched it was. He wouldn't stop whipping me, no matter how well I trotted. And he never spoke a word."

"And then?" I asked.

"Well, in the middle of the afternoon, after I'd been watered and rested on the edge of the marketplace, he drove me up the main road to his door. Of course, I remembered the house. I've recognized it every time we've passed it. And when I realized he was untying me from the cart, my heart stopped. He left me in bit and harness and whipped me into the hallway and then into his room."

I was wondering if this wasn't forbidden. But what did it matter? What could a pony do when such things occurred?

"Well, there was the bed we'd made love in, the room where we had talked. And he made me squat low, on the floor, facing his writing desk. And then he sat down at the desk and looked at me as I waited. You can imagine how I felt. That position is the worst, squatting, and my cock was unbelievably hard, and I still wore the harness, my arms bound tight against my back, and the bit with the reins over my shoulders. And he was picking up his damned pen to write!

" 'Drop the bit,' he said to me, 'and answer my questions just as you answered them once before.' I did as he said, and then he began to interrogate me about all aspects of our existence: what we ate, how we were groomed, what were the worst trials. I answered everything as calmly as I could, but finally I was crying. I couldn't control it. And all he did was write down the things I said. No matter how my voice changed or how I struggled, he kept writing. I confessed that I loved the pony life, yet it was hard. I admitted that I didn't have the strength that you have, Laurent. I told him you were my idol in all things, that you were perfect. But I longed for a stern Master still, a loving and stern Master. I confessed everything, things I didn't even know that I still felt."

I wanted to say, "Tristan, you did not have to tell him. You could have concealed your soul. You could have taunted him and insulted him." But I knew this was no good for Tristan, this line of thought.

I kept silent and Tristan went on with his account.

"Then the most remarkable thing happened," he said. "Nicolas set down the pen. And for a moment he said and did nothing but gesture for me to be quiet. Then he came and knelt before me and put his arms around me, and he broke down. He said that he loved me, had never stopped loving me, and these months had been agony for him. . . ."

"Poor boy," I whispered.

"Laurent, don't make fun of it. It's serious."

"I'm sorry, Tristan, go on."

"He kissed me and embraced me. He said that he had failed me when we had left the Sultanate. That he should have whipped me for my confusion in not wanting to be rescued and guided me through it—"

"It's about time he realized that."

"And he wanted to make up for it now. He wasn't allowed to take off my harness—there was a stiff fine for that and he had to respect the law—but we could make love together, he said. And we did. We lay on the floor together, as you and I did in the Sultan's bedroom, and I took his cock in my mouth as he took mine. Laurent, I've never known such pleasure. He is my secret lover again and my secret Master."

"What happened after that?"

"He drove me out again into the streets, and thereafter he kept his hand on my shoulder, and when he whipped me I knew that it was giving him pleasure. Everything was magnified. I was exalted again. Later, in the woods near his manor house, we made love a second time, and before he put the bit back in my mouth he kissed it lovingly. And he told me that all this must be kept secret. That the rules regarding the village pony stock were very, very strict.

"Tomorrow we're to lead his team when he goes to the country. We'll be tethered to his coach for some time almost every day, and he and I will have our secret moments when we can."

"I'm happy for you, Tristan," I said.

"But it's going to be so hard, Laurent, waiting for opportunities with him. Yet it's thrilling, isn't it, never knowing when they will come?"

I never worried about Tristan after that. And, if others knew of his renewed love with Nicolas, they did not seem to mind. When the Captain of the Guard came round to talk to me, he said nothing about it and treated Tristan just as affectionately as before. He told us both that Lexius had been taken out of the castle kitchen almost immediately and he now served the Queen on the Bridle Path every day. The fierce Lady Juliana had also taken a liking to him and was having a hand in his training. He was becoming an exceptionally accomplished slave.

"So now I don't have to worry about either Lexius or Tristan," I thought.

But all this set me to thinking again about love. Had I ever loved one of my Masters? Or was love elicited from me only by my slaves? Surely I had felt a frightening love for Lexius when I'd whipped him in his chamber. And I felt love, profound love, for Jerard now. In fact, the harder I whipped Jerard with my hand the more I loved him. Maybe it would always be so with me. The moments in which my soul yielded, in which everything formed a complete pattern, were moments when I was in command.

But one strange contradiction to this troubled me. It was Gareth, my handsome stable-boy Master. As month passed into month, I grew to love him too much.

Every night, Gareth spent some time in our stall, pinching my welts, scratching them with his fingernails as he complimented me on what I'd learned, or how well I'd done, or passed on to me the praise of some generous villager.

If he thought that Tristan and I hadn't been whipped enough that day—and this was common when we were not the last two in a team—he marched us out to the training yard, a large place at the opposite end of the stable from the other yards, and there he whipped both of us along with other neglected ponies until we were good and sore, having us all run before him in a small circle.

All detailed matters of grooming for Tristan and me he attended to personally. He scrubbed our teeth, shaved our faces, washed and combed our hair. He clipped our nails. He trimmed our pubic hair and oiled it. He oiled our nipples to soften them after the pinch of the clamps.

And when we were put in the fair day races for the first time, it was Gareth who calmed us as the screaming and cheering crowds unnerved us, Gareth who hitched us to the little chariots we had to pull and told us to be proud as we strived to win.

Gareth was always near.

On those rare occasions when we were to have some new style of harness or rigging, he put it on us himself, explaining it to us.

For example, after we had been in the stables about four months, high collars were introduced, much like those we'd worn briefly in the Sultan's garden. They were stiff to hold the chin high, and it was impossible to turn the head while wearing one. And this Gareth liked very much. He felt they added style, and provided better discipline.

As time passed we wore these more and more often. And the reins of our bits were run down through loops on the sides of these collars, so that our heads could be pulled more effectively. It was difficult at first to make turns in these collars. We could not turn our heads even a little as we had been used to do. But soon we did it well, in the manner of real horses.

On glaring hot days blinders were strapped on us that partially shaded our eyes, only allowing us to see a little of what lay directly before us. It was comforting in a way, yet it made us run at a more dogged and clumsy pace, because we were completely dependent upon the coachman's commands for guidance.

We were fitted out with ornamental harnesses for festival and fair days. On the anniversary of the Queen's Coronation, all ponies wore leather dripping with fancy buckles, heavy bronze medallions, and jangling bells, and it weighted us down and gave us a new awareness of our bondage, as if we needed it.

But, in truth, our rigging was so much the same that

the smallest change could be used as a punishment. If I showed the slightest sluggishness or sulkiness to Gareth, I was made to wear a longer, thicker bit that disfigured my mouth and made me miserable. An unusually large and heavy phallus was always used at least twice a week to remind us how fortunate we were to have smaller ones the rest of the time.

And skittish, uneasy ponies were often completely hooded in leather, their ears stuffed with cotton. With only their mouths and noses exposed for breathing, they trotted along in silence and darkness. And it did seem to calm them beautifully.

The times it was done to me as a punishment, however, I found it completely demoralizing. I cried from start to finish of the day, terrified at being unable to hear or see and whimpering every time a hand touched me. In blind isolation, I was more vividly aware of the picture I made than ever before, I think.

But, as time passed, I wasn't too often punished, and it became more and more of a catastrophe of the heart when I was, Gareth sparing me nothing of his disappointment and temper. I was too deeply in love with Gareth, and I knew it. I loved his voice, his manner, his mere silent presence. It was for Gareth that I showed my best form, did my best trotting, bore stiff punishments with heartfelt contrition, obeyed with quickness and even joy.

Gareth often complimented me on my handling of Jerard. He would come into the yard to watch. He said the added whipping made Jerard more animated and frisky. And I enjoyed the praise.

But, no matter how strong this love for Gareth became, the special love for Jerard grew as well. I became more and more tender with Jerard after the paddlings, kissing him and suckling him and toying with him in ways that weren't too common in the pony recreation yard. I feasted on his body for the whole hour. And, on those days when he wasn't put out for me to play with, I had little trouble finding obedient substitutes. It was amazing the pain I could inflict with my bare hand.

In fact, sometimes I wondered at my passion for whipping the others. I loved it as much as I loved to be whipped. And in my secret heart I dreamed of whipping Gareth.

I knew that if I whipped Gareth then the love I felt for him would boil over. It would be beyond my control or recall.

That never came to pass.

But I had Gareth. Perhaps he had had a lover in the early months; I was never to know. But by the end of the first half of the year, he was slipping into my stall and lingering there, and behaving restlessly and strangely.

"What is troubling you, Gareth?" I asked finally, getting the courage to whisper to him in the dark. He might well have whipped me for speaking, but he didn't. He had moved my hands to the back of my neck so that he could rest his head on his folded arms on my back. I rather liked it, him resting there, the feel of him against me. He was running a lazy hand through my hair. Now and then his knee would nudge my cock.

"Ponies are the only real slaves," he murmured dreamily. "I prefer them to the daintiest Princess. Ponies are magnificent. All men should be given the chance to serve as ponies for a year of their lives. The Queen should have a fine stable at the castle. The Lords and Ladies have asked for it often enough. They could go for little rides in the country with ponies in splendid rigging. There should be a fine academy for the ponies, and more races, don't you think?"

I didn't answer. I dreaded the races. I was a frequent winner, but it was as frightening a thing as any that I'd ever been made to do. It was performing for amusement again, instead of work. I liked hard discipline and work.

There was that knee again, against my cock.

"What do you want from me, beautiful boy?" I asked softly, using the phrase he often used for me.

"You know what I want, don't you?" he whispered.

"No," I said. "If I did, I wouldn't have asked."

"The others will make fun of me if I do it," he said. "I'm supposed to use the ponies when I choose, you know. . . ."

"Why don't you suit yourself and not worry about the others?" I asked.

That was all the urging he required. He dropped down on his knees and took my cock in his mouth, and soon I was roaring towards a finish in sheer bliss. "It's Gareth, my beautiful Gareth," I kept thinking. Then there was no thought at all. He snuggled against me afterwards, telling me how fine I was, that he loved the taste of it, my juices. When he slipped his cock into my backside, I came close to paradise again.

And though this happened often, his delicious mouth pleasuring me, he was just as stern a Master afterwards, and I was three times over his shuddering slave, crying at his slightest word of disapproval. Now, when he was angry, I thought not only of his handsome face and pleasant voice but of the mouth sucking hard on me in the dark. I cried frantically whenever he scolded me.

Once I stumbled while pulling a handsome equipage, and when he got wind of it he had me spread out on the stable wall, and he whipped me with a broad leather strap until he wore himself out. I was shuddering in misery, not daring to rub my cock against the stones for fear I'd come. When he released me, I knelt at his feet kissing his coarse rawhide boots over and over again.

"Don't be clumsy like that again, Laurent," he said. "It discredits me when you are clumsy." I was crying with gratitude when he let me kiss his hands.

When spring came round again, I could scarcely believe nine months had passed. Tristan and I lay together in the recreation yard, confessing our fears to each other.

"Nicolas is going to the Queen," Tristan said. "He is asking to purchase me when the year is out. But the Queen is not pleased with his ardor. What will we do when these days come to an end?"

"I don't know. Maybe we'll be sold back to the stables," I said. "We're good steeds."

But it was like all our conversations of this sort—pure speculation. All we knew was that the Queen would consider our cases at the end of the year.

And when I saw the Captain of the Guard, when he came into the stables and sent for me and let me talk to him, I told him that Tristan was desperate to return to Nicolas, and I was just as desperate to remain where I was.

After the life of a pony, how could I bear anything else?

He listened to me with obvious compassion.

"You're a credit to the stables, both of you," he said. "You earn your feed twice and three times over."

"More than that," I thought, but I didn't say so.

"The Queen may grant Nicolas's wish, and as for you, it would be the natural thing for you to be given over for another year. The Queen's more than pleased as it is to hear that you've both quieted down and behaved yourselves. And she has plenty of new playthings to content her at the castle."

"Is Lexius still with her?" I asked.

"Yes, she's frightfully hard on him, but it is what he needs," said the Captain. "And then there is a lovely young Prince who wandered into this Land and threw himself upon her mercy. Said he was told of the Queen's customs by Princess Beauty. Imagine that. He begged not to be sent away."

"Ah, Beauty." I felt a sudden stab of pain. I don't think a day had passed that I'd not thought of her in her velvet gown, a flower held in a gloved hand, its petals looking all the more delicate for the fabric that pinched it. Gone forever into propriety, poor darling Beauty. . . .

"Princess Beauty to you, Laurent," the Captain corrected me.

"Of course, Princess Beauty," I said softly, reverently.

"As to what will happen," said the Captain, going back

to the question at hand, "there is Lady Elvera, who asks about you constantly."

"Captain, I am so happy here . . ." I said.

"I know. I shall do what I can. But continue to be obedient, Laurent. You have another three years to serve somewhere, I am sure of it."

"Captain, there is one more thing," I said.

"What is it?"

"Princess Beauty. . . . Do you ever hear anything of her?"

His face grew a little sad, wistful.

"Only that she's sure to be already married by this time. The suitors were beating down the door."

I looked away from him, not wanting to reveal my expression. Beauty married. Time had not made me miss her less.

"She is a great Princess now, Laurent," said the Captain, teasing me. "You are having disrespectful thoughts, I can see it!"

"Yes, Captain," I said. We both smiled. But it wasn't easy. "Captain, grant me a favor. When you do hear for certain that she has been married, don't tell me. I would rather not know."

"That isn't like you, Laurent," he said.

"I know. How explain it? I knew her only a little while."

Coupling in the dark in the hold of the ship, her little face blood-red as she came beneath me, her hips pumping so ecstatically, she all but lifted my weight with her, off the floor. Of course, the Captain didn't know that part of it. Or did he? I tried to put it out of my mind.

Weeks passed. I couldn't keep track of them. I didn't want to know how fast the time was running out.

Then one night Tristan confided to me with joyful tears that the Queen was giving him over to Nicolas when the year was out. He would be Nicolas's private pony and sleep again in Nicolas's chamber. He was ecstatic.

"I'm happy for you," I said again.

But what would befall me when the moment came? Would I be put up on the auction block, and bought by some wicked old cobbler, and made to sweep out his shop while the ponies trotted past the door in all their glory? Ah! I couldn't think of it. I couldn't believe in anything else but this! Days following days. . . .

In the recreation yard, I devoured Jerard as if each moment was our last. And then one evening at twilight when I was just finished with him and pulling him up into my arms for a little tender nuzzling, I saw a pair of boots standing before me. And looking up, I realized it was the Captain of the Guard.

He never came out here. I went pale.

"Your Majesty," he said. "Please rise. I have a message of the greatest importance. I must ask you to come with me."

"No!" I said. I stared at him in horror, thinking madly that if I could somehow stop his lips the words wouldn't work their evil spell. "It can't be time yet! I'm supposed to serve for three more years!"

We had all heard Beauty's screams when she'd been told of her reprieve. I wanted to roar just as loudly now.

"I'm afraid it's true, Your Majesty!" he said. And, extending his hand, he helped me to my feet.

It was amazing, the awkwardness between us. And right there in the stables were clothes for me and two young boys, with heads bowed not to see my nakedness, who helped me to put the clothes on.

"Must this be done here!" I demanded. I was in a rage. But I was trying to hide my grief, my utter shock. I stared at Gareth as the boys buttoned my tunic and laced my breeches. I looked down in silent fury at my boots, my gloves. "Couldn't you have had the decency to take me up to the castle for this little ritual! I mean I've never seen it done right here on the hay-strewn floor!"

"Forgive me, Your Majesty!" the Captain said. "But this news couldn't wait."

He glanced at the open door. I saw two of the Queen's

most important advisers, both of whom had used me well at the castle, and now they too stood with bowed heads. I was on the edge of tears. Again I looked at Gareth. He too was about to cry.

"Goodbye, my beautiful Prince," he said, and he knelt in the hay and kissed my hand.

" 'Prince' is no longer the proper address for our gracious ally," said one of the advisers, advancing. "Your Majesty, I bring you the sad news that your father has died, and you are now the ruler of your Kingdom. The King is dead, long live the King."

"Damn it all," I whispered. "He was always an utter bastard, and he would choose this time to breathe his last!"

MOMENT
OF
TRUTH

THERE WAS no time for lingering at the castle. I had to ride for home at once. I knew my Kingdom would be on the verge of anarchy. Both my brothers were idiots, and the Captain of the Army, though devoted to my father, would now try to gain power for himself.

And so, after an hour's conference with the Queen in which we talked mostly war and diplomatic agreements, I rode out, taking with me a great amount of treasure from her and also some little lovely trinkets and souvenirs of village and castle life.

I was rather amazed still that all these cumbersome,

heavy garments went everywhere that I did—it was annoying not to be naked—but I had to be on my way, and I did not even glance at the village as I rode by.

Of course, a thousand Princes had undergone this sudden reprieve, this shock of clothing and ceremony, but few had had to take the reins of the Kingdoms to which they returned. There was no time for lamentation, no time to linger at a country Inn on the way and drink myself into a stupor as I tried to get used to the real world.

I reached my castle by the second night of hard riding and, within the three days that followed, put everything right. My father had already been buried; my mother was long dead. And what was needed was a powerful hand at the helm of government and I soon made clear to everyone that that hand was mine.

I flogged the soldiers who had abused the village girls in the few days of anarchy. I lectured my brothers and directed them to their duties with ominous threats. I had the army assembled for inspection and gave generous rewards to all those who had loved my father and who now came to me with the same love.

None of this was difficult, really, yet I knew that many a European Kingdom fell because a new monarch could not do it. And I saw the look of relief on the faces of my subjects when they realized that their young King exercised authority easily and naturally, that he directed all matters of government, both large and small, with great personal attention and force. The Lord High Treasurer was grateful to have someone to assist him, and the Captain of the Army went at his command with renewed strength with me at his back.

But when the first frantic weeks were over, when things quieted down in the castle, when I could sleep the night through without interruptions from servants and family, I began to think about all that had occurred. I had no more marks on my body. I was tormented by endless desire. And, when I realized I would never be a naked slave again, I could scarcely stand it. I didn't want to look at the trinkets the Queen had given me, see the leather toys that were of no significance to me now.

But I was ashamed afterwards.

It was not my destiny, as Lexius would have said, to be any longer a slave. I had now to be a good and powerful ruler, and the truth was I loved being King.

Being a Prince was just dreadful.

But being King was quite fine.

When my advisers came to me and told me I must take a wife and father a child to insure the succession, I nodded in agreement at once. Courtly life was going to devour me, and I should give it all that I had. My old existence was as insubstantial as a dream.

"And who are the likely Princesses?" I said to my advisers. I was signing some important laws as they stood about my writing table. "Well?" I looked up at them. "Speak!"

But even before any of the men said anything, one name suddenly came full force into my mind.

"Princess Beauty!" I whispered. Could it be that she had not been married! I dared not ask.

"O, yes, Your Majesty," said my Lord High Chancellor. "She would be the wisest choice without question, but she refuses all suitors. Her father is in despair."

"Does she now?" I said. I tried to conceal my excitement. "I wonder why she refuses them," I said innocently. "Go saddle my horse at once."

"But we should send an official letter to her father—"

"No. Saddle my horse," I said, rising from the table. I went to the royal bedchamber to dress myself in my finest clothes and to get a few other little things as well.

I was just about to rush out when I stopped. I felt a sudden invisible blow to my chest. And just as if the wind had really been knocked out of me, I sank down in the chair at my desk.

Beauty, my darling Beauty. I saw her in the cabin of the ship with her arms out, beseeching me. And I felt a surge of longing that left me naked as I had never been.

Other mad thoughts came back to me, of mastering Lexius alone in his chamber in the Sultan's palace, of having Jerard in my full possession, of the tenderness that came out of me in those precious moments when I looked at the reddened flesh beneath my open hand, the dangerous awakening of love for the ones I punished mercilessly, for those who were *mine*.

Beauty!

It took a surprising amount of courage to rise from the chair. And yet I was so eager! I patted my pocket where I had put the trinkets I was taking to her. And then I caught a glimpse of myself in the distant mirror—His Majesty in purple velvet and black boots, his ermine-trimmed cloak flaring behind him—and I winked at my reflection.

"Laurent, you devil," I said with wicked smile.

We reached the castle unannounced, just as I had hoped, and Beauty's father was jubilant as he brought us into the Great Hall. There had not been many suitors of late. And he was eager for an alliance with our Kingdom.

"But, Your Majesty, I must warn you," he said politely. "My daughter is proud and moody and will receive no one. She sits at her windows and dreams the whole day long."

"Your Majesty, humor me if you will," I answered. "You know my intentions are honorable. Merely point me to the door of her parlor and leave the rest to me."

She was sitting at the window with her back to the room, and she was singing softly to herself, and her hair, gathering the sunlight to it, looked like spun gold.

My sweet darling. The dress she wore was rose-colored velvet trimmed in carefully embroidered leaves of silver. And how finely it fitted her magnificent little shoulders and arms. Arms as juicy as the rest of her, I thought. So sweet to squeeze, those little arms. And let me see the breasts please, immediately . . . and those eyes, that spirit.

Again, the invisible and completely imaginary blow to my chest.

I crept up behind her and, just as she gave a start, I clamped my gloved hands over her eyes.

"Who dares to do this!" she whispered. It had a frightened, imploring sound.

"Quiet, Princess," I said. "Your Lord and Master is here, the suitor you will not dare to refuse!"

"Laurent!" she gasped. I let her go, and she rose and turned and threw herself into my arms. I kissed her a thousand times, all but bruising her lips. She was as gorgeous and pliant as she had been in the hold of the ship, as succulent and feverish and wild.

"Laurent, you haven't really come with an offer of marriage, have you?"

"Offer, Princess, offer?" I said. "I come with a command." I forced her lips wide with my tongue, my hands squeezing her breasts hard through the velvet. "You will marry me, Princess. You will be my Queen and my slave."

"O, Laurent, I never dared dream of this moment!" she said. Her face was beautifully flushed, her eyes gleaming. I could feel her heat through the skirts against my leg. And the surge of love came again, overwhelming and mingled with a maddening sense of possession and power. It made me hold her very tight.

"Go tell your father you will be my bride, that we will leave now for my Kingdom, and then come back to me!"

At once, she went to obey, and when she came back she closed the door after her and stared at me uncertainly, shrinking back against the wood.

"Bolt the door," I said. "We will ride out in a matter of moments, and I will save the having of you for my royal bed, but I want to prepare you for the journey properly. Do as I say."

She slid the bolt into place. She was a picture of loveliness as she approached. I reached into my pocket and drew out a pair of the gifts I had brought with me from Queen Eleanor, two small gold clamps. Beauty lifted the back of her hand to her lips. Charming, but futile. I smiled.

"Don't tell me I'm going to have to train you all over again," I said, winking at her, and kissing her quickly. I slipped my hand into her tight bodice and clamped the nipple firmly. Then I clamped the other. A shudder passed up through her torso to her open mouth. Such gorgeous distress.

I took another pair of clamps from my pocket. "Spread your legs," I said. I knelt and gathered up her skirt and reached up until I felt the wet naked little sex. How hungry it was, how ready. O, she was such a splendid darling, and one glimpse of her radiant face peering down at me, and I should go mad. I applied the clamps carefully to the moist secret lips.

"Laurent," she whispered. "You are merciless." She was already in appropriate misery, half afraid, half dazed. I could scarcely resist her.

Now I drew out a small vial of amber-colored liquid, one of Queen Eleanor's most important gifts. I opened the vial and savored the spicy aroma. But I must use this sparingly. After all, my tender little darling was not a strong, muscular pony used to such things.

"What is it?"

"Shh!" I touched her lips. "Don't tempt me to whip you until I have you in my bedchamber and can do it properly. Be quiet."

I tipped the vial and poured a bit of its contents on my gloved finger, and then I raised Beauty's skirt again and smoothed the fluid over her little clitoris, her trembling lips.

"Ah, Laurent, it's—" She flew into my arms and I held her. How she was suffering, trying not to squeeze her legs together, shivering.

"Yes, " I said, holding her. This was pure sweetness. "And it will itch in that manner all the way to my castle, at which time I shall lick it off, every last droplet of it, and take you as you deserve."

She moaned, her hips twisting in spite of herself as the

itching potion did its work, her breasts rubbing against my chest as if I could somehow save her, her mouth on mine.

"Laurent, I can't bear it," she said, breathing the words through her kisses. "Laurent, I am dying for you. Don't make me suffer very long, please, Laurent, you mustn't—"

"Shhh, it's out of your hands," I said lovingly. Once again, I reached into my pockets, and I drew out a delicate little harness with a phallus attached. She put her hands to her lips as I unfolded the phallus, her eyebrows coming together in a panic-stricken little frown. But she didn't resist as I knelt to slip the phallus into her little bottom, to secure it well in her anus, and strap the harness around her thighs and waist. Of course, I could have put the itching fluid on the phallus but that would have been too harsh. And this was only the beginning, wasn't it? Time enough for that.

"Come darling, let's go." I said as I rose. She was radiant and utterly compliant. I gathered her up and carried her out of the parlor and down the stairs to the courtyard, where her horse was waiting with its ornate sidesaddle already in place. But I didn't place her on her horse.

I seated her on my mount before me, and, as we rode off into the forest, I slipped my hand up under her skirts and touched the straps of the little harness and the wet, tender little part of her that was mine now, all mine, clamped and itching with desire and ready for me, and I knew I possessed a slave whom no Queen or Lord or Lady or Captain of the Guard could ever take from me again.

This was the real world then—Beauty and I free to have each other and all the others gone. Just the two of us in my bedchamber, where I should envelop her naked soul in rituals and ordeals beyond our past experiences, our dreams. No one to save her from me. No one to save me from her. My slave, my poor helpless slave. . . .

I stopped suddenly. The blow to the chest again. I knew I had gone pale.

"What's wrong, Laurent!" she said in alarm. She held tight to me.

"Panic," I whispered.

"No!" she gasped.

"O, don't worry, my tender sweetheart. I shall beat you soundly enough when we reach home, and adore doing it. I'll make you forget the Captain of the Guard and the Crown Prince and everyone who's ever had you, used you, satisfied you. But it's just . . . just that I'm going to grow to love you so." I looked at her upturned face, her savage eyes, her little body writhing beneath the rich gown.

"Yes, I know," she said in a small, shuddering voice. And she sealed her mouth to mine. And in a soft, heated whisper, she said slowly, thoughtfully. "I am yours, Laurent. And yet I don't even know the meaning of the words yet. Teach me the meaning! It is only the beginning. It shall be the worst and most hopeless captivity of all."

If I didn't stop kissing her, we wouldn't make it to the castle. And the woods were so nice and dark . . . and she *was* suffering, my precious one. . . .

"And we shall live happily ever after," I said through my kisses, "as the fairy tales say."

"Yes, happily ever after," she answered, "and a good deal happier, I think, than anyone else could ever guess."